Parleys Quest
An Inspirational Burnrise Saga

By Troy C. Wagstaff

Tibble Fork Publishing
American Fork, Utah

DEDICATION

*This book is also dedicated to all those who have or are currently struggling with any type of chronic illness, especially a chronic pain illness or **fibromyalgia**.*

ACKNOWLEDGMENTS

My first and most important acknowledgment goes to my loving and supportive wife Colette, who in spite of my chronic pain and fibromyalgia has not only stuck by my side, but pushed me along to finish this project. She has also helped with this novel by lending her critical eye to the editing of this book.

To Makenzie, Brittany and Katelyn my daughters. Thanks for all the never-ending support.

Thanks to LaVerde Hope for line editing.

Table of Contents

Chapter One: Life And Death Odyssey

Acts of heroism are not premeditated for the glory of others, but rather, they are done by the desire to serve, defend and rescue others. CallahanWriter

Valentines Day 2008
Willow Creek Resort, Montana

Parley struggled in the frigid air to get the snowmobile started. He was surrounded by a hardy few souls who came to see him off. The temperature was below zero. Their breath hung in the icy air. The blizzard was past and the pale blue sky was filled with the remains of a few heavy gray clouds.

After a few more tries, the two stroke 1000cc engine, roared to life. Parley revved it several times and then let the motor idle as he reached out to his wife Miranda as she leaned in for a hug. The engine continued to rumble which gave the four remaining supporters cause for hope. Maybe their ordeal of being stranded so far up the mountain would be over soon.

Parleys' snow suit had a body camera mounted on each shoulder. He turned them on. He leaned over in his seat to kiss Miranda, one last time. This was no ordinary ride down a snowy mountain. He scanned the white horizon in front of him. All he could see from his vantage point was eighteen feet of freshly fallen snow with the tips of spruce and pines poking out at the crest of the pristine powder. The rest of the mountain side was covered. He was reasonably sure he could still see a slight depression of snow where the road was going down the canyon.

He licked his lips, tasting the lip balm he had recently put on as he suited up for this emergency rescue run. Even with a gentle breeze, he could still detect the dusty smell of his snow suit he pulled from his winter survival kit which he stored in a utility box in the back of his truck. All he could hear was the roar of his motor. *I wonder how stable this snow is? I hope I don't start an avalanche.*

Parley let out a deep breath which hung like fog in the frosty air. He slowly let go of the brakes inching his way to the crest of the parking lot where the canyon road met the parking lot. He took one last look around the mountainside to orient himself before plunging down the canyon on a road buried with fresh unstable snow.

With all the weak powder beneath him, Parleys' mind was focused on keeping his ski tips up and trying to stay ahead of any tidal waves of white powder. He knew that with all the fresh snowfall the risk for dangerous snow slides was high. This would be the most dangerous snowmobile run of his life.

Miranda, Art Nance the manager of Willow Creek Resort and a few others made their way into the warmth of the grand foyer where the massive two-sided fireplace was keeping the stranded guests and workers warm. Between the lodgers and employees, there were thirty-five people stranded from the Valentines Day celebration.

There was a winter storm warning in effect for Saturday the sixteenth. Everyone had plans to be out of the canyon before the big blizzard. No one knew it would come in early and no one could have guessed how much snow would fall. The forecasters were caught with egg on their face and were trying to explain how they missed the forecast.

The storm caught everyone off guard, including the resort. The food was running dangerously low. They were expecting a new shipment the day after Valentines Day. The storm cut their power and left them with little food. Luckily they were able to keep warm by the fireplace. They had plenty of firewood, but no electricity. With any power they couldn't contact anyone down below and tell them of their dire circumstances. On top of all that, they had two seriously ill customers. Since the storm came earlier than expected, they had no idea if more snow was on the way. No one knew how long they would be snowed in. Without communication they were beside themselves with worry and concern for the sick patient and the other patient with a broken leg.

The sick guest was a cancer patient who had planned a romantic dinner on Valentines Day with his wife. Then back to Bitter

Root City, for bed and his medicine. The other patient broke his leg by slipping on ice while helping to bring in firewood the morning after the blizzard. These two patients were in terrible pain and getting worse.

Parley was keeping a deliberate speed trying to anticipate the turns on the road going down the canyon. The side of the mountain was to his right and the steep drop off was on the outside of the road to his left. He was struggling with his desire to go fast versus the need to stay away from dangerous wide turns to avoid losing control.

With the unsteady snow conditions an avalanche was just waiting to happen. He wanted to be out in front if it did. The thirty-five-mile drive started out with a gradual descent. The urge for speed and the common sense for a controlled descent were at odds with each other and kept fighting within his mind as he crept steadily down the canyon.

The biting wind chill increased as his speed increased. Other than his face, he was warm. He had ridden thousands of miles on a snowmobile throughout his life. Many of those rides were taped with his body cameras and put on his blog. He was a professional blogger. The topic of his blog was outdoor sporting activities. Of all his snowmobile runs this one felt very different. He wasn't doing it for fun. It was a big gamble with a heavy responsibility. It would normally be too risky just for his web site. In this case peoples' lives depended on his successful run down the mountain.

He was confident in his skills. He knew if everything was stable, he could make it to town and get help for his wife and the rest. His primary concern was the unsteady nature of the freshly fallen snow. One bad move and he could be buried in the snow. He had to be on his toes.

His downward ride suddenly got steeper. He reviewed his strategy and nothing really had changed. Hug the mountain side close, avoid the open side of the snow-covered road and hope that the unstable snow drifts wouldn't be triggered by the loud noise of the snowmobile. God willing, he would make his destination safely and quickly. *I hope I can get help early enough so a daylight rescue could happen.* They likely wouldn't go after them in the dark with the snow so unstable.

Parley was well on his way down the thirty-five-mile run. He continuously scanned the horizon while keeping an eye out in the rear view mirror for whatever might be behind him, sometimes he wasn't sure if he was even on the road. The snow was so deep and he was on unfamiliar terrain.

He noticed he was starting to sink in the unsettled snow. He down shifted and tried to stand leaning backward in an effort to shift some of his body weight to the back of the snow beast. He pulled the handle bars back as much as he had strength for and gave the machine all the throttle it required. The ski tips stopped sinking and soon he was, easing down the road. He was back in control again, cutting a trail down the canyon. He looked over his shoulder again, checking for any sign of snow slides. Every so often he could see an avalanche on the horizon. *So far, so good.*

Thirty-five people were crowded around the double-sided fireplace in the main foyer trying to keep warm. "Miranda? Hi, my name is Nicole and that is my husband, Brian." She pointed to a sickly man huddled in a blanket. "He is the one with cancer. I really appreciate what your husband is doing for my Brian. . ." She paused to collect her emotions, her voice was cracking. "We both appreciate his willingness to go down the canyon. We're praying for him."

"Oh, thank you. It's nice to meet you." Miranda noticed that Brian was asleep.

"How's he doing?" asked a concerned Miranda. *He better make it with my Parley risking his life for him.*

"He's hurting pretty badly. He took the last of his pain pills this morning along with the last of his nausea medicine. He's out of his mind in pain. He's scheduled to take his next chemo pill tonight."

"What will happen if he doesn't get his chemotherapy pill?" asked Art who was standing nearby.

"The pill is just part of his chemotherapy treatment. I'm not sure what will happen, I think he'll be okay in the long run. It's the terrible agony that he's in right now that worries me. I can't stand to see him suffer like this. He's so sick."

Parley was making good time down the canyon. He was glancing over his shoulders every few seconds checking for signs of a snow slide. *So far, so good.*

As he continued his drive down the snowy canyon he got lost in the memories of snowmobiling back home around Lake Shaft. He called to mind the memories of racing his snowmobile throughout the thick forest of evergreens, aspens, and spruce.

He had countless memories around Lake Shaft in the wintertime. Those and other outdoor activities like fishing, hunting and camping had been recorded and posted on OutdoorParley.com. In fact, he had recorded more than a hundred hours of video this past fall and winter with the two body cams he was currently wearing.

If I get out of this alive, this run just might make for some of the best video I've ever posted on my blog. . . Why am I even thinking about that now? I should be focusing on living and getting out of this alive. Forget the blog Parley, geez.

Parley motored on down the canyon and taking the turns as fast as he could without running off the open side of the road and down the steep drop off. He looked over his shoulder again as he continued a step decent down the canyon road.

He rounded the next turn a little too wide and he got a glance of just how deep the drop off was. His heart responded by pounding deeper and faster than he could ever remember. He felt like he had just swallowed his stomach. He hugged the inside of the road. The descent was getting steeper as he got closer to the mouth of the canyon.

He looked at the sky and the clouds seemed to be getting lower again. *Maybe another storm is rolling in? Hmm. . . How far away from Bitterroot am I? Where do I go once I get into town? Hadn't thought about that. The closest building with lights on makes sense.* He looked over his left shoulder and still no snow slides. *I'm flying like an eagle down the canyon. This is my snow! Man, oh man, this is fun! I own this run!*

Parley was shaken from his confidence by a thunderous vibration and a roar of rolling thunder. Suddenly, as he felt the earth move. He noticed billowing snow surging down the mountain directly behind him. He turned forward and opened up the throttle, letting the snowmobile have all it could handle. He kept his eyes directly in front of him. He shifted all his weight to the inside curve. He leaned in hard around the turns. He couldn't afford to brake for any reason. He couldn't let the avalanche gain any ground. With avalanches, inches could matter.

He managed a quick glance over his right shoulder and saw what looked like a cloudy white column of snow erupting into the air.

Faster! Go faster! Gotta beat the snow! God help me please. . .Why am I doing this? I should be with Miranda. I could die doing this.

Parley tried revving the engine, but it was already going full throttle. He tried to position as much of his body weight to the front of the snowmobile as he could, hoping it would give him a little more speed. Inches matter. The engine whined as he tried to rev it up. He was pushing his machine to its limit. He had to live. He had to beat the snow.

As he maintained full speed, he looked over his shoulder to judge the distance. *A mile, maybe two miles behind me. . .I hope.* But avalanches can be deceiving. With all the thunderous snow pouring down, it could be a little closer than he thought. The only variable that Parley had any control over was maintaining top speed. He was still riding at full throttle and praying hard. He was going to beat the snow or die trying. He had no other choice.

Please Lord, don't let me die, please. Don't let me die. He was shooting downward on the steep slope being chased by thousands of tons of snow. As he continued shooting down the mountain side, he hit a bump and went flying into the air. He seemed to be soaring like a hawk. Everywhere he looked, he felt like he was floating in slow motion. *This is strange. . .So weird.* He was surprised. It was like he and the snowmobile were perched on the wings of eagles as he seemed to be soaring through the air.

The avalanche rumbled closer to him, or was it tumbling below him, he couldn't tell. It was a blinding white everywhere. He had no point of reference.

He held on tight to the handlebars. He noticed the ground was rising up to meet him fast. Yet everything was so slow. He wasn't surprised, he wasn't confused, he was just drifting through the air getting closer to the snow cover ground. His snowmobile landed hard. The snow cat bounced several times. The only thing he was positive about, was that he had managed to keep his grip on the handle bars. *Amazing! How did that happen?* In fact, not only was his grip secure, the snowmobile was still going full throttle. On the last bounce or two, the machine sped off down the trail.

How did I not just crash? He looked behind him again and it looked like waves of snow were nearly on top of him. He looked forward again and saw flat land. He was now able to see past the mouth of the canyon and into the valley. He was nearly at the end of this wild odyssey and maybe his life. *Am I going to die? Will they find my body in the spring?*

Parley was managing to stay just ahead of the avalanche as the road leveled off. The distance between the snowmobile and the avalanche was closing in. He could feel the pounding of the snowy death as it grew closer. He could hear the roaring avalanche over the sound of his snowmobile.

Abruptly he could smell the two stroke, 1000cc engine overheating. He started to worry that he wouldn't make it. It was instinct to stop the motor for fear of burning out the engine. He couldn't stop. He couldn't even slow down. If he did, the cascading snow would cover him until the spring thaw. Inches matter. Looking over his shoulder, he saw a raging wave of white fury bearing down on him.

Parley wasn't a mechanic, but he knew that the knocks and pings from the motor meant something was very wrong with the motor. *Please Lord, please keep the motor going.* Scanning the horizon, he noticed some flashing red lights far off in the distance. *Strange.* He noticed his snowmobile was slowing down, it started to lurch forward, sputter and then lurch again. Then he heard the grinding sound of metal scraping metal. Miraculously, he kept going forward. The snowmobile engine started to spit black smoke, but it somehow kept going. Slowly, but still moving forward. The snow was starting to pile up around him.

The exhaust of black smoke was that last thing Parley saw before his lurching snowmobile sunk its ski tips into the snow with enough momentum to cause the machine to somersault several times, causing Parley to fly through the air landing hard head first about ten yards away from the broken snow cat.

Parleys' mind recalled the acrid smell of black smoke before comprehending that all he could see was nothing but darkness. His head was pounding. He was confused. *Am I blind? I can't see anything.* Parley felt an unfamiliar sense of panic and dread wash over him. His cheeks were freezing and throbbing. His face was bleeding, he could feel something wet run down his cheeks or was it melting snow? He was disoriented. He didn't know if he was upside down or right side up in the crusty snow.

Instinctively blinking his eyes, Parley felt his eyelids scratch against something coarse and ice cold. As he tried to blink, he saw a flash of something grayish white. His body gasped for air as he quickly realized he hadn't been breathing for a while. His body needed air now. As his lungs tried to expand, he felt a pain so sharp and so intense that he couldn't finish inhaling. His brain commanded him to gasp the air. The pain demanded him to stop breathing. He tried to compromise and breathe short, shallow breaths. That was doable, barely. Even small gasps made him feel like his body was being flattened by a waffle iron. His arms were throbbing. With every beat of his heart a fierce ache surged throughout his bones. It was worse when he tried to move his arms. It was eerily quiet. All the Parley could hear was his heart pounding and the occasional gasp he took between the ache.

Time seemed to stand still. He couldn't pass out because the icy coldness continued to revive him. His body finally overcame the cold and he faded off. He was awakened by the sound of metal scraping against the frosty snow. Soon he heard muffled voices in the distance. He could see some faded orange light around his eyes.

"Help–" he passed out again.

Chapter Two: Time And Chance Happens

The race is not to the swift or the battle to the strong, nor does food come to the wise or wealth to the brilliant or favor to the learned, but time and chance happens to them all.
The Preacher

February 2008
Bitterroot, Montana

As Parleys' eyes slowly fluttered open, he knew time had passed, but he didn't know how much. He didn't know where he was, but he was no longer cold. He started to blink deliberately trying to adjust his eyes to the bright light. He took a deep breath only to feel the pressure of a vice grip squeeze around his chest. Breathing deep was impossible.

He heard what sounded like a distant intercom voice, he couldn't make out what the voice was saying, but he was certain it was a woman crackling over the speaker. There was no sound coming from the television, which was hanging from the wall.

He noticed a hissing sound somewhere around his face. He couldn't figure out what it was. *Is it a bee or a fly?* His throat was dry and irritated. Instinctively he tried to wiggle his nose as he tried to raise his hand to swat the bug away. As he tried to lift his right hand, he noticed his arm was weighed down with something heavy. It hurt to move. He felt disoriented. *Where am I? What's-going-on? What is that buzzing sound?*

He was confused and frustrated. Whatever was buzzing around his nose was driving him crazy. *Why can't I move my arm?* He tried his left arm only to realize something was really wrong. His left arm was in agony and it seemed to be restrained like his right arm.

Where am I? What's wrong with me? He was feeling uncharacteristically afraid. He was never afraid of anything. Now he was in some strange room, stark in appearance and strange odors wafted through the stale air. He could hardly breathe through the pain.

Feeling a growing sense of panic, he stiffly turned his head to the left only to see a faded, but clean white wall. Painfully, he turned to his right as far as his neck would allow, there she was. Miranda! Finally, something familiar. "Miranda," he tried to say, but all he did was cough and wheeze. The sound of Parley trying to clear his throat caught Miranda's attention.

"You're awake! How are you feeling sweetie?" she asked.

"Where am I?" Parley managed to ask in a scratchy whisper.

"You're in the hospital, sweetie."

"Why? What happened?" Parleys' lips were dry, his throat sore and his voice raspy. He coughed again.

"You got caught in an avalanche coming out of the canyon. You got hurt."

He was still trying to raise his arm to swat away whatever bug was stuck in his nose. "Oh ya." His awareness was slow but improving.

"Water." His voice still rough. "Water," he asked again.

Miranda helped him sip water from a cup. He coughed again and then took another sip.

"What time is it?" asked Parley.

"It's 6:00 PM. You've been in and out of consciousness since last night."

That didn't make sense. He felt like he had lost time.

"Mmm. . ." Parley was trying to move so he could adjust his back, he groaned in agony and realized he was stuck.

"I'm so glad you're awake. How are you feeling?"

"Why can't I move my arms? What's going on?"

"They're broken."

"What do you mean they are broken? Which arm is broken?"

"Both of your arms are broken."

"Everything hurts. Why is there so much pain?"

"You also have some broken ribs and a broken coccyx."

"A coccyx?"

"That's your tail bone sweetie. The very last part of your spine."

"I need to scratch my nose. "It's driving me crazy," Parley complained. "There's a fly buzzing around in my nose." Parley was growing desperate.

"That's not a fly. You have an air tube going into your nose."

"What? Why? Pull it out."

"I'm not going to pull it out. Besides, part of the tube is taped on. "

"It's driving me crazy." Parley thrashed his head around on the pillow, trying to wiggle the hose out of his nose. "Come on. . .Can't you get it out of me? Help me," Parley demanded.

"Let's call the nurse and see what she says," responded Miranda as she pressed the Nurse Call button on the side of his hospital bed. In the two minutes it took for the nurse to come to his room, Parley had fallen back to sleep.

After Miranda decided to spend the night with Parley, they brought in a couple of big white plastic bags stuffed with Parleys' snow suit and clothes he was wearing while going down the mountain.

After a while the musty, moldy smell of his snow suit caught Miranda's attention. She pulled the snow suit out of the bag. It was cut up, from the paramedic cutting it off of him. She would take it to the dumpster outside and throw it away. The smell was oppressive. *Why couldn't he have washed this snow suit at least once a year? At least I can throw it out now.*

Before throwing it out, she went through the rank snow suit to look for his wallet or anything else important. One of the body cameras fell to the floor. She picked it up and started looking for the other one. She knew he always used two or more cameras. *I wonder if it is even in this bag. Maybe it got lost in the avalanche.* A minute later she found the other camera still clipped to the right shoulder of his snow suit. She separated his clothes putting the damaged clothes in a smaller bag and took them, along with the foul snow suit outside and got rid of them.

I wonder if he recorded the rescue run down the mountain?
Once she got back to Parleys room curiosity getting the best of her,
she plugged the camera into her laptop to see if he turned on his
cameras. He did, and it was interesting. Interesting and terrifying.
She sat back in her chair and got comfortable. She adjusted the
laptop and watched the most scary video she had ever seen.

Most of the footage was spectacular. What made it so scary
was the realization that Parley was the one filming it all. This was a
visual proof of the danger he went through for three dozen perfect
strangers.

There were many times when the left camera caught
glimpses of the steep drop offs giving her a sense of how deep they
really were. She could see how close he had come, to running off
the open side of the road to certain death. She saw the sky, clouds
and snow as he tumbled through the air. She saw the cameras
getting covered with avalanche snow. She saw the cameras go
dark. Even though she couldn't see anything but dark shadows, she
could hear the sound of Parley scraping around under several feet
of icy snow. Then everything went quiet and turned a quiet gray. A
little while later she heard the scratchy, crunchy sounds of metal
scraping against the crusty snow. She heard mens voices yelling
and shouting as they dug her husband out from under the deep
snow.

I'm surprised the camera's survived the crash. Not only did
his body cameras capture his thirty-five-mile run, they also captured
Parleys' rescue from the avalanche.

The cameras kept rolling and captured, from Parleys
perspective, him getting put on a stretcher and into the helicopter.
The cameras, both caught the same thing from different angles.
They filmed the paramedic in the helicopter work on Parley. Then
the video went dark and then light again as the paramedic was
cutting off the snow suit. Next all she could see was one camera
pointing at the floor of the helicopter, but she could hear the
paramedic talk to Parley with the sounds of the helicopter in the
background and occasionally the pilot. It caught a little of the
emergency room before it stopped recording.

"What's wrong honey? Why are you crying?" Parley struggled to get his words out between painful breaths.

Miranda wiped her eyes and gathered her thick blonde hair past her ears. She forced a smile.

"Hey you, you're awake. How are you feeling sweetie?" She wiped her eyes one last time.

"I feel like my boat is crushing my chest," he gasped. "It hurts to breathe." He winced. "Why are you crying?" He was concerned. Sweat was beading on his forehead.

"I was just watching the footage from your body cams. They got the whole thing. . . You could have been killed."

"I wish I had been. I doubt death would be this bad." Parley was a rugged outdoors kind of guy and very tough. Miranda knew he had to be in a lot of pain for him to complain like that. The nurse brought in lunch for Parley. After he ate, Miranda put her laptop on his hospital tray table and positioned the screen so they could both see the video. Parleys face looked beaten up with some nasty bruises.

They watched the first video. Parleys puffy eyes popped open when he got a taste of just how dangerous that run really was. They watched the second one which showed the rescue run from a slightly different angle exposing more of the danger and steep drop offs. The footage was chilling. Parleys' stomach flopped as he contemplated how close he came to flying off the edge of the road. Miranda had wet eyes.

In an attempt to calm herself, Miranda said, "That video is going to make a great post on your blog. . . You are going to post it, right?"

"Yeah," Parley took a deep breath. "Yeah, as soon as I get my arms back. As soon as I can breathe easier."

"Wait a minute. We got nothing but time on our hand's right now." Miranda said. "I know how to edit digital files. I can get the video ready to post and you can dictate whatever you want for the article. I'll be your fingers on the keyboard. No reason to wait."

"That's a good idea. Thanks." He tried taking a deep breath and the pressure it made on his lungs caused him to winch in pain and cough at the same time. He went on to say, "You can post the other file on your blog and we can do one of those cross blog posts."

"Now you're talking. Here you are, battered and bruised and still have your Midas touch. You're my hero," Miranda said with an exaggerated smile.

"Oh geez." Parley tried to turn his head away playfully only to be reminded that he hurt all over.

Both Parley and Miranda were professional bloggers. They made a good income writing articles and posting videos of their interests on their respective blogs. For Miranda, it was mostly cooking original recipes.

They had been writers for as long as they had known each other. They met in journalism school. Parley grew up wanting to earn a living somehow in the great outdoors. When he got to high school, he discovered that he liked to write creating a second interest. He looked for ways to combine his two passions.

Miranda grew up cooking. While other girls her age were learning how to bake bread, she was way ahead of them inventing her own recipes. She had even gone to chef school for a while before attending college. She realized while taking culinary arts classes that she didn't want to be a chef, but she did want to earn a living through her passion for the culinary arts. She decided she would like writing about food and cooking. She tried it out by submitting a few articles and original recipes to food magazines. Each submission was published so she pursued writing and met her husband during their first journalism class. They dated through the rest of their time in college.

After graduating, they both had success as contributors to various magazines as they worked for the family business in Lake Shaft City. Parley was part of the Burnrise family that owned the Burnrise Family Resort at Lake Shaft which was only a few miles from town.

When blogging became a thing on the internet, they both recognized the potential in their fields and they each created a blog. As blogging got popular on the Internet, their web sites took off like a wildfire. Soon they were charging for advertising space. Parley would record himself fishing or hunting or any other outdoor activity he participated in. He would post the videos to his website, OutdoorParley.com. He also wrote countless articles related to his outdoor interests.

Miranda would post original recipes with pictures to MirandasHomestyleGourmet.com, but what made her outrageously successful was to video tape her, while cooking using her original recipes. With her shoulder length blonde bob and expressive deep blue eyes, she was a natural in front of the camera. Her energy and passion were engaging. She had, over the years been asked to make guest appearances on local cooking shows and to act as a judge for cooking competitions. They also had a unique angle in their blogging business. They did a thing they called cross posting. Parley taped himself catching a fish and then put a link to Miranda's blog to see how it was cooked. Miranda posted a cooking video with her preparing freshwater fish or game and link to Parleys' blog to see how it was caught. It was a very successful program.

After posting the rescue run video and article on Parleys' site, she posted a video and an article explaining the story behind the run, how she and thirty-five others were stranded at Willow Creek. Occasionally she posted non food related videos on her blog and this was clearly one of the exceptions. She had just uploaded the last video when they heard a knock on the door. It was Mr. Schmeider, the hospital administrator. He came into Parleys' room and gave them astonishing news.

Bitter Root City was a small town and the rescue of the people at Willow Creek Resort was big news. The reporter who wrote the first story about the rescue, put it on the wire and other news outlets picked it up.

The story of a man riding a snowmobile thirty-five miles down a dangerous canyon to save thirty-five people was considered a good news article. That local reported talked up Parley making him out to be the greatest daredevil since Evel Knieval tried to jump the Snake River Canyon in Idaho. Within a short time, other new organizations picked it up and within twenty-four hours, twelve reporters from around the country converged on the small town hospital looking to interview Parley. They had already talked to other survivors and the manager of Willow Creek Resort. The reporters were clamoring to talk to Parley.

"I told them I am bound by privacy laws and couldn't tell them anything about your condition," said Mr. Schmeider. "That's why I'm here. I want to know what you would like to do about the situation?"

"Are they here now?" asked Miranda.

"No, I sent them away and told them to call in the morning."

"Do they just want to know my condition? If that's all then go ahead and tell them, I don't care."

"They are also hoping to talk to you, to ask you a few questions. But you are not under any obligation to talk to them."

"I don't want to talk to them. You can tell them my medical status. I don't care about that."

"That's what I'll do then. I'll swing by tomorrow morning and check up on you before I talk to them," said Mr. Schmeider. "See you tomorrow."

"Okay, bye," Miranda waved.

"I keep forgetting to ask," Parley said. "How did things turn out for that guy who had cancer?"

"He was in terrible agony when we were rescued. He looked like he was going to die. He was hospitalized for just one night. They were finally able to get his pain under control and they got him back on track for his chemotherapy."

"What about the guy with the broken leg?"

"They kept him in the hospital until this morning. I guess that means he's doing all right."

"I just had an idea. . .What do you think about having that Administrator guy, Schmeider, tell all the reporters to go to our web sites and they can see our videos. They can ask questions through the blogs. We can post my condition daily until interest wears off. It might help promote our blogs, what do ya think?"

"Sweetie. That's a great idea. With all of the narcotic's you're on and you still have that golden touch."

"I am starting to get tired. If you're up to it, could you write a post on my injuries and post it. Or, well, I guess it can wait until tomorrow."

"I can get that article written. There's nothing else to do here."

Within three minutes Parley was asleep only to be awakened a half hour later by a nurse who needed to listen to his heart and take his blood pressure. *Geez, the hospital is not a place to be if you want to rest.* Parley was able to go back to sleep.

The next morning Miranda talked to Mr. Schmeider and gave him both URL's. Parley was making great headway. They took him off morphine drip and put him on pain pills. The pain was being well-managed which was a good sign the doctors said. They expected to release him the following day.

A little more than two days had passed since telling the reporters they could get all the information they needed from their blogs. Miranda checked out the visitor statistics of their blogs. She was astounded to see a jump in views to the tune of almost one and a half million views. After Parley got back from getting one last set of x-rays, she told Parley the great news. He wanted to see the stats himself. She looked it up and put her laptop on his lap. She refreshed the screen and now the daily views were just less than two million. They checked Miranda's site to see over two million views. They realized some people watched the video several times, but considering it was a long video they figured most people wouldn't watch the whole thing more than a few times.

"This is so awesome. I would have never dreamed of anything like this. If we're careful and do a lot of followup posting, we might get a big chunk of these viewers to be regular followers." Parley gave a satisfied smile.

"This could be another major stepping stone for our web sites. Maybe we can look into increasing our ad rates if we can keep a bunch of these visitors," added Miranda.

"This could be huge."

A few hours later the doctor gave him the go ahead to be discharged.

Chapter Three: A Time To Sow

To every thing there is a season, and a time to every purpose under the heaven. . . a time to sow, and a time to harvest and a time to build up. The Preacher

June 2008
Lake Shaft, Wyoming

Looking out over the shimmering still waters of Lake Shaft, Parley noticed the breathtaking horizon of the rising and falling water on the smooth beach. Beyond the waterline was a wooded forest with scattered switch grass and wild flowers in the foreground. Tall spruce and maple trees along with a smattering of aspen trees provided the dramatic background, framed by a soft blue sky and calm reflective blue water.

It was a tranquil morning with only three fish in his cooler. The fish were large, but three fish after four hours of fishing was considered a slow day for him. He didn't care. This morning was turning into a transcendent morning. For as long as he could remember, Parley always found himself impressed with the grandeur of God's creations. These dramatic scenes of natures beauty created the greatest cathedrals known to man.

Parleys' dad took him and his older brother Nick fishing all the time when they were young. As they held their fishing poles in their hands and surveyed the serenity of the woods from the vantage point of the fishing boat, his dad taught them about Gods grand creations of nature and man. It was easy to believe in a benevolent God when one was taught with the loving kindness of a caring father in the middle of Wyoming's garden of Eden.

Not only was this view breathtaking, Parley could just detect the faint smells of cedar and pine wafting over the water a hundred yards away, another reason that this was Gods country. This remote area was free from any type of pollution. This was a place where you could not only see some of the best forest in the world but you could still smell it. You could almost taste the thick, rich smells of the forest. It was nature's harmony at its best.

Parleys' tranquility was disrupted by a sudden jerk on his fishing pole. He was quickly brought back to reality with a fish tugging on his line.   As he was landing the large rainbow trout, his cell phone began to ring. By the time his fish was secured in the cooler, it stopped ringing. He cast his line out for a chance at another big fish. Hopefully a record breaker. He sat back in his captains chair trying to adjust his five-foot eleven inch frame. *I need to get a better chair.* He was mesmerized as he gazed at the tall cottonwoods across the channel in a nearby forest. He was stunned for the thousandth time at the quaking leaves of the aspen trees. It only took the gentlest breeze to make those leaves quake and flutter.

His phone rang again bringing him out of his deep contemplative mood.

"Hello?"

"Hey sweetie, how's the fishing?" asked Miranda.

"Just pulled in my fourth fish of the morning."

"Little slow today?"

"Yeah, a little."

"Bert called me because you didn't answer your phone. Art Nance came down from Willow Creek looking for you. He spoke to your Dad and Nick. He told them the owner of the Willow Creek Resort wants to honor you for saving the lives of his employees and guests."

"Really? Why? That's. . .I'm not the hero type– "

"You saved thirty-five people, that's heroic."

"Come on, we've talked about that. I could have kept everyone fed and warm until the spring thaw. It was only for the cancer guy and the broken leg guy that I went down that canyon."

"It doesn't matter. Anyway you look at it, you saved lives and that makes you a hero."

Knowing he wasn't going to win the argument, Parleys' dark brown eyebrows arched as he sighed. He ran his hand through his wavy dark brown hair. Even though he didn't want to admit it, technically she was right. He had saved two lives and saving anyone is a heroic thing. He took a deep breath, "So what else did Art have to say?"

"They wanted to invite us and some of our family and friends to their resort on the Fourth of July for an all day celebration in your honor. They are hoping to invite all the people you saved back to the resort to help celebrate."

"We can't do that. It's Independence Day, our biggest holiday of the year."

"That's what Bert and Nick told him."

"So what did Art say?"

"Well. . .That's where the story gets interesting. They really want to honor you, but they also want to use the whole thing as a publicity event for their resort. So Art is going to see if the owners are flexible enough to do something at our resort."

"When will we know what they say?"

"That, I don't know, but Art is still here and your Dad wants you to come back now and help him deal with it."

"Since the fishing isn't all that great. . . I guess I can come back."

"Good. Bert wants me there as well, so I'll meet you at the Café. Love you sweetie."

"I love you too, babe." Parley put his phone back into his pocket and took one last long look at the reflected rays of the sun bouncing off the endless ripples of water that made up the surface of a calm lake. He reeled in his line and stowed everything away while making a note to himself to start blogging about the breathtaking scenery of the lake and surrounding forest. He realized it was odd after all these years of blogging he seldom wrote about the lake itself and all its beauty. The vast majority of his writings were about hunting, fishing, hiking, camping and boating, but not about the lake itself or the surrounding forest.

As he was making his way to the dock, he squinted to cover his coffee brown eyes from the air as it whipped pass his face. He had forgotten his sunglasses. As he made his way, he reflected about his blog and how successful it had been. He was able to make a lot of money through advertising. The blog had been helpful to the resort. People came from all over the country and the world to vacation at the resort. He advertised and promoted the Burnrise Family Resort on his blog for free. It was payback for his parents allowing him and Miranda to work for them while they got their preferred career underway as writers.

He had a responsibility to provide for his family and he had a responsibility to his parents and his brother in the way of the family business. He was pulling up to the dock and saw Nick waiting for him.

Nick helped Parley unload his fresh catch of the day. Miranda didn't need the fish so they took them to the Café kitchen. "Any word from Art about that silly award?"

"Not yet," Nick responded, "but when I walked out here a few minutes ago Art was on the phone with his boss."

"So what are going to do? Are we just going to have our monthly meeting at eleven?"

"As far as I know. Hank and Rita are on their way. Dad will want to hear what Art's bosses have to say. We'll need to make a few adjustments if they agree to honor you here."

"I don't really like the idea of an award. We always emphasize the military and the veterans when we celebrate Independence Day. I'm not a vet and this isn't a military honor," Parley protested.

"You're right, but it is still a heroic thing you did. You deserve this honor."

"Hey boys, Art just got off the phone with his boss and they have agreed to make the presentation here, during the festival on opening day."

Parley was glad to see Art and went over to shake his hand. They sat down for a cup of coffee. Art proceeded to tell Parley about the honor they wanted him to have for his help in rescuing everyone from the snow storm. They thought there was eighteen feet of fresh snow, but experts later said twenty-five feet of snow had fallen on the mountain. The avalanche buried Parley in twelve feet of snow.

Parley and Art were interrupted by Miranda. "It's so good so see you Art," Miranda said as Art jumped to his feet and met Miranda for a friendly hug.

"Art, let me introduce you to two of our closest friends. Art, this is Hank and Rita Standing Elk. Hank and Rita, meet Art. He is the resort manager we told you about."

They all shook hands and exchanged greetings. Hank and Parley had been friends since they were in elementary school.

Bert came by and interrupted their reunion to remind them it was time for their Board of Directors meeting at eleven. Earlier Art had been invited to spend the night at their resort rather than drive back to Montana all in one day so he excused himself and they made plans to meet for dinner at the Café.

They held their Board of Directors meeting in the back room. The Burnrise Family Resort was a five-generation family business. Each generation had left its mark on the family business. One of Bert's legacies was organizing it into a corporation. Bert and Betty, the parents, were the majority stockholders and their sons Nick and Parley along with their wives were also stock holders. That meant their Board of Directors consisted of six people. They wanted an odd number for voting reasons, so they invited Parleys' best friend, Hank Standing Elk, to sit on the board with a minor stock ownership. Hanks wife, Rita, served as their corporate lawyer and she attended all the meetings.

Hank ran a medical clinic on the Washakie reservation as an Advanced Registered Nurse Practitioner, ARNP. Rita ran a legal aid office on the reservation. They were considered family by the Burnrises.

They held monthly board meetings to cover all corporate business, plan for the upcoming month, and assess their yearly goals among other things. The majority of the June meeting was to prepare for the upcoming Independence Day holiday. The fourth of July was their biggest holiday. They were a very patriotic family. Bert was a decorated Marine and POW during the Vietnam Conflict. Nick and Parley never served in the military. Parley tried to enlist only to be turned down for medical reasons. He had two pins in his leg. Nick married very young.

Parley had given up his objections about the Willow Creek honor and went along with everything they said. Their meeting lasted for three hours and turned into a lunch meeting. After the meeting finally ended, Parley slipped away to work on his blog. He needed to edit a few videos and write a few articles. He also needed to come up with an outline for all the work he needed to do for videotaping the entire four-day Independence day celebration. Bert, Nick and Parley, were all responsible for one separate fishing derby during the four-day celebration. They would all work together for one major fishing tournament as well. He was hard at work when his concentration was shattered by his cell phone ringing.

Miranda was calling him to remind Parley about their dinner appointment with Art. The kids and Art were all waiting at their table. Parley was there in less than five minutes. He had been on the go since five in the morning putting in twelve hours so far. By the time they were done with dinner and many fish stories from Parley and his son Ted, Art was very interested to try the fishing on Lake Shaft. Ted and Emily were twins and very much alike with one major exception. Emily hated fishing. She hated the smell and she hated the taste of fish, but she did like to hunt.

They all went on the families big boat except Emily. She went over to her grandparents' house and spent the evening with them. Everyone else enjoyed an evening of fishing. Between the four of them, they pulled in twelve big trout and four large mouth bass.

"I like the name you gave your boat," said Art. "The Family Boat." The name of The Family Boat was painted on the side of the boat near the back end in a shade of orange paint.

"We get a lot of comments on the name. It suits us well," responded Parley.

Lake Shaft was fed by spring runoff, three rivers and hundreds of natural springs. Many of those springs were hot mineral water springs which cause the deep lake to offer some shallow warm water areas perfect for bass and a lot of cold deep water perfect for trout.

It had been a typical day for Parley although he didn't go on a guided fishing trip that day because of the business meeting. Long days didn't bother Parley, in fact, the busier the better was one of Parleys' mottos.

Once Parley relaxed in bed, he quickly dropped off to sleep at one minute past midnight. It was a long day for Parley. Fourteen hour days were normal. An eighteen to twenty hour day during the summer wasn't unusual.

Chapter Four: The Fishing Eagle

I see God in the wooded hills and the rolling ocean waves.
I see God in the faces of the young and in the wrinkles of the old.
I see God in the ripples of the pond and the majestic mountain
peaks.
I see God in the little things you do.
CallahanWriter

June 2008
Lake Shaft, Wyoming

Parley was finally on the lake and situated just south of
Volcano Island. He was agitated for getting a late start on the day.
After taking a deep breath to calm himself, he took a breath and
focused on getting his cameras ready and everything set up. He
watched the gentle morning breeze cause the leaves on the nearby
aspen trees to quake. In spite of him playing catch up all morning,
the breathtaking scenes surrounding him were powerful enough to
slow him down as he caught glimpses of the surrounding beauty of
nature.

He finally got his fishing pole ready to cast into the gently
lapping waters of Lake Shaft. It was a good day to go fishing. As his
hook faded into the water, so did his guilt of sleeping in. Normally
he was on the water around six o'clock in the morning.

It was unusual to have his body betray him like it had this
morning. When the alarm went off at five, his body wouldn't
respond. Miranda gave him a good shove and told him to turn off
his alarm. All Parley remembered of that morning was the shock to
see his alarm clock displaying 6:30 a.m. Somehow, he lost an hour
and a half. He was late. He jumped out of bed and rushed down to
the lake.

He had been so frantic in getting dressed and out on the
water that it wasn't until he settled in with his line cast that he
started to realize he was feeling a little under the weather. Parley

was never sick. It took him a while to recognize a dull achy sensation in his lower back. As he focused on the discomfort in his lower back, he could trace that unusual feeling to his hips and thighs. He wondered if he was sick or hurt? He didn't feel like he had a cold or flu, but his muscles in his lower back, hips and thighs seemed to be experiencing a dull ache. He couldn't remember the last time he had been sick. All that he could be sure of was that he didn't feel his usual one hundred percent. He shrugged off the uncomfortable feeling.

He looked out at the nearby shoreline with the water rhythmically bringing up shallow waves and dropping them on the beach. The morning smell of the wet loam of the nearby forest wafted out to greet him. The cawing of nearby seagulls caught his attention. He looked to the northern sky over the island and saw several seagulls dashing and darting through the air as they seemed to be playing an aerial game of tag. Parley thought about his life and how blessed he was, being able to earn a living in the great outdoors. *Life doesn't get much better than this.*

Suddenly he felt the tip of his pole bend and the fishing line grew taut. Catching a fish made a good life better. Parley gladly threw his thick, 185 pound frame into catching the first fish of the morning. *It doesn't get better than this. . .*

In less than three hours he had caught his daily trout limit. He still had time before he was due back at the docks. He called Miranda to see if she would like any bass or catfish. She did. He drew up his anchor and went to a warm, shallow part of the lake. He dropped his anchor and within minutes the cameras were ready and his baited hook had sunk to the bottom of the lake.

Lake Shaft was a deep lake. The average depth in the main parts of the lake was eighty-one feet. Some places had been measured at more than one hundred and twenty feet.

Parley was feeling sluggish. Within a half hour he had two catfish and one largemouth. As he put his line out again, he had a thought cutting his trip short and go back to the resort. He couldn't remember ever cutting a fishing trip short. Many a time he would limit out and stay on the water to read or he would motor around the lake to take landscape photos. Today, something was off in the way he was feeling. It was confusing because he was never ill. He couldn't remember how it felt to be sick.

His back and hips felt like they were on fire from the inside out. The throbbing sensation radiated into his thighs. He found himself rubbing the palm of his hand into his thigh trying to get some relief. *This is weird. Where did this pain come from?*

It occurred to him that there might be some aspirin or Tylenol in the first aid kit he kept in his fishing boat. He discovered both aspirin and Tylenol. However, the aspirin was two years past its expiration date. Luckily the Tylenol was still current. He dry swallowed two pills. *What have I done to injure my back and legs?* After thinking about it, he could find no reason for the pain.

How long will it take for the medicine to kick in? He pulled out his thermos and poured himself a cup of coffee. He settled back in his captain's chair and let his mind drift away. The memory of meeting his wife in journalism school came to mind. His heart skipped a beat when he reminisced about their first few dates.

He hadn't had a nibble in almost an hour and was wondering if he should pack it all in for the day or try one more spot. He put his coffee cup back on the thermos when he heard the distant sound of a hawk overhead. He quickly grabbed his handheld camera. He had tried for more than twenty years to get the perfect footage of a hawk or eagle catch a fish and fly away. He had seen the spectacular occurrence many times, but he had never been able to catch it on film.

He was looking into the sky through the viewfinder of his video camera in the direction of the screeching hawk. Parley saw a big bird flying in narrowing circles. *This has to be him*. Parley pressed record. The bird started his gradual descent as its circles grew smaller. Then suddenly he realized that he had a bald eagle in his sight. *Wow! A bald eagle. Oh-my-gosh! A bald eagle. Don't lose it Parley, don't you lose it.*

The eagle started his descent in earnest. It was heading straight down. As it grew closer to the water Parley was able to determine that it was a fully mature eagle, a massive bird. The king of the sky. So far, so good. He had the eagle in his sights. Suddenly there was a splash and out of that splash were two large feet of the bird with its talons firmly gripping a big lake trout, or was it a rainbow? No matter, he could zoom in later to see what kind of fish it was. He caught the bald eagle flying off to the west over the island. *I did it! Yes, yes! I did it!* He was almost positive he got it all on in the frame. He was going to play it back and check when his attention was drawn to his blending fishing pole. He reeled in a seven-pound catfish.

He watched the video from beginning to end and verified that it was all in frame and the entire sequence was filmed. He went back to fishing and daydreaming. It wasn't until he started back to the resort that he realized the Tylenol wasn't helping the pain. The pain in his back steadily inched up his spine invading the other muscles. He could feel a deep pulsing sensation in the small of his back. The agony made him worry that if he bent over his spine would snap. In spite of this painful flare up, he was in a good mood. This was one of his better fishing trips in recent memory. Some random achiness wasn't going to bother him.

His cell phone rang. It was Miranda. He was anxious to tell her the big news about finally getting complete video of an eagle catching a fish on Lake Shaft.

"Hey babe."

"Hi sweetie, I got some awesome news."

"So do I, but you called so you go first."

"I just got off the phone with a TV producer from TAN."

"What's TAN?"

"True Americana Network."

"That sounds vaguely familiar. What is it?"

"It's a cable network. They specialize in TV shows and movies that celebrate Americana."

"So what did the producer have to say?"

"This is the big news," Miranda said excitedly. "The producer saw my blog and she noticed how we frequently cross post when I cook the fish you have caught that day or the game you hunt. She looked over both of our blogs and came up with an idea about using that format to create a TV reality show for their network."

Parley felt himself get excited as he had a feeling where this was going, but he didn't want to get his hopes up.

"So what does this all mean exactly?"

"The producer wants to talk to us about creating a pilot episode to present to the network executives. She's hoping it could become part of their line up."

"That sounds incredible."

"So, when are you going to be done fishing?" asked Miranda.

"I'm on my way back right now."

"How about we meet at café for a late breakfast?"

"Yes. Great idea. See you in about twenty minutes."

Parley was on his way back to his private slip when he realized he hadn't mentioned his video to Miranda. *Oh well, a chance to be on TV, that may be more important than his fishing eagle video.* He was glad that he didn't have one of his guided fishing tours scheduled. He was anxious to get all the details from Miranda.

Three hours later, Miranda and Parley were on a phone call with Sue Rigby, the producer with TAN. Sue explained that before the network executives would approve the show they would need to film a pilot episode and see what kind of response they got from their audience.

Parley and Miranda agreed to film the pilot. They also told Sue about Lake Shaft and the Burnrise Family Resort and the big upcoming Independence Day holiday. Miranda also mentioned the award Parley was getting.

Sue thought the Independence Day weekend would be the ideal background for the pilot. Miranda and Parley knew that trying to make a pilot during the middle of their most hectic four days of the year would be tough, but they were not afraid of the challenge.

This Independence Day was going to be a six-day affair since the fourth of July fell on a Friday. The crew from TAN was coming in on the evening of June 30 to get acquainted and to assess the lay of the land. The Burnrises had three house boats for rent and they also kept a private family owned house boat. They would put the crew from the network up in their private house boat. They were prepared to bend over backwards for the crew hoping to do everything possible to win them over for a series. As luck would have it, both Parley and Miranda had a light load for the first three days of the festivities and they planned on doing a lot of filming with the crew on those days.

Chapter Five: A Big Day

Two are better than one; because they have a good reward for their labor. For if they fall, the one will lift up his fellow: but woe to him that is alone when he falleth; for he hath not another to help him up. And if one prevail against him, two shall withstand him; and a threefold cord is not quickly broken. The Preacher

Independence Day Weekend 2008
Lake Shaft, Wyoming

Parleys' alarm came crashing down on his dreams. He was roused back into reality. The recurring dream of catching a world record trout was put on hold for another night. As Parley was fumbling around to turn off his alarm he felt a strange sensation. As he tried to get out of bed, he tried to figure out what he was feeling. He had a headache. His neck felt achy, thick and stiff. He felt groggy and unrefreshed and wondered if he was feeling sick? Parley was a morning person and normally got out of bed easily. Not today. He felt stiff all over.

"Are you all right sweetie?" Miranda has sprung out of bed with her usually vitality.

"No."

"What's wrong?"

"I don't know. I'm stiff and achy, all over," Parley stretched his arms and let out a deep moan as he tried to work through the strange sensations.

"My body doesn't seem to want to get out of bed" sighed Parley.

Miranda was surprised and concerned. Parley had boundless energy. He was always strong and reliable. *How can Parley be sick? He's never sick.*

"I'll shower first," Miranda said anxiously. "That'll give you a few more minutes to wake up. Maybe whatever is bugging you will go away when you get up and move around. We can't be late for our big day."

"Miranda, what does it feel like to have the flu?"

"What do you mean? Like a head cold or stomach flu?"

"Both or either, I don't know. I'm feeling achy and gross all over. I feel. . ." Parley was struggling to find the word to describe how he was feeling. "It's like I feel an achy thickness in my neck and spine all the way down to my lower back and hips. Is that the flu?"

"It could be, maybe. The last time I had the flu I felt achy all over, especially in the neck and shoulders" answered Miranda as she made her way to the shower.

"I don't feel like I have any energy." Miranda could hear the frustration in Parleys' voice.

"Are you going to be able to make it to work today?"

"Wild horses couldn't keep me away. Nothing can get in the way of today. Maybe a cup of coffee will perk me up?"

Both Parley and Miranda were the type of people with energy to burn. For Parley, working sixteen to eighteen hours a day in the summer season wasn't unusual. They could both put in a twelve or fourteen-hour day and find the energy and motivation to take the kids water skiing, fishing, or hiking, at the end of the day. For Parley to complain about his health was almost humorous because he didn't know how to feel sick. He had been sidelined from injuries and broken bones, but he couldn't remember being sick. Growing up, Parley had never missed a day in school from sickness.

Parley was still feeling groggy and out of sorts as they were pulling into the resort parking lot That concerned Parley. He was always feeling strong and healthy.

Parley and Miranda went into the café and saw Bert, Betty and Nick already sitting down at their table with Sue, Holly and Adam from the cable network. Once their introductions were made, they scanned the menu and ordered before engaging in conversation. As they were getting to know each other breakfast arrived. The conversation slowed as they started to eat.

"I noticed this 'Betty's Worlds Famous Hot Chocolate' on the menu last night," said Holly as she held her mug in her hands, "I thought I'd order it this morning. I'm so glad I did. It's spectacular. No wonder it's world famous."

"It is fantastic," Adam said to emphasize every word. "I've never tasted anything like this."

"Oh poop. I ordered Coffee." Sue was disappointed. "Now I want to taste this hot chocolate after all that raving." Betty slipped away quietly and within two minutes returned with an empty mug. She put it down before Sue, filling it with the mysterious hot cocoa. She put the pitcher of hot chocolate down near Holly and Adam.

"There you go," Betty said. "I am rather proud of this family recipe."

Sue picks up her cup and blows on the rich dark creamy liquid. She takes a sip and then another followed by one more. "This is spectacular. Thank you so much Betty for getting me some of this, this heavenly brew. I've never drunk anything so good. Oh, this is good."

The breakfast meeting was nearly over and they all agreed they would film at least two or more segments of Parley fishing and Miranda cooking the fish. They also wanted to film as much of Parley and Miranda's involvement with the Independence Day Festival throughout the weekend. Sue suggested there was potential for an additional segment or separate documentary on the resort. Which would likely include footage from the weekend celebration. That would be in addition to the catching and cooking idea they were there to pursue.

As they were breaking up their meeting and going off in their different directions to prepare for the day Parley went by the outfitter store and picked up a bottle of aspirin and Tylenol. *I hope these are strong enough to help with all this achy soreness.*

Sue decided she wanted at least one fishing trip to include both Miranda and Parley fishing together. They used to fish together frequently, then when the kids came, they weren't able to fish together as much. They set Miranda and Parley up with a clip on microphones and earpieces. Holly went with Parley and Miranda while Sue and Adam would be on the second boat filming.

They were told to act naturally and be conversational. Holly was there to ask questions and direct the conversation. Since Parley and Miranda had filmed hundreds of videos in the past, Sue was comfortable with how they would respond talking to a camera. As they were passing Volcano Island on their way to the first fishing spot, Holly asked Parley about the Island.

"Volcano Island is the top of an ancient volcano. We have a lot of natural springs around here. Many of them feed Lake Shaft along with the snow melt and the three rivers. The volcano heats up a lot of the underground water, creating a lot of natural hot springs."

They say it is an active volcano because of the way it heats up so much of the underground spring water. A few of the shorelines around volcano Island are made up of volcanic rock and there are a few decent beaches as well.

The natural hot springs that drain into Lake Shaft creates a very unique fishery. The lake is deep and cold, which is great for trout, but the warm, shallow parts of the lake are great for bass and catfish. This allows the lake to provide a large range of freshwater fish.

Parley paused to catch his breath and sip on some coffee. It was perfect timing because their fishing poles both got a strike within a few seconds of each other. They were good size trout and put up a good fight. Soon they each had a big lake trout splashing and bouncing on the bottom of the boat.

After their lines were back out in the deep lake, Miranda asked Parley how he was feeling. She had noticed him wincing and letting out a few moans when he was reeling in his fish.

"I'm not feeling too good," he said, "that achiness from this morning is still bothering me. The Tylenol seems to help a little, but not completely." Parley shook his head, "I can't seem to shake it."

"Maybe you have the flu," Miranda suggested.

"Sounds like the flu to me," said Holly.

"Nonsense, I never get the flu."

"How is that possible? Everyone gets the flu at least occasionally," remarked Holly.

"Not me."

"That's true," agreed Miranda, "but, if it's not the flu, then what is it? What's causing you to feel so lousy? Is it all pain or are you having any other symptoms?"

"That's a good question. I've been trying to ignore it, whatever it is. I feel achy, I have a headache. . .But no sore throat, no upset stomach and I'm not at all dizzy."

Miranda and Holly were both perplexed at what Parley might have. Then out of nowhere Miranda shouted excitedly, "I got one! I got another fish!"

"Set the line. . .Good job, good job. . .Work it on in here. There you go. . . You got it."

An hour later, the two of them had caught 14 fish to the tune of about thirty pounds. Sue was commenting through their two-ways about all the great footage they had.

"Holly, how much longer do you want us to stay out?" asked Miranda as she noticed how miserable Parley looked. Holly talked back and forth with Sue. Sue joined the conversation asking Miranda, "how many fish do you need for your recipe?"

"I have more than enough to cook for you and your crew along with my extended family."

"How about we boat around the lake for a little while and film some of this spectacular scenery before we go in?"

"Sounds good. Want to follow us?" asked Parley.

"Lead the way," answered Sue.

Two hours later they were back at the resort and Miranda was cooking up a storm with Adam filming her every move. Holly acted as Miranda's assistant. Miranda was tearing up a storm with her stage presence. Her energy was intimidating to Holly. The camera loved her every move. Parley had to attend to some last minute details for his fishing derby in three days. He was annoyed with his body because he wasn't use to being impaired by poor health. He hadn't paid this much attention to his body in more than ten years. Except for a few months ago when he had to take some time to recuperate from his broken arms and ribs in the snowmobile accident. He felt fatigue come along to join the aches and pains.

There were enough fish to film two cooking sessions. Holly

was interviewing Miranda as she cooked. Some questions were about her recipe or technique. Other questions were about Miranda to even out the footage. "When did you realize you wanted to be a chef?" asked Holly.

"Ever since I was a little girl I loved to cook and thought I wanted to be a chef until I took some cooking classes. I decided that being a chef wasn't as much fun as I thought it would be. I still wanted to make a living with food and figured out that I could write about food. I had many articles published in food related magazines. But it wasn't until I started to blog that I really hit my stride with these cooking videos."

"Do you compete with any of these original recipes?"

"I have, but not too much. My blog and my work at the resort keep me busy. I do judge a lot of competitions around Lake Shaft and around the state."

Holly snuck a taste of one the trout recipes and by the time she finished praising the taste, she thought she may have gone overboard and didn't sound too professional. *They can always edit that part out.*

A few hours later they all gathered around three big tables under the first pavilion to eat the fish feast Miranda had prepared from the day's catch. Sue had several cameras set up around the pavilion to catch several angles of the crowd eating these gourmet recipes. Sue was partially amused and partially impressed that Bert took charge of the gathering and started the family dinner off by saying grace. *It just might add some flavor to the show.*

The next day Parley went fishing without Miranda. It was a successful trip in spite of how crappy Parley felt. He managed to catch his limit in less than two hours. Once the fishing was done and delivered to Miranda, Adam and Parley went back out on the lake. Parley took Adam on a guided fishing trip so Adam could catch some fish. They filmed this expedition with Parleys' cameras since it wasn't anything Sue was interested in. Both Parley and Nick acted as fishing guides for hire several days a week during the summer months. They were also hunting guides in the fall and spring. Adam was in for a great surprise. He caught his limit of trout in three hours. They went over to some shallow water and both caught a few catfish before coming back in.

Parley wasn't anxious to receive the award and have the spotlight shining on just him, but Adam made sure they got back in plenty of time for the award ceremony.

Sue was anxious to film Parley receiving an honor from the Willow Creek Resort for saving all those lives. She felt like it would add to the sales pitch she would make to the executives. Having a bonafide hero, who has a very successful outdoors blog that partners with his wife's very successful cooking blog and then this wonderful resort providing the perfect backdrop for TV series. She had high hopes and a lot of confidence in her idea for this show.

Sue was amazed at the level of energy required for Parley and Miranda to keep up such hectic pace balancing their blogging career with the demands of their responsibilities with the resort and family. While interacting with Miranda and Parley, Sue picked up on a major underlying attitude they both seem to share and that was their kids and a strong sense of family. She was looking forward to meeting their two children this afternoon at the award ceremony. She was told that they were thirteen years old and twins. A boy/girl set of twins. She wondered what a couple of young teenagers from a small town in Wyoming would look like. How would they behave?

Parley was constantly on the go. Just the way he normally liked it. "The busier the better," he always said. That was until now. This flu-like thing was weighing him down. He was beside himself. He felt groggy or some kind of fatigue. He seemed at ache all over and he couldn't seem to shake it. It was unfamiliar territory and he was grateful he had the energy to work through the flu or whatever ever it was.

With Adam in tow, Parley made his way from the back room where he had just washed up, to the pavilion where the ceremony was being held. He met up with Miranda, Ted and Emily. Parley was embarrassed and shocked at how the pavilion was decorated. There was a small platform with a podium on it. The TAN cameras were set up. Parley and Miranda both had been involved in similar events through promoting their blogs over the years, but they were not the featured guests, just part of the various programs. The fact that the spotlight would be focused solely on Parley made him feel uncomfortable. He was by nature an unassuming man who was willing to promote their web sites. But that's where it ended. He understood the need for promotion, but this was honoring him. There was always a fine line he tried not to cross, trying to keep his personal life private from his public life that was displayed on the many videos posted on his blog.

He had agreed to the ceremony as a means of publicity for their blogs. But the way things were set up, he felt it had crossed the line by a country mile.

Nick stepped onto the stage and called for everyone's attention. The crowd quickly responded and many took a seat. There was standing room only under the pavilion.

"On behalf of the Burnrise Family Resort, I am honored to welcome you all here. We're gathered here at the request of Art Nance, the manager of Willow Creek Resort in Montana. You are all aware of my brothers heroic rescue of the guests and employees of the resort in that massive blizzard in February. The owners of the resort wanted to honor Parley for what he did. So, please welcome Art Nance."

Nick's introduction was followed by a hardy round of applause. Art took the stage and stood behind the podium. He joined in the applause and gestured his clapping hands at Parley.

"Thank you all for coming here and supporting your local hero. On behalf of the owners of Willow Creek Resort I am here to honor Parley Burnrise with an award for his heroic rescue of the thirty-four guests and employees. If you haven't already, you can go to his web site, OutdoorParley.com and watch a video of his harrowing and heroic run down that dangerous canyon. He was willing to sacrifice his life for people he didn't even know. I guess that's what makes Parley a real hero– "

The crowd applauded in agreement with what Art had said. Parley surprised himself by blushing. Miranda put her arms around Parley and gave him a big hug. Emily joined in the hug. Ted awkwardly patted Parley on the back. Bert and Betty were standing on the other side of the pavilion. They joined in with the applause. They beamed with pride.

When the applause died down, Art asked Parley to join him on the stage. As Parley made the short walk, the crowd erupted with another round of applause. *This isn't right. I don't deserve this applause.* Parley rubbed the muscles in the small of his back to try and relieve some of the throbbing that was radiating up and down his back.

Art began to address the audience again. "There was substantial damage done to the hotel, enough to require considerable construction work. When it is completed in late August or the first of September, the owners are going to name the refurbished building after Parley Burnrise. There will be a plaque in the foyer that is an exact duplicate of the plaque shown here." When he said that, the cover that was draped over a stand was drawn away, revealing a rich cherry wood plaque embellished with a large inscribed bronze plate on one side and a picture of Parley on the other side. The crowd gave another round of applause.

Art went on to tell the group what was on the plaque. "The story of his rescue is described at the top. Below that are the names of everyone he rescued." Parley was embarrassed by the award and the applause. "Additionally, here is a binder that contains letters of thanks written to Parley by everyone that was at the resort when he made that dangerous run down the mountain."

For the first time since the ceremony started, Parley went from being embarrassed too being touched. Art handed Parley the binder. "Lastly," said Art as he handed an envelope to Parley, "here is an all expense-paid voucher for you and your family to any of the Willow Creek properties in North America."

As those that were gathered gave one last round of applause to Parley, Art shook Parleys' hand. He was followed by Miranda and the kids coming to the stage to congratulate Parley. Meanwhile, the TAN cameras were rolling and Sue Rigby was feeling like she had discovered a gold mine. *The executives are going to eat this up. Look at those kids, clean cut and proud of their father. You don't see that much anymore.*

Finally, after a long and exhausting three days, it was Independence Day, Parleys' favorite holiday after Christmas and the single biggest and busiest day of the six-day celebration. Parley was dragging everywhere he went. It was the one day they didn't go fishing. The day got off to an early start with a formal flag raising ceremony. That was followed by an early morning breakfast buffet. There were non stop activities all day long. Parley was wishing he was on the boat. At least that way his feet wouldn't be full of burning, prickling pins and needles. He was very confused and very sick. *How can the flu hurt my feet? Maybe I don't have the flu, maybe I should think about going to the doctor when this is over?*

He didn't know how to deal with this flu bug or whatever it was. He didn't have experience being sick. He tried taking a lot of over-the-counter medicines. The only thing that made sense was to crawl in bed and rest, but that would have to wait for another day, maybe another life time.

The fourth of July was one event after another. This day was being filmed because Sue thought it would help sell the series even though it wasn't directly related to fishing, hunting and cooking between Miranda and Parley. Sue was hoping she could manage a network special or a documentary on the Burnrise Family Resort in addition to the reality show they were working on.

Everyone one was looking forward to the evening. The Burnrise patriotic celebration was known throughout the region. People had been pouring in all day long anxiously waiting the evenings patriotic pomp and circumstance. There would be a full military color guard to retire the flag, followed by an Army Reserve brass band putting on a concert. The concert would be followed by a patriotic fireworks display with patriotic music blaring from massive speaker system placed all around the grounds. Part of the show included pyrotechnics on the lake.

Parley had some alone time for the first time all day. He was resting in his unfolded chair waiting for the fireworks and noticed the camera wasn't on him. It had been both fun and stressful being followed by a camera for four days. He didn't mind a camera on him for a few hours in the morning when he went fishing, but all day long? Even though there were more than a thousand people spilling out over the grounds and on boats near the shore, he felt like his privacy had been restored. *I hate the flu, or being sick. I can't believe I am looking forward to some down time.* He was brought out of his thoughts when he heard the first whistling sounds of sky rockets shooting through the air exploding above, with red and blue colors cascading from the night sky. Then the sounds of the first patriotic song filled the air. From then on, the music and the fireworks were synchronized.

It was a festival for the senses. The strains of patriotic fervor filled the air with breathtaking explosions overhead and the smell of black powder from the exploded fireworks. The excitement in the crowd was palpable.

After the grand finale Parley remained seated while everyone else got up and proceeded to the campgrounds or the nearest exit. Parley felt strange and out of sorts. Normally he would be up and mingling with his many friends and customers. Now all he could do was respond to his body's demand for rest. His feet were sending signals to his brain to stay off of his feet. He felt like he was being held hostage by his body and their selfish demands. Twenty minutes later he was approached by Sue.

"I have seen thousands of firework shows in my life, but I can't remember a more spectacular one than what I saw tonight. I was. . .It was. . . Well, spectacular."

"The Burnrise family has always been patriotic. The Fourth of July is our family holiday. . .Not to mention that it's always been a big summertime promotional for the resort. The fireworks have become a great investment."

"This whole resort thing that your family has going on here is the epitome of Americana. I'm going to make a presentation with all this video we have for another show. Maybe it would be a documentary or maybe another reality type show. But it would feature your resort and all the things you offer, all the activities you folks do throughout the summer and throughout the year. Your family has done a remarkable job building up this venue like you have."

Chapter Six: Lost

For what hath man of all his labour, and of the vexation of his heart, wherein he hath labored under the sun? For all his days are sorrows, and his travail grief. The Preacher

January 2009
Lake Shaft City, Wyoming

Parley was in the throes of agony. Every muscle in his body was overcome with painful muscle spasms. As the technicians tried to pull his aching body from the stretcher to the solid x-ray table, he was suffering all the more. That table was as hard and cold as a slab of granite.

Why is this happening to me? I'm supposed to be healthy and strong. I need to get up and walk out of here.

"Mr. Burnrise, I need for you to hold your left leg, right here," said the x-ray technician as she moved his left leg into an unnatural and painful position. "Don't move it. . .That's good Mr. Burnrise, hold that position. Take a deep breath and hold it. . .Hold it. . .– " A loud hum and clanking sounds were heard. "Good job, thank you. You can breathe now." *Why do they make it hurt and then expect you to hold your body in such a painful position? How's this going to make me any better?*

Parley went through what seemed like a never-ending series of painful poses for numerous x-rays. He didn't feel like he should be in the Emergency Room, much less be getting all these x-rays, but when Sue Rigby called the ambulance to pick him up, his fate was sealed. He would have rather been driven to town and allowed to call his own doctor rather than go through all the fuss of an ambulance ride and the misadventures of an ER visit.

Parley was the type that didn't care for doctors or hospitals. If his wife or children were seriously hurt and sick beyond his ability to help them, he would rush them to the proper medical care. As for himself, there was seldom anything that was so serious he needed to see a doctor, much less a trip to the hospital.

As they wheeled him back to his room in the ER, he could hear the heavy wheels on the bed clank and rattle as they bounced over uneven seams in the long hallway. He could smell the sterile air with the scents of a disinfectant wafting through the hallways. It seemed so clean and dry. He opened his eyes on the way down the corridor only to be blinded by the bright fluorescent lighting. *If I'm not injured or sick enough, they'll make sure I am by the time they're done with me.*

They pushed his rolling bed through the double doors of the ER. The thud of his bed hitting the doors jarred him ever so slightly, but it was enough to send penetrating shock waves of pain though the core of his legs up into his spine. *Maybe this is the right place for me.*

Miranda reacted to the noise of the doors. "There he is, Parley!" She ran up to his bedside and grabbed his hand, pulling his arm closer to her side of the bed. "Are you okay? What's wrong? Are you in much pain? You don't look very well," Miranda rambled on urgently.

"I don't think I am as bad off as it might seem," replied Parley.

Miranda didn't believe him. She could see the pain and frustration in his eyes. His mouth was saying one thing and his eyes something different.

The nurse got him situated in ER Room 3 where he would wait for the Radiologist to read the x-rays and send the information to the ER doctors. It was a busy night so they expected he would have to wait a while. The nurse asked him if he needed anything while they waited for Radiology to read the x-rays and send the results to the ER doc.

"Coffee, please. I'm cold. I'm freezing down to my bones."

"All right. I'll be right back. I'll get you a couple of warm blankets that we can wrap you in," the nurse added.

"Excuse me nurse, would it be possible to call our family doctor. Dr. Wilson?"

"You're in luck. Dr. Wilson is on call and is in the ER with another patient. I'll tell him you're here."

The nurse brought Parley a cup of coffee and helped him sit up so he could drink it. Parley was miserable and groaned with every movement his muscles made. The pain let up when they stopped adjusting him. He barely had enough strength to sip his coffee. After several sips he was exhausted and laid back and closed his eyes to rest. This overwhelming pain he was experiencing seemed to draw the energy out of him. Or was it the lack of energy causing him to hurt all over? As he was resting, he thought back over the last seven months. It had been a long, miserable and complicated seven months.

After the successful Independence Day celebration, being honored by Willow Creek for his snowmobile rescue, and filming the TAN pilot, he had spent four weeks lying in his bed and his recliner. He was exhausted and he ached over almost all of his body. When the mystery illness first came on, everyone thought it was the common flu bug. But after a full two weeks of bed rest, the doctors ruled out the flu yet they never really figured out what was plaguing him.

The symptoms ebbed and flowed. Frequently he felt he was almost better only to have the symptoms flare up again. He had a lot of agony and hurt in his lower back, hips and legs. Sometimes his feet would flare up in a prickling pain. Sometimes his neck would ache. Headaches were frequent.

August slowly and painfully rolled into September. The True Americana Network was busy getting the pilot ready to air. They decided on a name for the show, From Catch To Plate. Parley and Miranda had no control over the name. They were all right with it. The pilot aired the second week of October and it was a great success. The executives ordered twelve episodes. Thanks to Sue's foresight, they had enough video to make at least one more episode. They had to quickly make plans for nine or ten more segments.

As they had expected, both of their blogs had a big surge in viewers and they also picked up several thousand new followers on each of their blogs. Both of the rescue videos went viral again along with the Fishing Eagle video. Parley was feeling conflicted with his poor health. He had prayed many times for a blessing of good health. He was grateful for the success of the pilot, but wondered why he wasn't being blessed with better health. He hadn't been out fishing in three and a half months, not since the Fourth of July celebration. He hadn't been able to post anything. If it hadn't been for Miranda's willingness to edit some videos from his archives and post them, he wouldn't have had anything for his new visitors to see. Miranda was terribly busy herself with being a mom, working on her own blog career and working with Betty at the resort. Adding Parleys' blog to her responsibilities was pushing Miranda nearly to her limits. She figured she could keep up the pace for a few months. After all, Parley couldn't be sick forever.

Because of the late airing of the pilot, they had missed several of the main big game hunts. By the end of October they had managed to shoot a couple more fishing episodes and an elk hunt. The freezing cold weather was difficult for Parley. He had done many late season frigid hunts throughout his life and the cold never bothered him before. Whatever was bothering him didn't like to be in cold temperatures. Now it was the beginning of November and the needed six more episodes filmed. The problem was that Parley was completely spent. He had no energy and he was in g pain writhing. It made no sense to be in such pain when there wasn't anything wrong with him, according to the several doctors they went to see.

He managed one more hunt just after Thanksgiving. Now they only needed five episodes. Sue was getting worried. They were behind their filming schedule. She was glad of the successful premiere or the executives might have canceled the show given just how far behind they were. She offered to fly Parley to Chicago to see a doctor, but Parley couldn't comprehend getting on a jet he was so miserable. Underneath his outward optimism he felt a sense of foreboding. Whatever was wrong with him was mysterious. The doctors all said there was nothing wrong with him. Besides the pain and fatigue, he didn't feel quite right inside. He didn't know why. He just knew it wasn't right. He had every reason to be positive and no reason to worry about his future. But he was. December rolled around and Parley wasn't able to film anything the entire month.

Now it was January and they had been out filming a pheasant hunt trying to catch up in their filming schedule. His quiet reflection was interrupted when good old Dr. Wilson came strolling into his room.

"Good heavens, my boy, what are you in here for?" asked a friendly old man with thin white whiskers dotting his wrinkled checks and chin. Dr. Wilson was seventy-seven years old and as spire as a younger sixty-year-old.

"I was out filming a pheasant hunt with the TAN crew and started having some kind of seizure in my thighs and lower back. I think it was a seizure. All my muscles seemed to be in a spasm at the same time and then they just gave out. I dropped right where I was standing. Some of the guys had to help me get up."

"How long did that episode last?" asked Dr. Wilson as he jotted a few notes down on Parleys' chart.

"It seemed like forever, I think one of the guys said it was a good five minutes or so. I really don't remember."

Dr. Wilson looked at Miranda. She shrugged her shoulders. "I wasn't out there with them. I was getting ready to film my part, cooking the pheasant, when he got back. Miranda then went on to explain to Dr. Wilson what had been going on since July with the fatigue, the pain and the other symptoms."

"All the specialists said there was nothing wrong with Parley." Dr. Wilson examined Parley and told him that the x-rays were all normal, but given his current pain and his history of the last several months he wanted some more tests done including an expansive blood panel and a CT-scan on his spine. A few minutes later there was a knock on the door.

"Hello Mr. Burnrise. My name is Angie and I need to draw some blood."

"Be careful. I'm in enough pain as it is," replied Parley.

Just as the technician had finished drawing the eighth vile of blood another technician from radiology came in to take him back to radiology for a CT-scan.

Three hours later he was diagnosed with Lumbar Radiculopathy. This diagnosis explained the sharp pain in his lower back, hips and thighs. It also explained his legs giving out. Parley was confused with himself. He was happy to have a diagnosis, but he was unhappy that he was legitimately sick with an illness. But then he thought that with a real diagnosis, they could finally start treating him and hopefully salvage the show. They only needed enough tape for four more episodes.

Chapter Seven: Give It All You Got

Trust in the Lord with all thine heart; and lean not unto thine own understanding. In all thy ways acknowledge him, and he shall direct thy paths. Proverbs

January - February 2009
Lake Shaft City, Wyoming

It was well past midnight when Parley got home from the pheasant hunt, by way of the emergency room. Dr. Wilson gave him a cortisone injection near the spinal cord while he was in the ER. He was then sent home with muscle relaxers for the spasms. He was also given care instructions that included rest and physical therapy. He got home and barely made it up the stairs before collapsing into his bed. He slept deep and long, or long compared to what he had been getting. He slept for six hours before a crushing, ripping, burning sensation opened his eyes and demanded that he get off his back. He was left in a hazy stupor. Stiffly and slowly, he made his way to his den.

Later in the morning, Sue Rigby called Miranda to check on Parley. She was anxious to know how he was doing. Miranda explained what Lumbar Radiculopathy was and how it affected Parley. Miranda also went on to say that according to the doctor, it would take at least six weeks of rest and physical therapy to heal, maybe more.

There was no chance of any more filming in January so Sue and the production team left. Parley started the week off by resting for a few days. He followed the doctor's orders and went to physical therapy. The therapist worked out a daily program of exercise and scheduled Parley to attend therapy twice a week.

Knowing this was a big break for him and Miranda, Parley was frustrated and a little scared he might not have it in him to overcome whatever this mysterious illness was. There wasn't time for him to be sick and go through physical therapy, but he knew he needed to put the time into his therapy, time they didn't have. Sue had hinted that the executives were not going to be happy about the delay in filming on an unproven show. *I've got to get better. This can't be happening to me. Everyone is relying on me.*

Sue called Miranda two weeks later to check on Parley. She also told Miranda that some of the executives were happy with the show. It was the most popular debut of a show in the network's history. There were rumors of authorizing a second season. On the other hand, some executives were unhappy with the filming schedule and wondered if the Burnrises were capable of doing a second season when they were so far behind in the production schedule for the first season. This news added more pressure on Parley. With more pressure came more frustration. Parley wasn't showing any signs of improvement. Parley wasn't used to being held captive by his health. Miranda went on to tell Sue that the doctor said that while many respond within six weeks it can take some people three months or more to heal. Sue was a little worried with that news. The executives were anxious to get the last four episodes in the can.

In a desperate attempt to make everything work, Parley redoubled his efforts in spite of the agony he was in. He soaked daily in the mineral hot springs after his workouts. The old Indian folklore said the mineral hot springs had magical curative powers. His dad was a believer. It made no scientific sense, but Parley was willing to try everything he could, hoping it would help. He noticed a temporary benefit from the hot water, but a few hours later the aches and spasms would return. He was able to maintain his renewed effort for ten days before the fatigue swallowed the last of his energy.

It had been a full month since Parleys' trip to the ER when Sued called again. She had managed to put off the executive in charge of production by a week, but now he was chomping at the bit wanting a hard fast filming schedule for the next four shows. Parley and Miranda were on speaker phone so they could all three talk.

Parley explained to Sue that in spite of his best efforts there was no improvement. He had still had no energy and he was in a constant state of agony. He had even received a second cortisone shot and had started seeing a chiropractor. He was soaking twice a day in the hot springs.

Sue explained they needed a certain amount of time between filming and the air date and even though the executives demanded the filming schedule start the day after Presidents Day, Sue knew they could get by, barely by, if they started three days later on Friday. That would give Parley eight more days to heal.

"Sue, I have a terrible question, what would happen if Parley can't be ready by then? What if it takes him two or three months before he is recuperated enough to work?" Miranda asked.

"This is one of the parts of my job I hate, especially when dealing with great people like you guys. Those kinds of things are covered in the contract. There are penalties up to and including termination of the contract if there is a breach of contract on your side. It might be a good idea to have your friend Rita, review your contract for you so you know the details and what options, if any are available to you legally."

Parley looked at Miranda with despair in his eyes. Miranda tried returning a look of hope. She wasn't very convincing. Miranda took a deep breath and asked Sue, "what now? Where do we go from here?"

"If you think there's a chance of making the deadline, then let's set up a filming schedule."

They were in the middle of scheduling when Miranda stole a glance at Parley. She noticed he was grimacing from the pain caused by trying to adjust himself in his chair. He couldn't seem to get comfortable. When she saw the look on his face, she had that overwhelming sense of foreboding. She was feeling like this effort to schedule was a waste of time because he probably wouldn't make it by the twentieth. *I could be wrong, after all, he doesn't know how to fail.*

Thirty minutes later they had a firm filming schedule that was perfectly reasonable if Parley could carry his load. Miranda wished she could carry his load, in fact, she had an idea. They hung up the phone and Miranda helped Parley up the stairs to his den. She got him settled in his recliner and sat down on the love seat to the left of the recliner.

"Hey sweetie, I had an idea come to me about how we could handle the fishing side of the filming schedule. I was thinking even though we don't normally fish together that often we could have me in the boat with you and I could run the boat and do everything you normally would do. That way all you'd need to do is let the cameras capture your handsome face as you hold on to the fishing pole. Do you think that would help?"

"Hmm, It might help a little. Right now it seems like an impossible dream to climb into the boat and sit in my captain's chair. The rocking of the boat and thumping of the waves, makes me think that my back would crack in two." Parley took a deep breath. "I know how important this is to you and I will say this much, I will do whatever I possibly can to make this work. I don't want to let you or the family down."

"Oh sweetie, I didn't mean to add more pressure on you. I know you'll do your best. You always do. I don't expect you to be superman. I don't know what is going on with your health, but I do know that if anyone can beat it, it would be you. If we have to lose this TV deal for the sake of your health then we will and we won't feel sad about it. Your health is way more important than the show."

Later that day Miranda called Rita to ask about the contract and the possibility of Parley not being able to fulfill it. Rita explained that their contract had a few allowances for termination. The show could be cancelled. There could be a death or unexpected catastrophic circumstances preventing fulfillment of the contract. There were penalties in place if there was willful misconduct preventing completion of the contract. Rita felt like his health condition would allow them to void the contract without penalties. Parley was happy to hear that. However, he was more concerned about the potential loss to their blogs and the loss of reservations for the resort.

Chapter Eight: Breaking Point

If you only have something to hope for, you have a reason to live.
Unknown

July 2011
Lake Shaft City, Wyoming

As Parley gazed mournfully over his backyard, all he could see was a lawn and garden in total disrepair and overgrowth, just like his life. His grass used to be green and his garden weed free. Three years later, his life, like his backyard, was in total disrepair and overgrown with pain and weeds. His yard looked like it suffered from neglect. While he had neglected his yard, he hadn't neglected his life. He had been to countless doctors receiving no diagnosis and no lasting help. Three years later he still suffered and he still had no answers.

He knew the source of his gardening problems, but he didn't know the source of his health problems. One thing he had learned over the last several years was to appreciate the little things. Parley was grateful to be standing on the deck behind his grill with a spatula in hand. He was having a decent afternoon with the mysterious pain and fatigue ever so slightly at bay. He was trying to advantage of the sunny blue sky by grilling some gourmet hamburgers Miranda had made. The air was fresh with the feeling of the sun beating down on his perma-tan skin.

He had just finished turning the burgers when he jumped at the sound of firecrackers going off in the front yard. He smiled. *It's probably Ted and his buddies lighting the last of the fire crackers.* The crackling and popping sounds of the fireworks called to mind the big Fourth of July celebration three years ago when he received the award from Art and the Willow Creek organization. That was the same week when TAN filmed the pilot of the From Catch To Plate TV show. He sighed as he remembered the success and failure of that time in his life. Now he wished he could do something as simple and basic as mowing the lawn or catching a fish.

When it was all said and done, they managed to tape seven episodes of the TV series before having Rita cancel the contract. Not only did they lose their TV series, they lost the potential of the other shows Rita was interested in. He couldn't film anymore. His mysterious illness, whatever it was, wouldn't allow it. In the two months that the seven episodes aired both his and Miranda's blogs were exploding with new visitors and the reservations for the Burnrise resort nearly doubled.

He flipped the burgers one last time before slapping a slice of cheese on each patty. He closed the lid of the grill and jumped back into memory lane. He was sad and proud when he thought of the twins. As he thought over the last few years he was grateful for the choice's Ted and Emily had made in spite of his absence from their lives. Before getting sick, he would take the kids out on the boat almost every day during the summer. They would fish or water ski. Sometimes they would go on family camping trips on Volcano Island or the nearby forest. He enjoyed spending time with the Church's youth group taking them camping or water skiing.

When Parley and Miranda were engaged, they decided their kids would be their second most important priority, second only to their marriage. That commitment was easy because Parley considered his wife and his children to be his closest friends. He genuinely enjoyed their company. The last few years Parley was all but absent from their lives. He just didn't have the physical capacity to spend time with them other than the occasional movie or game.

Miranda was working furiously on her own website. At the same time she was trying to edit and post videos from Parleys' archives to post on his blog. She had been trying hard to help keep Parleys' blog going for the last couple of years. They didn't want to lose the momentum of all the new followers since his rescue run and then the TAN series. She was burning the candle at both ends, causing the candle to melt in the middle.

He turned off the propane grill and scooped the hamburgers onto the serving plate and covered it with tin foil. He yelled at Miranda and the kids. "Burgers are done!"

He had to sit down. His energy was quickly draining from him. He had been on his feet a little too long. As he watched Ted and Emily walking out through the sliding glass doors each carrying a serving plate of food and teasing each other, he was grateful for his twins. They had recently earned their driver's licenses. They were only too happy to run errands for him when it involved driving the car somewhere. That was a big help to him. They all were seated and ready to eat. They all bowed and Parley was happy to feel well enough to say grace.

A half hour later, as Miranda, Emily and Ted were cleaning off the table the phone rang. Ted answered it. Within two minutes the kids were on their way out of the house. Miranda brought out root beer floats for dessert. "You look awful sweetie, is the pain back?"

Parley just nodded. He hurt too much to speak, even to say 'yes.' He thought regretfully how he was not creating good memories for his kids over the last few years. He was afraid the only memories they would have of him would be running errands for him and bringing food to him. He thought back to his growing up years and all the great memories he had with his brother Nick and his parents. He wished his kids had been able to have such memories.

As Parley and Miranda were watching a movie, he looked over at his wife of seventeen years. He was amazed that she was able to spend time with him. She was always busy, but somehow she always managed to make time for him and the kids. *How does she do it?* He was feeling guilty about just how hard she was working and her involvement with his website. Maybe it was time to stop posting to OutdoorParley.com. It would take away one big responsibility for her. He knew being sick was a big burden on her. His blog another. He decided it was time to let go of his blog. He couldn't afford to let her get burned out. She was working hard to pick up his slack with the kids. While his first thought was that of gratitude, it was quickly replaced with anger. He was frustrated and angry at the toll his illness was taking on his wife and kids. *If it was just me that was suffering, it might be easier to handle. . .All this physical pain and then all the emotional baggage. It seems to be too much to handle. It has to stop. I've got to tell her to stop posting to my blog.*

"Miranda babe, can we pause the movie?"

"Sure, what's up sweetie?"

"I've been thinking over the past few weeks about all you are doing. I don't know how you do it, but I really think it is time to let go of my blog. You don't need that additional pressure on you."

"So what are you saying, no more posts to your blog?"

"For now, yes. You have so much going on. . .We can't afford to let you burn out."

"But letting go of your blog. . .OutdoorParley is your life's work. Are you sure?"

Miranda didn't say anything for a minute or so. Parley looked at her and could see the wheels turning as she was thinking.

"Do you realize what will happen to your life's work if we stop regular posting?"

"I've been thinking about that very thing. It's not fair to you for me to be so sick all the time. Much less have you dealing with my website. You've got to pace yourself. It really is time to let go of my blog. I don't like that idea, but I think it's the right thing to do."

"Wow." Miranda was stunned. They had worked hard to build their blogs up and to let go of his was a monumental decision and a sad one at that. "Okay. I see your point. It will be nice to have one less set of deadlines." She got up from her chair and slid down next to Parley on the sofa. They snuggled for as long as Parley could endure it, which wasn't for long. Miranda was dealing with a conflict of emotions, on the one hand, she was grateful for one less deadline. On the other hand, she was scared. This was a big step that represented a lack of hope for the future.

Time crawled by ever so slowly. Every day that passed by served to defeat Parley a little more. Every day that crawled by took a little more hope from him. He felt defeated, depressed and hopeless. Sometimes, when he had the energy, he tried looking up his symptoms on the Internet. If the doctors couldn't or wouldn't diagnose him, then he would have to do what they couldn't. In the process of researching chronic illnesses and pain on the web, he ran into groups of people on various social media websites. In these groups, the members would talk back and forth, giving support to one another. He was at first shocked when he saw that some of those conversations dealt with the idea of suicide. At first Parley thought the idea of suicide was terrible. But after a while he began to see things from a different perspective. He realized how desperate people could entertain desperate measures. He started to wonder if he was that desperate?

At first, the idea of killing himself seemed preposterous. He had no idea how one could do that sort of thing. He started to feel he no longer fit into his life. He had lost his old life and had not been able to replace it with a satisfactory life in the present. How could he continue to live his life based on who he used to be? He had no viable life to look for other than a life filled with senseless agony, never-ending pain, constant fatigue and sleep deprivation.

Would suicide give him the rest and peace he couldn't find in his new life? *Am I really thinking these thoughts? I shouldn't be thinking like this. Come on Parley, you're better than that. Right?* He wasn't so sure anymore. Life was rude and insensitive. It just kept on going without him. It didn't slow down. It just raged on regardless of how he was doing.

The whole concept of committing suicide would have seemed so impossible a year ago, but now seemed possible in the midst of fatiguing lonesome despair. As he started to entertain the idea of a permanent pain-free sleep, he chastised himself. There was no way he could do it. Time inched along slowly and with agony. The doctors were useless.

He frequently made a pros and cons list in his mind regarding the idea of killing himself. Every time he made a mental list, the pros always outweighed the cons. He knew his life insurance policy would pay out in the event of a suicide. He felt like, in the long run his wife and children would be better off without him. He felt that all he really was to his family was a millstone hanging around their neck. Parley detested the idea of being at anyone's mercy. He despised the idea of being under someone's care. He had a lot of pride.

Oh Lord, why are you hiding from me? I need you. Please help me. Each thought he had seemed to conflict with the next thought. Nothing seemed to make sense anymore. *Confusion, conflict, and chaos, this is my life now.*

He was disappointed in the absence of the Lord in his life. If all his future held for him was nothing but pain and no energy, what kind of future was that? Not a future he wanted. Surely the Lord would understand.

~

Nick had gotten a license to raise pheasants and needed to pick up some feed and supplies for his new hobby in Cheyenne. Parley decided to tag along.   Before leaving, he had managed to go to the ATM and withdrew five hundred dollars.

When they got to Cheyenne, Nick found his way to the specialty feed and grain store. He invited Parley to go with him.

"I mainly wanted to come here just to get out of the house and have a change of scenery. I don't think I have the energy to go with you. I have a book. I'm happy to stay behind."

"Are you sure? I'm going to be a while. This list will take me maybe two hours, maybe a bit more."

"Thanks, but I'm doing well to do this much. Don't worry. I'll be fine hanging out in this nice new cab. I like your truck and these seats are amazingly comfortable. Go on, don't worry about me."

Shrugging his shoulder, Nick said, "all-right little brother. Call me if you need anything." Nick shut the door and walked across the street to the first of three stores he needed to visit.

After Nick had been gone for a good ten minutes, Parley slowly and carefully slipped out of the cab onto his unstable and pain filled feet and started his quest with a slow agonizing walk. He had done his research and knew generally where the seedy parts of town where, at least according to the newspapers and other Internet sources. He was going to attempt to buy drugs off the street. He was looking for Lortab or Percoset. If the medical community wasn't going to help him, he was left with no other choice. He couldn't live this way. He wasn't even sure he could make the walk.

He had just turned a corner into one of the worst streets in town, at least by reputation. It wasn't a terrible street, mostly just old homes and buildings. There were a few abandoned buildings and a couple of houses boarded up. There was an old, worn out, but functioning diner, two blocks down the street. Parley had never done anything remotely like this and didn't know what to expect. He wasn't sure this would even work.

As he painfully shuffled down the first block, he noticed weeds growing out of the cracks on the sidewalk and potholes all over the faded asphalt roads. Everything looked old and worn out. The only redeeming quality of this neighborhood was the sun filled sky above. Other than that, nothing. *They ought too bulldozed this neighborhood and start over. But why do I even care? I won't be around much longer.*

He was dragging as he came upon the second block. After a few more agonizing steps he saw the run down old diner he was looking for. He past another boarded up house. He noticed a redheaded young man who could be a college aged kid standing in front of the dilapidated old diner talking to a woman. Parley noticed that across the street from the old diner, there was a boarded up old fashioned gas station. The kind of gas stations they had before convenience stores. *Is this diner the only building on this street that is still functioning?*

Looking at the redheaded kid, Parley thought, *that seems strange. . .Oh, maybe she's buying drugs, that is in the area where they say a lot of drugs are sold. What do I know? I've never done anything like this before. What do I say to that kid? Hi, I'd like to buy some drugs please. Hmm.*

This was all new to him, but that interaction seemed strange. At least he hoped so. In spite of his research, he wasn't sure how to go about buying drugs. He was now coming up on Old Ma's Diner. There were more weeds in the parking lot than cars. Old Ma's diner looked dingy and worn on the inside and out. He looked at that light complected, clean-cut red head standing calmly with his hands in his pockets on the sidewalk in front Old Ma's.

Parley nodded his head at the kid. He returned the nod.

Parley didn't know what to do or what to say. *What the heck, I've got nothing to lose.* He knew there was going to be risk involved.

He approached the young man hoping he was a drug dealer. He didn't know how to behave on the seedy streets of Cheyenne so he just asked the kid, "do you know, by any chance where a guy could buy some pain pills?"

"I might have a few. Anything in particular?"

"Lortab or Percoset. Does it matter?"

"Only got Lortab"

"How much?"

"Five bucks a pop."

"Five dollars for one pill?"

"Yeah."

"Wow."

Quickly doing the math in his head, Parley said, "I'll take one hundred pills. That's five hundred dollars right?"

"Right."

The transaction was surprisingly easy. To Parley it seemed about like buying a hot dog from a street vendor at the county fair. But it wasn't illegal to buy hot dogs. He hobbled painfully away.

Parley altered his route back to the truck to make sure that there were no police officers watching him ready to pounce on him and arrest him for buying drugs. The pain in his legs and lower back was so intense he thought they might be almost numb. With every beat of his heart he could feel more energy drain away.

There was a local Shakes and Dogs fast food joint near the parking lot where Nick's truck was parked. He went inside and ordered lunch. Sometimes eating made him feel a little better. He had a light jacket on with his stash of illegal drugs in his pocket. He sat down to eat his lunch and to try and relax. He was nervous. He had never broken the law in his life other than the occasional speeding ticket and he hadn't received one of those in twelve years.

He reflected on his crime spree, *That dealer didn't look like any dealer in the movies. He looked more like a college student than a hardened criminal.* If it wasn't for the tattoo's on the kids' arms, Parley would have thought he was a choir boy. Parleys' hamburger was gone and he was finishing up his fries and milkshake when in walked a Cheyenne police officer in a dark navy blue uniform. The broad chested officer seemed to walk in slow motion as he walked through the door and into the foyer where he gazed around the dining area of the restaurant. The police officer caught Parleys' eyes and they held the stare for what seemed like hours. All the while Parleys' heart was pounding so hard it almost hurt. Parley quickly looked away from the policeman. He had five hundred dollars of illegal drugs on him and there was a huge police officer, fifteen feet away from him.

Just then, in walked another police officer from the other side of the foyer. He too seemed to saunter in slow motion glancing around the room like the first officer. *Be cool, relax. Breathe slow and act natural. Act casual and drink your milkshake and casually look away, that's it Parley. . .Be cool.* Parley tried to follow his own directions, but he felt like he was falling apart inside. Every move was awkward. *Why were there two police officers? Was one for back up? What if they arrest me? They probably would want two or more officers for a drug arrest. How do they know I have illegal drugs on me? Did they follow me?*

After the longest two seconds passed, the police officers turned their attention to the cashier and ordered their lunch.

Trying not to be obvious, Parley released a sigh of relief. He wished his heart would stop beating so violently. *What if those policemen can hear my heart beating?* He gathered his garbage in his sack and dropped it in the receptacle on his way out. His legs and feet were on fire and his back was so sore he walked hunched over. "Here, let me get that for you sir," said the first police officer as he opened the door for Parley. "Thank you officer." He hobbled out of the restaurant.

Parley was only in the truck for twenty minutes when Nick showed up with a big paper sack from Shakes and Dogs.

"Hey Parley, I got us some food. Hungry?"

"Um, yeah, yeah, sure." Parley wondered how he could eat

another lunch, as he reached for the shake Nick handed him. "Thanks." *I can't eat another bite I'm so full. How did I get myself into this* mess?

They started to eat in silence. *I'm a criminal, I'm a criminal, . . . I'm really a criminal. What have I done?*

Chapter Nine: Parleys' Secret

We are the author of our own happiness. We are the painter of our own beauty. We are the thinker of our own future. CallahanWriter

July 2011
Lake Shaft City, Wyoming

The throbbing abyss that Parley was falling into was getting deeper each day. Parley felt that without hope, there wasn't much to live for. *Why is this happening to me? What have I done to deserve this? Isn't there something, anything I can do to get rid of all this suffering?* Anything he tried to do served as a reminder to him of his limitations. He couldn't watch his favorite hunting and fishing shows on TV anymore. When he first got sick, those shows served as a motivation to get well as fast as he could and get back to his active life style. However, when he realized he wasn't getting any better, but in fact, getting progressively worse, they became a source of anxiety reminding him of all the things he could no longer do. He was angry that those guys were living their dream while Parley was hopelessly sick and constantly miserable.

Gone were the days he would wake up at three or four in the morning to travel a hundred miles to a lake where he would spend the day fishing for his blog. Gone was the endless energy and strength that allowed him to work eighteen hour days.

Parleys' relationship with the Lord was becoming strained. He had always been a good and faithful member of his Church. He donated money and service to his Church. He spent many a joyful hour on Lake Shaft taking the youth water skiing or fishing. He offered members of his Church access to Elk Farm Island. Parley always had a bible in his tackle box. He loved to read the account of the creation when he was enjoying the breathtaking vistas in the middle of the lake.

Many times he felt God's presence while reading from the good book in the middle of nature's cathedral. These were times more special than attending a good bible thumping sermon at Church on Sunday morning. He never doubted God's existence and that was part of the strain in their relationship. Why was God allowing him to suffer without help? Why didn't God lead him to someone who could diagnose his painful condition? Parleys' patience in Gods time frame was weakening.

"Where is God now, when I really need Him?" Parley would ask himself frequently. Parley had a difficult time concentrating on anything for any length of time. His prayers suffered as did his daily reading of the good book.

A couple of days after Parleys' 'crime spree,' he found himself in the middle of his worst day in last three agonizing years. He felt lonely all the time. Even with Miranda and the kids around, he still felt isolated because no one could understand his pain, it pushed him further into a chasm of loneliness. He felt an isolation from the rest of the world. It didn't help that his friends were falling away. Even though he was alive, he wasn't enjoying life. In addition to the pain and insomnia that racked him over the coals of despair, he was always fatigued. It took all the energy and emotional stamina he had to push the buttons on the remote control.

Parley was thinking. . .Was the pain, making him suffer more or was his suffering making him hurt worse? It was a vicious cycle with no beginning or no end. In his desperation, he remembered the narcotics he had stashed away in the drawer of his end table.

As he fingered the pills through the plastic baggy he thought how rude he had been with Miranda and the kids before they had left for church. He felt bad for all the demands he placed upon them. He was angry at the way he had been so short tempered with them since becoming so sick. The sicker he became, the more intolerant of himself he became. What was worse, he wondered, the agony he suffered or all the hurt he caused his wife and kids? In the past, he had taken great pride in the way he treated his family, and seeing to their needs. Now, instead of giving he was taking, maybe even robbing them of happiness.

He felt like he was now at the end of his rope. His suffering was causing his family to suffer. They didn't deserve to be treated this way. *Why me? Why is this happening to me? I'm a good person, why me? Am I a good person? Did I do something to bring this onto myself?*

While he had been very successful in his life, he still had dreams that hadn't been met. He dreamed of the ambition he once had to catch a rainbow trout in all fifty states. He thought of the desire he once had to write the great American novel. Now his primary dream was just to be able to go fishing, even if it was just casting a line off of the dock. He was not living. He hadn't been living for a long time. He had merely been existing for a year or more. His memory was failing him frequently. When you can't do what you love and you begin losing some of those precious memories of your past, there isn't much to look forward to. *Who wants to look forward to forgetting?*

He looked at the bag of pills he had recently bought from a clean cut college looking drug dealer in Cheyenne. Now he finally had a chance to make up to his family for all he had put them through the last few years. Surely they would thrive without his dead weight holding them all back. Finally, they would be rid of his dead weight dragging them down. As Parley thought about this, he felt a sense of relief come over him. Surely, this was a far better thing for him to do. He would free himself and his family from the suffering he was going through.

He dumped the pills on his bedside table. He wondered if he should write a note telling Miranda why he was doing what he was doing. The reality of killing himself was catching up to him. He paused what he was doing and sat back in his chair. After a wave of debilitating agony swept over him, he contemplated the moment that he was in. He thought of his family and while he contemplated his love for them and their feelings for him, he wondered what impact killing himself would have on them. Would it be any better or worse than the state he was already in with the never-ending agony of his pain and fatigue?

He had no control over his life. The affliction he was in, hurt his entire body at times. He felt that he was nothing more than a stump on his recliner. The doctors gave him nothing to hope for. He was tired of the pain and of not having any control over his life. He was receding into a hopeless chasm of darkness. He felt like he was being punished for doing something, he just didn't know what he was being punished for.

He thought it was odd that his future rested on the pills in the palm of his hand. Overdosing on pills isn't a bad way to go, he thought to himself. *I might as well get on with it. My pain is only getting worse.* His aggravation continued as the thought came to him about whether to write Miranda a suicide note. Miranda had sacrificed a great deal in her life to take care of Parley along with taking care of the kids by herself. He found a notebook within his reach. He opened it to a blank page. *What should I tell her?*

He stared at the blank page. He was surprised at the feelings he was having. He felt a deep sense of mourning. He realized he was mourning the loss of his family. *They're not dead, so why do I feel this way?* Parley believed in a life after death. Now he was wondering if this feeling he was having, this mournful feeling would go with him to the other side? This mournful feeling all of the sudden seemed to hurt worse than all the physical pain he was going through. He was feeling hollow inside, like someone had ripped out his heart leaving a void that could not be filled. This was an agony he had never felt before. He felt out of control, more than at any other time in his life. A frightening sense of loss was boiling over inside of him.

In his hand he held his future in the form of little white tablets. The power over life and death, over pain and peace, but if this sense of loss and despair was what he would be feeling on the other side there would be no peace. *Is this feeling worth getting rid of the physical pain? Is it worth the control I will finally have over my life?*

For the first time in this pain filled period of his life he realized there is something worse than the pain, the agony of not having his family with him.

Parley let out a sigh as he stiffly stood up. He held onto the end table long enough to make sure he had his balance. He took a deep breath and started the longest walk of his life, the walk to the master bathroom. Parley noticed tears in his eyes as he slowly made his painful walk. He was feeling pain and hope at the same time. He hadn't had a sense of hope for so long he couldn't remember that last time he felt hopeful. The closer he got to the toilet, the stronger the feeling became. From out of nowhere the words to one of his long forgotten, but favorite verses came to his mind, "I know the plans I have for you. . .Plans to prosper you and not to harm you, plans to give you hope and a future."

As the little white pills swirled around the toilet bowl on their way down the drain, he felt that sense of control he was looking for. He had not been able to feel any sense of control since he was afflicted with pain. Now he felt control as he got rid of those little white pills of death. The gentle refrain of words from the Gospel of Matthew came to his mind as he shuffled painfully back to his chair. "Come unto me all ye that labor and are heavy laden, and I will give you rest. Take my yoke upon you, and learn of me; for I am meek and lowly in heart: and ye shall find rest unto your souls. For my yoke is easy, and my burden is light."

The pain was putting up another wall of fuzziness in his mind and he wasn't quite sure what the passage from Matthew meant right there, right then, but it gave him hope. He sat down in his chair and let out a loud moan. He thought about Miranda and his children. He felt their love and he felt something else, something warm and complete. *I don't think I'll tell Miranda about this. She might worry if she knew what a near miss this was.*

Chapter Ten: Hope On The Horizon

There's a saying that say's you can't see the forest through the trees. That idea is also true with pain. You can't always see the beauty through the pain. Pain can be so debilitating and so encompassing that it clouds your view of everything around you.
Unknown

May 2012
Washakie Reservation, Wyoming

Miranda got out of bed and put on her bathrobe. She glanced around the master bedroom as she was looking for her slippers, she was appreciating the mauve dominated earth tones. She found one slipper hiding behind a large terra cotta Native American vase with decorative sticks in it. She smiled as she remembered the give and take when remodeling their bedroom. Parley wanted it to be less feminine. Miranda added an antique fly rod on the wall above the king size bed and put some twigs and sticks in some vases. Parley came home that evening and saw the sticks and fly rod and was perfectly happy. She loved it too.

She found her other slipper under her side of the bed. She liked the decorative twigs and the fishing pole and she got all the feminine touches she wanted. She enjoyed the outdoors a great deal, but she also enjoyed refined tastes. This style of decorating gave her what she wanted and kept Parley happy. He could never understand the need to keep a room used for sleeping all fancy and nicely decorated. Men.

Parley was starting to stir when he heard Miranda go down the hall banging on Ted's bedroom door. He wondered why they still needed the morning wake up ritual, after all the kids were almost done with their junior year of high school. *They ought to be able to get out of bed when the alarm went off.*

"Wake up Ted." Miranda then banged on Emily's door.

"Wake up Emily. Hurry kids." She started down the stairs to get breakfast ready. *What would I do without her? I hope I'm not burning her out being sick for so long. Geez, I've got to get this figured out. There has got to be some kind of medicine I can take. There's no way I can be this sick and in this much pain forever.*

Another morning and another battle to get going. Parley had to fight his way through the morning stiffness, pain and fatigue to get out of bed. Then he slowly put on some sweat pants and a T-shirt to limp, hunched over to his den only to take an unrefreshing twenty minute nap.

His den used to be a joint home office for both Parley and Miranda. Over the three years of being in a mysterious pain and fatigue, he took over the home office. It became his sanctuary. He found the recliner was the most comfortable place to rest. They left the love seat in the room and took out Miranda's desk. Parleys' desk, gradually developed mounds of papers and books and eventually it looked like a pile of junk. Parley claimed that the heap was organized chaos. Occasionally he would pull something out of the pile to prove his point.

The more time Parley spent in the den the more the den evolved around his needs. The den had a side table with a lamp. The bookshelves remained even though its only use was to collect dust. Nick brought over a mini fridge and microwave which they put with arm's reach of his recliner. As it evolved into a living space, Parley would spend more time there because it was reasonably comfortable. As Parleys health declined, he spent more time in the den. He would take most of his meals there and even Bert, Nick and Hank would sometimes come over and watch a football game or an outdoor show. They thought it was good for Parley to have company. Parley was frustrated watching people play games, hunting and fishing reminding him he had evolved into an invalid. He appreciated their company and since he didn't have the strength to do anything else, he watched the shows they wanted to watch.

After Parley got settled in, he heard his son Ted lumber up the stairs to say goodbye. He brought his Dad a cup of coffee. "Thanks son, for the coffee, I love you." Ted grabbed the remote that was just out of Parleys' reach and handed it to his dad. "I love you too, Dad." He then flew out of the den and jumped down all six stairs, rocking the hall from his hard landing. Parley shook his head in dismay at his son's roughness and smiled at the sensitivity of his son at the same time.

"Bye dad," Emily cried out, "I love you." She dashed out the front door. "Bye honey," Parley yelled back, but it was too late for her to hear.

Time was painfully slow and contradictory. He couldn't sleep at night. He survived on cat naps during the day. His tail bone hurt so badly he couldn't sit, but his thighs and feet hurt so much he couldn't stand. The noise from his kids easily annoyed him. He tried to overlook their annoyance as long as they were getting along. Sometimes he succeeded.

It made no sense to him he could be so tired by night time and yet not sleep more than one or two hours in a row all night long. He had seen a few doctors specifically for his insomnia. That was the only symptom the doctors seemed genuinely interested in. Over the span of six months he was prescribed several different sleep medications. None of them worked. In spite of their interest, the doctors were unable to fix his sleep problems.

The day squeaked slowly by. The next morning made another repeat performance. In spite of the crippling stiffness, he managed to get out of bed. With his bathrobe and slippers on he slowly fumbled his way down the six stairs to the kitchen, moaning with every step. Miranda was sitting at the kitchen table reading the newspaper and sipping her cup of coffee.

"Hey sweetie, how are you feeling?"

"I feel like. . .Well, you know, aching, pounding muscles, excruciating pain, the usual," responded Parley sarcastically.

"At least you're down here for breakfast, instead of in that cave of yours. That's always good," she said optimistically.

"I don't know how I managed to get down those stairs? I barely managed to get my robe on," Parley shook his head.

Parley was miserable almost every minute of every day, there were so few pleasures left for him, one of them was food.

Between his reliable friend food and the fact that Miranda was incapable of cooking anything bad, Parley had steadily put on weight since his long bout with chronic pain.

"What would you like for breakfast sweetie?"

"Just warm up whatever you made the kids," he replied.

"We just had oatmeal and eggs." She put some water in a pan and turned on the stove.

Parley buttered a piece of toast still on the kitchen table and sipped his coffee as he waited for his breakfast. He twisted and groaned, trying to get comfortable on the kitchen chair. Minutes later his breakfast was served. He enjoyed his breakfast while pushing away the frequent reminders of his ever increasing waist size. He had been eating like he normally did, but instead of being constantly on the go he had been confined to bed or a recliner all day long.

"This is fun sitting at the kitchen table eating breakfast, just like old times." Miranda beamed. "Feel like doing anything today? Maybe you could rest a few hours and then we could go for a ride or catch a movie?"

Parley thought for a moment. Really, he analyzed the question. He was in the habit of analyzing how he felt and how he might be feeling in the next several hours when trying to make a decision. "That sounds fun," he hesitated, "I just hope I don't let you down."

"I know the drill. I won't be upset if you can't end up going." One of the things they both struggled with was making plans to do something and at the last minute Parley wouldn't be able to go. Their combined social life had been virtually nonexistent lately.

"Let's give it a try," Parley responded. "Why don't we try for a slow boat ride around the lake? It's a long shot, but what the heck?"

Three hours later they were on the boat and Miranda was piloting the water craft toward the area between Volcano and Wild Wind islands. Lake Shaft had three Islands. Volcano, Wild Wind and Elk Farm. The Wild Wind was located at the north end of the lake near the Washakie Reservation. Elk Farm was a private island owned by the Burnrise Family Resort located on the south tip of the lake near the resort. They were licensed to keep a private elk herd on the island. It was closed to fishing and hunting. They used the elk ranch to supply elk meat for the restaurant. Volcano Island was the biggest of the three islands and the only one open to the general public. It was located dead center of the lake. The deepest part of the lake was 127 feet. The widest part of the lake was three miles wide.

In spite of the jarring pain on Parleys' back, he was enjoying himself and the little burst of energy he was experiencing. After a while they turned off the motor and let the boat drift while they warmed up their lunch and enjoyed the view while they ate.

Parley was enjoying the warming spring temperatures as the morning gave way to the afternoon. The fresh pine scented air was intoxicating to a man who was being held a prisoner for the last three years in his den. The boat gently rocked to the rhythm of the waves. They were looking at some densely forested shoreline on the east side. They were close enough to feel a breeze come off the mountains. The leaves of the aspen were quaking in the gentle wind. The spring time scent in the air was one of Miranda's favorite things about fishing.

From out of nowhere Parley felt a powerful thickness in his chest. The pressure seemed to be swelling and receding, swelling and receding as the boat was rocking in the waves. It was impossible for Parley to take a deep breath. The painful sensation in the center of Parleys' chest panicked him. He clutched his chest with one hand and held onto the armrest of the chair.

"Something's wrong, it's hard for me to breathe," Parley gasped with a tone of fear as he was trying to get Miranda's attention.

"What's wrong?" Miranda asked with horror.

"My chest. . . It's tight. . .Hurts. . ." Parley managed to breathe with quick, shallow gasps. "Heart attack?"

Miranda was stung with shock as she stood looking at him. They were isolated in the middle of the lake. They could call for help, but it would take far too much time for help to respond. They had to make a run for it. Either to the reservation or to Lake Shaft City only to drive another twelve miles to the ER. Then, from out of nowhere her mind mechanically assessed the situation. *He needs a doctor now! We're five miles closer to the reservation than to the resort.* The clinic is a block away from the marina.

Parley was still clutching his chest with a look of terror smeared all over his face. He was trying to breathe. Parley wasn't used to being afraid of anything, but he had never had a heart attack before. By now Parley was bent over as he held his chest. Sweat was dripping from his reddened face.

"Parley. We're going to Hanks clinic. Sit down and hold on," Miranda said with sternness. She picked up her phone as she made her way to the helm. She called the clinic.

"Washakie Medical Clinic, how can I help you?"

"White Flower this is Miranda Burnrise. I am on my boat, Parleys' having a heart attack. We're closer to the clinic than the hospital. I'll be there in a few minutes, please have Hank waiting for us at the Marina."

"We'll be there."

Miranda clicked off her phone and started the boat's engine with a roar. Within seconds she was at full throttle racing toward the reservation.

Every time the boat hit a wake with full force, Parleys' back exploded. Still, he clutched his chest. Now that a few minutes had passed the shock waves of pain made his head hurt. He was breathing just a bit easier, even though his chest was squeezing Parleys' lungs. Parleys' best friend, Hank Standing Elk, was an Advanced Registered Nurse Practitioner, ARNP, and ran a medical clinic on Washakie Reservation.

This isn't supposed to be happening. I'm not supposed to be dying. I'm too young for a heart attack. In the midst of his agony Parley caught the irony of the situation. About a year ago he had his "near miss," thinking he wanted to die. Now, all he wanted to do was live. *Please God, help me live.*

The same excruciating sensation that gripped his chest was now working its way from his sternum to both sides of his ribs. *Oh no, it's spreading, I must be dying. Why is this happening to me? What have I done to deserve this?*

Miranda saw through her wind swept hair the cautionary buoys and slowed down so she could pull into the clinic's slip safely.

"Miranda!" yelled Hank as he waved at Miranda and ran up to the boat, grabbing at the rope to help tie it down. "What's going on?"

In just minutes Parley was at the clinic. It had an emergency room that consisted of one bed, two exam beds and an office.

By now the death grip had moved past his ribs and was putting pressure on his back. He felt like his entire torso was in a vice grip. His breathing was quick and shallow because the pain was so fierce and the muscles were too tight.

Parley was laid out on the emergency room bed hooked up to oxygen while White Flower, the medical technician, was putting in an IV into Parleys' right arm.

Miranda was explaining what was going on with Parley as Hank was checking his vitals. They quickly hooked up an EKG to Parleys' chest. Hank examined the results. "Oh thank the heavens above. The electrocardiogram, looks good. White Flower, take his blood pressure again."

"What does that test mean?" asked a frightened Miranda?

"It means that from this read out his heart is healthy. It's not likely a heart attack." Hank went on to ask a series of questions to both Parley and Miranda. He noticed some involuntary muscle movement on Parleys back while he was examining him.

After a few more tests' Hank said, "I think I know what's going on here." Hank ordered some blood tests. White Flower drew the required vile's of blood as Hank started to explain. "I think Parley is having heavy some spasms. I'm fairly certain his heart is just fine. I've given all the tests we can do here on the Reservation. I think Parley is having muscle spasms that started at his sternum and it spread to his ribs then his back. How are you feeling now buddy," Hank asked?

"It's letting up a little," he gasped, "I'm breathing easier."

Hank washed his hands and went to the coffee pot and

poured himself a cup of coffee. "Do either of you want something to drink?" asked Hank.

"I'd like some water," responded Parley.

"Nothing for me," answered Miranda. "I wish you could be Parleys' doctor," Miranda said wistfully. It was nice to see someone really take an interest in Parley and his pain."

"I can see him as a patient."

"You can?" Miranda asked quizzically.

"Yeah, sure, why not?"

Miranda noticed that Parley had fallen asleep on the exam table. She picked up a tissue and dabbed the beads of sweat off his forehead.

"Well, were not Indians for one thing and we don't live on the Reservation?"

"Oh, so that's it. Ha," Hank let out a soft laugh.

"What? What are you talking about?"

"All this time I wondered why you guys didn't come to me with all of Parleys' medical problems and all this time you thought I couldn't practice medicine off the Reservation."

"You can practice medicine off the Washakie reservation?"

"Sure, of course I can. I'm licensed by the state of Wyoming, not from the Reservation. I can practice medicine anywhere in Wyoming."

"Oh. My. Word!" said Miranda emphasizing every word as she sighed. "All this time we were wishing we could bring Parley to you and we could have. We should have just asked. Oh-my-heavens."

"Well, then, can you be Parleys' doctor?"

"Yeah, I can treat him."

"He's going to be so happy when he wakes up."

"Excuse me Hank, you have a patient," said White Flower.

"White Flower, bring Miranda the new patient paperwork please. Excuse me Miranda. I'll be back after this patient."

Miranda went to work filling out enough forms to buy a car with. Parley woke up while she was turning the fifth page over.

"What are you doing?"

"I'm just about done, filling out new patient forms."

"Why?"

"You're Hanks new patient."

"I am? How? We don't live out here and we're not Shoshones."

"I just talked to Hank about that and it turns out he can treat you."

"Really? I thought Hank couldn't practice medicine outside of the Indian Reservation?"

"Yeah, well he can. He's licensed through the State, not the tribal council."

"Really? Hallelujah."

Chapter Eleven: All Gave Some And Some Gave All

Trust in The Lord with all thine heart, lean not to thine own understanding. . .and He shall direct thy path. Proverbs

May 2012
Walter Reed National Military Medical Center, Maryland

"Gunny? Wake up Gunny," the recovery nursed said loudly as she gently nudged his shoulder. "Andy, wake up!"

Annabel, the recovery nurse, checked his vitals and added the new set of numbers in his chart before trying to wake him up again. Andy was coming out of eight hours of surgery.

"Wake up Gunny. Wake up," Annabel said sternly. Andy started to stir and let out a barely audible groan. "Andy, can you hear me?" Andy moaned and tried to move his legs. They didn't seem to want to move. He was agitated. The effects of the anesthesia were still playing tricks on him. He managed to open his eyes for a moment and look around with a look of confusion on his battle-hardened face.

He had a blank stare, not knowing where he was. Not knowing that he was state side at Walter Reed. Everything was fuzzy white and blurry. He couldn't seem to focus beyond the fuzz of his eyelashes. Then, in the faded chalky white horizon, he saw three boys turning a corner around a bleak and broken wall. Sounds of distant gunfire filled the air. They were walking in the direction of his men beneath his sniper's perch. He was providing surgical cover for his platoon who was going door to door down below. His orders were to eliminate anything that threatened his men. He was in communication with the forward operating base (FOB).

These boys shouldn't be walking around out here. They could get killed. This is a war zone! I thought this war was supposed to be over.

"HQ, be advised, I have three boys approaching south-

southeast about fifty to sixty yards from the platoon. One appears to have a shoulder mounted rocket launcher. Another has a rifle. . . Looks like an AK-47."

"Copy that."

Gunnery Sargent, Andy Zimmerman was a decorated war hero who was coming out of surgery on what remained of a leg that had been partially blown off in an IED explosion in Iraq.

To the nurse, Andy seemed agitated, but that was normal when coming out from under the effects of general anesthesia. "Gunnery Sargent Zimmerman, wake up!"

Andy's eyes were closed, but his eyelids reflected rapid eye movement and his lips were pursed and tense. He was yelling at the top of his lungs in his haunted flashback at the three boys to turn around and quit advancing on the intersection where his buddies were heading. His spotter was telling him to focus, and HQ in his ear piece was telling him he had a 'go' on the approaching target if they looked like they were going to open fire on his boys.

Turn around kids, Judas priest, turn around!

The next thing that played out in Andy's dull aching flashback was being in the U.S. Army Hospital in Landstuhl Germany. He was in shock. The surgeon just told him that his leg had been amputated.

"Andy Zimmerman. . . Gunny, wake up, it's time to wake up. The surgery went very well. Andy, can you hear me?" Annabel could see his eye lids flutter as he let out faintly audible groans. "Squeeze my hand if you can hear me." Weakly, Gunnery Sargent Zimmerman squeezed the nurse's hand. "Good Andy, good job. Can you wake up Gunnery Sargent? Open your eyes."

Andy's head was starting to move from side to side as he tried to clear his head from the unwelcome flashbacks. He was fishing the Turtle river near his home in southern Georgia. It was the first time his Dad had let him go fishing alone. He was fourteen years old. He could smell the water and the scent of decaying grass and leaves on the ground. He baited his hook and as soon as he cast his fishing line out into the river, he heard the startling sound of a high-powered rifle going off. It startled him so much he almost dropped the fishing pole. His pole jerked. He started to reel in his line. The more he reeled it in, the lower his heart sank. *Stupid kids. That stupid idiot kid! Why did he do it? Why?* His orders were clear, if anyone threatened his marines, man, woman, or child, he was to shoot them. This wasn't the first time he had shot a child. In fact, it was his third time.

It was always the same story. He was in his sniper perch looking out for his buddies on the ground. Sometimes it was a woman, other occasions kids would approach his me with a weapon of some kind and he would have to take them out. Every time he was following orders and every time he was cleared. One time it was a woman and a child. They each carried a grenade in their hand. They pulled the pins and hid the grenades under their clothes and started running toward his marines. He took them both out saving his men and haunting his dreams.

The second time an eight or nine-year-old boy was running toward an Army squad with a grenade. He had pulled the pin and started running at them as he prepared to throw the handheld bomb. Andy's .50 sniper round took him down long before he was within range of the soldiers. Now he could regretfully add a third child to his total. *I hate this war, why did I even come over here?*

"Andy, wake up," Annabel drew out each word. Andy's eye flew open, wide open and he was breathing heavy, as if he had been woken from a nightmare, which he had. Thin layers of sweat were forming on his forehead. He started to cough from the irritation of the air tube that went up his nose and down his throat. He couldn't swallow. He was frightened and confused.

"Do you know where you are Andy?" He shook his head no.

"You're at Walter Reid. If you're in pain press this red button," the nurse handed him a small tube like device with a red button on top. Andy immediately pressed the button and within seconds was back asleep.

With the nurse goading him, he woke up every few minutes. She tried to keep him awake a little longer every time he opened his eyes. He was back into the deep black hole of nightmares that only combat veterans know. The smell went from a sterile disinfecting aroma in the recovery room to the dry, sandy smell of the desert. Acrid fumes were penetrating the smell of the dry sand. The first thing he felt in that black abyss was the penetrating pressure in his leg from an IED explosion. He heard short bursts of automatic gunfire being exchanged between him and his fellow survivors and the enemy trying to finish them off. His memory was reminding him of the deep throbbing sensations pounding from both legs every time his heart beat, it felt like his legs would explode. He felt weak. Everything was growing dark. Everything was ebbing away. "Andy! Wake up!"

Confusion. *What's going on?* Andy wondered. Another memory shot through his mind. Smelling breakfast food in the cafeteria. Andy heard scattered cries from people in the lunch room. "Oh no! Look at that!" Andy looked at the big screen TV and saw a replay of a jetliner crashing into one of the Twin Towers. Another flash, the first Twin Tower was collapsing in front of everyone in the cafeteria. He could taste the eggs in his mouth. "What is happening?" That was eleven years ago. Andy was confused. *Why am I in so much pain? What's happening in New York? Why do my legs hurt so bad?* Nothing made sense. In an instant, Andy's mind was in Iraq, Germany, Georgia and Maryland.

The terrorist attacks on September 11, inspired Andy to join the Marines after he graduated from college.

"Andy. . . Gunny, wake up."

Andy groaned.

"Good, good, vital signs are okay." The nurse updated his chart.

A few minutes later Annabel said, "Wake up Andy, time to wake up." He started to respond to Annabel's tough encouragement.

He had lost his right leg and his left foot from an IED in Iraq. He had just come out of surgery on what remained of his right leg. They had to do some repair work that they hadn't been able to do in Germany. During his last surgery, the surgeon found a cancerous growth woven high in his right thigh because of that, the surgeon had to remove more of his thigh in the process. He sent a sample to the lab to confirm the diagnosis.

"Gunny! Wake up Gunnery Sargent Zimmerman," Annabel said with the tone of a Drill Sargent and almost as intimidating.

"Mmm. . ." Andy was still moaning. Confused, he turned his head back and forth sideways, struggling to open his eyes while he tried to orient himself.

"Andy!" called the nurse, "where are you?" she asked. There was no reply, but Andy was making an effort to look around on both sides of his bed. Andy let out a loud groan as he tried to sit up. With the passing of another hour he was finally doing well enough to go to the ICU.

During his first night in the ICU, he was awakened every hour while the nurses checked his vital signs and otherwise looked in on him. Andy made it through the night. He was alone in the ICU. He had no family. He was an only child and his parents had both passed away while he was in college. His parents were also only children and so he had no cousins, uncles or aunts.

He looked around at his room and things started to make sense. He wasn't sure where he was. He had been in a hospital in Landstuhl Regional Medical Center. He was fairly certain he had left that military hospital, but the room he was in looked similar to Landstuhl hospital room. Maybe all military hospitals looked alike, he wondered. He was confused and in pain.

He looked around the room and saw a blood pressure cuff on him. He also saw an IV line with the morphine drip taped to his right hand. There was an oximeter on his index finger. He realized that there was an oxygen tube going into his nose and down his throat.

Just gazing around his new room was tiring. The Marine hero fell back to sleep only to be awakened by a loud voice that turned out to be the doctor. He looked over Andy's chart, asked the nurse a few questions and then turned to look at Andy. Andy's eyes were open and he looked white and frail.

"How are you feeling Gunny? Pretty bad I guess?"

That's a stupid question. Andy had no desire to try and talk. When he tried to speak with the tube down his throat, he coughed and choked. He blinked at the doctor. "Let's take that tube out, and maybe he'll feel like talking." Together, with the nurses help, the tube was quickly removed and replaced with an air hose wrapped around his head and placed under his nose.

"Better now? How are you feeling Gunnery Sargent?"

"Terrible. Hurts, so bad," Andy's voice was throaty, he coughed again.

"I wish I could give you something stronger for the pain. I hate to see you suffer any more than you already have. You're on the biggest dose I can safely give you. Trust me. The pain will start to let up. These ICU nurses are great."

The doctor left his room and the nurse followed him. Andy was left alone. He groaned when a dull throbbing wave of pain hit him. The agony was unbearable. *It's not taking the edge off.* He let out an agonizing cough. He hurt all over.

"Dear God," Andy prayed, "Please help me with the pain. It hurts so bad. Help me please. I'll suffer whatever I need to, but I think this pain is going to kill me. Just give me enough help to get through this, please. My trust is in you. . ." Andy begged the Lord for help. His mind started to fade as he felt himself peacefully slip into a deep sleep.

As he was drifting to sleep, he went through that short twilight period between being awake and asleep, where he thought about his injuries, being shot was like a tickle compared to the effects of losing a leg and a foot. He felt angry that he was a double amputee, and at the same time he somehow felt grateful that his unintentional sacrifice contributed to both his freedom and the freedom of his nation.

There were many ways he could have lost his leg and foot and it would be just as painful, but he was privileged to lose them in the service of his country.

Chapter Twelve: Patience

Be not wise in thine own eyes: fear the Lord, and depart from evil my son, despise not the chastening of the Lord; neither be weary of his correction. For whom the Lord loveth he correcteth; even as a father the son in whom he delighteth. Proverbs

June 2012
Lake Shaft City, Wyoming

After four weeks, the last of the medical records, Hank had been waiting for finally arrived. Parleys' file was large and extensive with all the MRI's, CT-scans, x-rays, blood tests, ultra sounds, EKG's and other diagnostic records. No one doctor had ever assembled all of the records in one place. During that time, all Parley had for medicine was the muscle relaxer Hank sent him home with and a week's worth of pain pills which were long gone.

The first week after Parley saw Hank, he had taken both the muscle relaxers and pain pills Hank had given him, Parley had felt some improvement of the pain, but it was never gone completely. The muscle relaxers made him very sleepy. He spent fifteen to eighteen hours every day asleep or so groggy he couldn't do much.

The last three weeks, the pain was back in full force. He was still sleeping longer and continuously groggy. There were long periods of time when he was so hazy that he couldn't remember if he was asleep or awake. At first he was grateful to be sleeping, then he got tired of constantly sleeping.

Another one of the downs he experienced over those four weeks was the loss of his last three advertisers for his blog. He had a hunch they would be gone soon, but when it happened he was despondent. For over a year his posts were slowing down and the last six months he was lucky to post two or three articles or videos a month. The last two months he had posted nothing.

After he lost the last of his advertisers, he decided in a hazy stupor to forget about the blog. He was mad and depressed. But after a while he found he still had the nagging feeling to post to his website. Maybe he could mount a comeback? He tried to write an article or edit a video, but he found he was worn out from the constant pain. He was constantly fatigued and he couldn't concentrate.

White Flower called Parley to tell him Hank had all the records assembled and having looked over them, he was ready to see Parley again. The only problem was trying to decide how to get to the reservation. The boat ride would, most likely cause Parleys' back to hurt as the boat bounced through the waves. Driving to Washakie reservation would take four times as long the way the roads were laid out. Driving might not be much better than the lake. Parley decided a clear shot to the reservation would be best because it was so much quicker.

As luck would have it, the weather was mild and the lake calm. The boat was skimming the water and Parley would have been enjoying himself if he hadn't been weighed down with the despair of losing his last three advertisers. Now he brought in no money. He was feeling worthless. After all, one of his biggest life goals had been achieved and then ripped away from him. Now what did he have? Just a life of unexplained sickness and pain. He couldn't even work as a guide for the resort. His whole life had been about work and family. He couldn't work and he felt like he was a drain on his family. He was in too much pain to enjoy the kids or be a part of their life. His life's work had been flushed down the toilet.

He was constantly tired. He thought about Hank and wondered if he had any idea what was wrong with him. Parley wondered if Hank could treat him when so many other doctors had failed.

Then Parley thought about one of the questionnaires he and Miranda had filled out in Hanks office a month ago. He was surprised at how much was wrong with him. His main complaints had been ceaseless pain, constant fatigue and insomnia. But after filling out those forms, he realized how the constant terrible pain had made it nearly impossible to understand how many other things were wrong. He had stumbled over his feet a few times. He brushed if off until the wording of the questionnaire made him rethink it. He realized he had some degree of trouble with balancing and overall coordination.

He had been having night sweats on and off over the last few years and it was getting worse. Lately he had woken up a few times drenched in sweat. He had so many other things to worry about that he ignored the other lesser issues. One of the most recent problems for Parley was his mind. He seemed to be forgetting a lot of things. He also seemed to have trouble concentrating. Maybe these issues were a big reason why he had fallen so far behind with his website.

But the primary problem was still the pain and agony that racked his body. If Hank could get rid of the pain, he would learn to deal with the other health issues. He thought back at the 'near miss'. He was grateful he chose to live.

Miranda slowed to wake speed, they pulled into the slip reserved for the clinic. White Flower was there to pick them up. Within a few minutes they were in the clinic.

"Parley my friend, how are you today?" Hank looked Parley over, from head to toe. "Never mind, you look like death warmed over. I'm sorry you don't feel so good."

Parley managed, with great effort, to raise his head and look Hank in the eyes. In that glance he noticed Hanks close-cropped hair and shiny dark skin, but more importantly, he noticed Hanks eyes and smile. His eyes spoke volumes and they sent a message to Parley that he had never seen before in the almost thirty years of friendship, the heartache of seeing Parley racked with so much pain and hope he would do everything in his power to make Parley well once again.

"Here you go, sit in this chair," Hank said, pointing to a new recliner. "We just got this chair in last week. I have several patients with chronic pain like you have and I had the budget so I got a chair that is easier for them to get comfortable with. I know you use your recliner a lot, that's what gave me the idea."

Parley was impressed. "So what do your patients think of

this nice chair?"

"You're the first to use it."

"You used the phrase 'chronic pain' describing your other patients, what does that mean? Is that what Parley has?" asked Miranda.

"'Chronic,' is when you have a condition beyond a certain amount of time. In this case pain. It can be a diagnosis, but it's usually a symptom. When you have pain, you have a symptom. Pain is designed to tell the body that something is wrong. That could be from a broken bone to a burst appendix to a headache. Usually the symptom of pain is accompanied by other symptoms which allow us to narrow down what's wrong with our patients when they're sick."

"So how did those muscle relaxers, and those pain pills work for you?" Asked Hank.

"The muscle relaxers made me so tired and sleepy that I was hardly able to enjoy the reduction in pain from the pain pills. Those muscle relaxer pills make me sleep almost all day long even when I shouldn't be sleepy. The pain pills seemed to lower the intensity of the ache," explained Parley. "Other than that, it's still about the same."

"From a scale of one to ten, with ten being the worst pain imaginable how would you describe your pain without the pain medicine?"

"Well. . ." Parley thought for a moment. "I'd say when the pain is at its worst. It would be a ten."

"So with the narcotics, what was your pain like?"

"It was still bad, but noticeably less than before I took the pills. I guess I would say it got down to a seven. Maybe a six. I was so groggy from the muscle relaxers that I couldn't pay as much attention to the pain."

"There are a lot of muscle relaxers and we can try another one so you won't be so groggy. Going without sleep is bad and too much sleep isn't good. But we'll keep on trying. In the last three weeks could you tell if the muscle relaxers were helping the pain?"

Parley had to think hard on this one because he felt it had, but not as clearly as he thought it should. He then went on to explain. "The pain was pretty much just as bad, I think the difference is that while taking the muscle relaxers I never seem to have had a. . ." Parley was trying to think of the right word. "I guess the way to explain it would be that while my muscles still hurt, I haven't had any muscle spasms. The pain was still there, maybe at a nine or nine and a half, but I haven't had my muscles seize on me since taking the muscle relaxers."

"Then we will try another muscle relaxer to find one that gives you some relief without making you so sleepy."

Hank picked up Parleys' chart and made a few notations. Then he started to explain what he had learned from compiling his chart. "There are a lot of things I know you don't have. Whatever is wrong with you is going to be determined by a process of elimination. I'm afraid to say that most of the obvious things, the easiest things to treat, you don't have. It would be nice to have a run of the mill condition that causes chronic pain. It would be easier to treat."

"What about all the other stuff the doctors have said like the Lumbar Radiculopathy, the arthritis, the ankylosing spondylitis and I forget the other things they said were wrong. What about all that?" asked Parley.

"I agree with some of it and I'm not so sure with some of it. Even if everything they said was true, it wouldn't explain the type of pain you're having. Arthritis would probably be the closest thing to the kind of pain you have, but the arthritis you have is localized. I want to do some more blood tests to check for Epstein Bar Virus, Cytomegalovirus, Lyme Disease and several other more obscure illnesses."

"I want you to try this new muscle relaxer, give it five days. If you're still sleepy then call me and I'll call in another prescription for a different muscle relaxer. Also, go to the hospital and get your blood drawn. Make an appointment for ten days with White Flower. We'll see how you're doing and see what the blood tests say."

"I was hoping for something with more substance than this," complained Parley.

"I hear you sweetie," Miranda butted in, "but Hank is being far more proactive and thorough than anyone else has been."

"Yeah, I guess you're right."

"The thing is Parley. Pain is a symptom of so many things. It's not really the illness or condition, but rather it's a symptom of an illness or condition. We have got to determine what that condition is and that requires a myriad of tests."

"Well," Parley took a long, deep breath, "I guess I understand that. Does the fact that the pain pills made my pain go down mean anything?"

"It means that they are working to reduce your pain. The problem is, is that we can't just mask the symptoms. If we do, we may never get to the root of the problem."

Parley was angry and frustrated, not as much with Hank, but with life. *Why me? Why is this happening to me?* Parleys' voice started to crackle as little as he said, "this pain and fatigue and insomnia. . .They are ruining my life."

Hank was a little taken back at this show of emotion from his best friend. "I know you are hurting and I know this is bad, but isn't that just a little extreme?"

"No, it's not," Parley blurted. "I just lost my last three advertisers to my blog. I haven't been able to post anything for months. I'm not guiding anymore. I can't do anything."

Hank glanced at Miranda, who nodded her head in agreement with what Parley said.

"I'm sorry. I didn't realize it was that bad. I should have known. We haven't done much together in a long time. There's no excuse."

"You and Rita have been really busy– "

"No," said Hank. "That busy thing is just a poor excuse."

"I can't make up for the past, but I swear to you buddy, I will do everything I can to get you better."

The ride home across the lake was rough. The waters were choppy and the boat bounced around as it skimmed the white caps. It was otherwise a pleasant day in the lake. Parley knew he should be enjoying the weather, he always did, but this time he was too miserable to care about the lake, and the surrounding beauty.

Day after long day passed. Day after day Parley was secluded in his den on his recliner. He ate his meals in the recliner. Other than to answer the call of nature, he spent days on end and nights on end in the easy chair.

The day of his next appointment came. He finally took a shower. As he was sitting in their boat on their way to the Reservation, Parley was thinking about how much time had passed since he last saw Hank. He felt like he was lost in time. He knew how many days had passed, but it didn't feel like it. Time seemed to have lost meaning.

They got to the Reservation harbor and noticed Hank sitting on the dock waiting for them. Miranda guided the boat into the slip. Hank tied the boat off. "I thought I'd meet you guys here. It's that much less energy Parley has to spend getting in and out of the boat. Besides, I've been stuck in that clinic all day and the weather is so nice. . .Of course, if you want to go to the clinic we can."

"I like it here well enough and I like the idea of not having to get in and out of the boat," responded Parley.

"So the test results came back and they're all negative, meaning that now, with all the other tests and these last results I can say that there is no good reason for you to be in constant pain." Hank saw a disheartening look come over Parleys' face when he finished talking.

"But there are still options and by that I mean that I have been doing some research on other reasons for pain that are not so obvious. A couple of them are fibromyalgia and chronic fatigue syndrome. I don't know them well enough to treat them, but there are a few things related to mental health that we should try. Oh, and by the way, I am going to a seminar early next month and it's about treating chronic pain. I should know a lot more when I get back."

"So what do I do for now?" asked Parley in a dejected tone.

"How did that muscle relaxer do?"

"About the same, maybe a little improvement."

"I am going to give you another muscle relaxer to try and I am going to give you a couple of pills to take for anxiety and depression. I know that might not excite you, but I really feel at this point we need to see if it will help. I can tell you're depressed and who wouldn't be if they were in your shoes suffering the way you are." Parley didn't have any more argument left in him, so he didn't say anything.

Chapter Thirteen: The Price Paid

May the peace of God always fill my heart, and the love of God forever hold me tight. May the Spirit of God flow through my life, and the joy of God uphold me day and night. Irish Blessing

June 2012
Walter Reed National Military Medical Center, Maryland

Several days passed by for Andy in ICU and so did some of his post operative pain. At least enough to be taken off of morphine and put on a pain pill. It was his fourth day in the ICU. Things were going well enough for Andy. Later in the day he would be transferred to a room in the post surgery unit. Once he was settled in, he immediately fell asleep from the exhausting agony that came from switching rooms.

The nurses didn't seem to care that he was exhausted. They woke him every hour to take his vital signs and they asked him how he was doing. He wanted to yell at them that all he needed was sleep, but he didn't have the energy. They woke him up again for dinner. He looked at the food and fell back to sleep.

Jeff Bellows, the social worker assigned to Gunnery Sargent, Andy Zimmerman came in after dinner. He wanted to tell Andy he had been nominated for the distinguished Navy Cross. The Navy Cross was the highest award that a Marine or Sailor could receive, short of the Medal of Honor.

Andy was asleep. Jeff sat down in a chair near Andy's bed. He decided he could wait for Andy to wake up while he looked over Andy's file and got to know this war hero better. He noticed that Andy, had received a Purple Heart and two Bronze Oak Leaf Clusters for being wounded three times in battle. The Gunny had also been awarded the Bronze star in his first combat tour and a Silver Star on his second combat tour.   He was already a highly decorated Marine. But it was still a high honor to be nominated for the Navy Cross. Jeff put down the file for a moment and noticed there were no flowers, cards, or balloons. No evidence of any visitors or family. He flipped through Andy's file to see that he had no extended family. His emergency contact was his last CO. He made a note to bring a plant or some balloons to Andy's room tomorrow. He went back to reading up on this hero. He noticed Andy's rapid rank advancement. He entered the Marines as a Private First Class. By the time he shipped out on his first deployment, he was a Corporal. He came back from his first deployment as a Sargent.

He consistently displayed excellent leadership and was well educated both scholastically and in his duties. That's what his evaluations generally said. His outdoor experience in his youth was helpful in his duties as an infantryman.

Andy didn't have the normal time in service for his rank, but he had everything else, in spades. He rapidly advanced in rank for his meritorious service and heroism. Most Marines, he met didn't begrudge him his rank advancement, especially if they met him in his dress uniform and saw his very colorful chest plastered with awards and ribbons. He was elevated to a Gunnery Sargent by the time he left on his third deployment. He always commanded the respect of those he worked with.

The next morning Dr. Marne entered Andy's room along with the Chaplin, Father Earl Friday and the social worker, Jeff Bellows. Jeff brought a nice potted plant, a Peace Lilly. Dr. Marne had called in the Chaplin and Andy's social worker. He thought that with the news he had to give Andy, he could probably use a support system.

"Gunny, I'm Dr. Marne from oncology. I have the results from the lab work done after your surgery. When they were operating on your right leg, they noticed a growth woven into your muscles. They removed as much as they could and then sent it to the lab for testing. I'm sorry to have to tell you, but you have cancer. They were not able to remove all of it due to the way the cancer was growing in your thigh. It's not a traditional tumor. It is woven throughout the muscle tissue of your upper thigh close to parts of your pelvis and hip. We need to run more tests to get a better idea of how extensive the cancer is. We know they were not able to get clean margins. We can't do anything yet, not until you have recovered more from surgery."

Dr. Marne paused to allow Andy to respond. Andy was listening intently to what he had to say. When the doctor paused, Andy looked around at the other two men and back at Dr. Marne. Andy felt as frail as he looked. He didn't like feeling so physically helpless. Feeling weak made him feel vulnerable. However, he was surprised at how strong he felt on the inside. He knew cancer was bad and he knew he would need to fight it, and he also knew that God was with him. He felt an inner strength. He couldn't sit upright, a reminder of his physical weakness. He was laying down looking up at three healthy, vibrant looking men. He felt small and insignificant in comparison. But he was a Marine, a tough Leatherneck. He felt God on his side.

"Okay, go on."

"Well," Dr. Marne was a little taken back by his response. He wasn't crying, he wasn't cursing, he was business like. *Maybe he doesn't understand.* "Well," Dr. Marne said, clearing his throat. "We need to give you a PET scan as soon as you feel strong enough to get one."

While Andy appeared calm on the outside, his mind was now running full steam or as much as the pain and the pain medicine allowed him to. He was temporarily able to forget the pain. He didn't know much about cancer, but he knew he needed to wage war against it. He was mentally committing himself to do combat against it. Because he was a Marine, it was second nature for him to fight. Fight the enemy and be victorious. He didn't have much energy or strength at the moment, but he knew he would heal and he would be able to give it a good match. He was feeling the Spirit of the Lord give him courage and strength. Between his leather neck toughness and willingness to engage along with his faith in God, he had every confidence he would beat this cancer. He wouldn't give up without a good fight.

"I'm ready for the scan, set it up right now. I intend to fight this enemy and God willing, beat it."

"It's only been six days since you were in surgery. You've

been blown up and had two major operations in less that two weeks time. It won't matter in the long term if you wait a week or two."

"What does a scan entail?" Andy asked. "Is it as bad as a surgery?"

"No, not at all," Dr. Marne saw where Andy was taking the conversation and paused as he considered his response. Andy spoke up again, saying, "I want the scan today and I want to start fighting the cancer ASAP! I know I'll be sick with the chemotherapy, heck, I'm sick now, if I'm sick for one, why not be sick for two problems at the same time, kill two birds with one stone. I can recuperate for both at the same time. I want to fight, don't hold me back doc."

"All right there, hold on, Gunny. I'll compromise with you. I'll set up the scan as soon as I can, but you won't be cleared for whatever treatment you need until you have had enough time to recuperate, or at least until you're physically strong enough to handle the chemotherapy. If you are weak going into chemotherapy, you will open yourself up to getting infections and catching everything that comes along, maybe even dying."

"So I'll get the scan today?"

"I said I'll set it up as soon as I can. Realistically, it could take a day or two, depending on how busy radiology is."

"I have your word then?"

"Yes gunny, you have my word."

"So how bad is this cancer?" asked Andy.

"Truthfully, it's bad. We know that the surgeon was unable to get clean margins, which means there is still a part of the tumor high up in your thigh muscles. The scan should tell us how much cancer is still in there and if it has spread."

"What I mean is. . .Will I be able to beat the cancer or will I be dying soon?"

"You are rather blunt, aren't you?"

"I am pragmatic and I also have faith in the Lord. I'll live if he wants me to live, I'll die if that's what he wants. So I don't see any reason to tip toe around. The more details I know the better I can talk with God about all of this."

This young man may just well beat this, if anyone can, it would be someone like him. There was something about the way Andy spoke that touched Dr. Marne. "I can tell you that the type of cancer you have, is discouraging, but until we scan it to see how big it is and to see if it has spread. . .Well, I can't tell you anything concrete. Like I said, I'll get that scan scheduled as soon as I can."

"Well, so now what? Do I just lay here until I get scanned?"

"I'm afraid that's all you can do, but it is important that you rest and eat and do everything you can to get strong. Fighting cancer is hard on the toughest people. Use that faith of yours to get all the spiritual, emotional and physical strength possible to fight this thing. A good state of mind is helpful in this type of battle. That's why I called in Jeff and Father Friday. They may be able to give you some support during this difficult time."

"Thanks doc."

"You're welcome, and thank you for your sacrifice in battle, you're a brave man."

Chapter Fourteen: The Thanks You Get

A time to get, and a time to lose; a time to keep, and a time to cast away. A time to rend, and a time to sew; a time to keep silence, and a time to speak. A time to love, and a time to hate; a time of war, and a time of peace. The Preacher

June 2012
Walter Reed National Military Medical Center, Maryland

Jeff Bellows had decided to visit Andy rather than call him with the fantastic news. After all, Andy could use some good news and a visitor. As a result of the tests in radiology and the blood labs, they had determined just how bad the cancer was and their course of action. Andy was looking at rigorous chemotherapy and radiation therapy. Jeff wanted to share the great news that Andy's nomination for the Navy Cross had been approved. He thought this news might cheer Andy a little.

Jeff was walking down the long corridor and passed many rooms of brave men and women who had been severely injured in battle. His heart winced a little as he thought of their sacrifices on the battlefield and the pain they were all feeling.

The long corridor went from the post surgery ward to the oncology ward where there were many elderly veterans being treated for cancer along with several young servicemen and women. It was an expensive hospital to be in. The price for admission was the sacrifice made on the battleground or in serving your country in the military. It was an honor for Jeff to work in this hospital with these brave people.

Finally, he came to Parleys' room. Several of his personal belongings had finally caught up to him, one of which was his laptop. He was sitting up in his bed with his computer on his lap. He looked gaunt and pale. Yet, he also looked determined still wearing his Marine combat face.

"Gunny, hi. How are you doing this morning?"

"Sick as a dog and quiet as a log, Ooh-rah!"

Hmm, was that a unique Marine unit phrase? Jeff wondered. The military was loaded with expressions. He heard a new one every week. "I don't know what you just said, but it sounded positive, so I'll assume things are going as well as can be expected."

"Yeah, can't complain. I'm a little tired, but they say it's normal."

"I've got some great news, the powers that be, have approved your nomination for the Navy Cross and they will be making arrangements for the ceremony to be done here at Walter Reed."

"I wonder if they are doing that because they think I'm going to die?"

"Hmm, well," Jeff was caught off guard at Andy's bluntness. "I think they are doing it because you are going to be in here for such a long time. What else is there to do in this place than be honored for meritorious service above and beyond the call of duty?"

"That's cool. I guess. I don't have any family to invite. It doesn't really matter when and where the ceremony is. Might as well get it over with," responded Andy.

"You don't sound very excited about this award."

"I appreciate it, I guess. You don't think about awards when you're under fire. When you're in the hospital missing a foot and leg you realized that nice looking hunk of medal won't bring your body parts back. I guess it's nice having my work appreciated. That's all it really was. I was in the right place and the right time, or maybe the wrong place and the wrong time. I was just doing my job like any other marine would. Heck, a nice steak dinner and a couple of movie tickets would suit me fine, if they want to recognize me for doing my job."

Andy laid back on his elevated bed. He sipped from his glass of water. "I don't know about humble. I'm just being honest. The Navy Cross is nice and all, but really I was just doing what I agreed to do when I signed on the dotted line. Since college, I have known I wanted to make a living serving others. When the twin towers went down, I felt my calling come to me. A great way to serve my country and my fellow man was to fight for them. Not everyone is cut out to fight and to kill. I knew I would be.

"How did you know you could fight and kill before you even joined the military?"

"I grew up hunting and fishing. I have shot and killed countless deer, elk, boar, rabbits, squirrels and birds. I was taught to respect the kill. There is an integrity behind it. I enjoyed the hunt, but when it came time to shoot the prey. . .Well, I shot the animal knowing it would be put to good use. There was a respect in it." Parleys' voice faded off. He coughed a little.

"So, was the reality of your experience everything you thought it would be?"

"For the most part." Andy's voice was a little emotional.

"You said, 'for the most part'. What does that mean?"

"They teach you that you are shooting targets. You're neutralizing the target. You're not shooting a man. You're shooting a target. That's how I thought about it until I killed my first woman. . .And my first child. . .It's impossible to call a child a target. That's why women shouldn't be in combat. It's hard to call a woman a target. . .But when you have your orders and they are carrying a rocket launcher or a grenade and they're running at your guys. . .It's kill or be killed. You squeeze the trigger and two seconds later you see a woman in long flowing robes topple to the ground and it's your bullet that did it to her. . .She hits the ground hard and bounces and rolls and blows. . ." Jeff knew they were reaching his limit. He stayed quiet and let Andy squeeze his eyes shut.

Ten days later, Andy was sitting in a wheelchair being wheeled to the chemotherapy lab. As he was going in for his first treatment, he was wondering what it would be like when he lost his hair. He didn't have much hair to lose. His hair was cut high and tight. The standard Marine Corp haircut. They told him he would lose his hair most likely after the second treatment. Possibly as soon as the first treatment. Andy was surprised how good he felt after his first treatment. He expected to be very sick.

Andy felt well enough to eat dinner that evening. The nurse

in oncology told him not to eat his favorite food before chemo or right after because he would end up throwing it all up. He would probably come to hate what used to be his favorite food. He didn't understand, but he followed their advice. Father Friday came by to visit with him the evening after his first treatment.

"How are you doing my boy?" asked a friendly faced Father Friday.

"Oh, Father, come on in. I'm doing surprisingly well."

"Didn't you have your first chemotherapy treatment today?"

"I did."

"Well, I have to say that you are looking rather good."

"Thanks, I guess. I'm getting a little nervous about losing this pretty head of hair," Andy said as he rubbed his closely shorn head of dark blonde hair with his right hand. That gave Father Friday a good chuckle.

The nurse came in while they were talking to give Parley some medicine. "What am I taking?" Andy asked as him as he looked at a hand full of tablets and capsules.

"One of those is your pain pill, one is for nausea, the other is part of your chemotherapy. The other two are vitamin supplements," said Jacob the oncology nurse.

"I'm not nauseated."

"Hopefully you won't be. They have some really cool medicine to make chemotherapy a lot easier than it used to be. It's still bad, but with any luck and some good pills, it won't be near as bad as it could be."

"Well then, bottoms up," said Andy as he tossed the pills to the back of his mouth and washed them down with a 7-Up. The nurse also placed a box of lemon drops on Andy's bed side tray.

"What are those for?" asked Andy.

"Oh, didn't they tell you about lemon drops in the lab?"

"No. Why lemon candy?"

"Lemon drop candy is strong and a lot of chemo patients find that it helps them get the metallic taste out of their mouth. It also helps remove the bad taste after throwing up. Not everyone uses it, but a lot of people find that it comes in handy."

"I'll keep that in mind. Any other advice?"

"Yes, keep this tray with you for when you feel like you might vomit," said Jacob as he handed Andy a plastic yellow kidney tray.

"When will that happen? I'm feeling pretty good."

"It's different for everyone. You might not puke right away. From my experience, I've never seen anyone on a chemo protocol like you're on that doesn't throw up on the first treatment. Just saying."

"What if I throw up these pills I just swallowed, will that be a problem?"

"Not if you keep the medicine down for about twenty minutes or so. This is all a best effort thing. Small mistakes happen like timing between medicine and personal reactions. Cross your finger's gunny and hope." Father Friday said goodbye to Andy and left. Andy was feeling surprisingly good. He was enjoying the feeling of wellness and hadn't felt all that good until the last day or two. He was getting tired. It was a heavy tired, and it came on fast. He didn't want to waste the wellness feeling by going to sleep, but the desire to sleep was stronger than his strength to fight it. He slept deep and he slept well all through the first two nurses visits.

He was having a pleasant dream of fly fishing on the Brown river close to his boyhood home. He had got forty fish and was fighting another fish on his line when he felt an overwhelming wave of nausea engulf his body causing him gag and vomit in the brown river. He was doubled over and his stomach muscles were seizing. He gagged and convulsed as his dinner came back up. His forty trout starting flying out of his wicker basket and flying away. He was feeling warm and wet, but he hadn't fallen into the river. *Why am I wet?* The smell was revolting, it wasn't a fishy smell. There were beeps and whistles and strange mechanical sounds and chaos was everywhere. His eyes flew open. The river was gone. *Where am I? Where did the river go?* He was breathing hard. *Oh yeah. Walter Reed.* Andy had been yanked from his pleasant dream that had quickly turned into a nightmare. He was wet, the stench was awful and he felt nauseated. He realized that the prediction of him vomiting had occurred while he was asleep.

He was upset with himself. A nurse came in to check on all the beeping noise. "Looks like a bad accident. Don't worry gunny. We'll get you cleaned up."

"I was sleeping," Parley said, shaking his head, "and I woke up in the middle of throwing up, I feel sick."

"That's the good old chemo for ya. While its killing the cancer cells it's also killing some healthy cells. You can't win for losing with that stuff," Jacob said in a good natured tone.
Andy felt more sick than he had ever felt before. The room was rocking and Jacobs kindly voice was annoying him. *Will this ever end?* Sundance, another nurse came in to help Andy into the shower to clean up. This was the worst part for him.

Andy was normally a strong and sturdy five feet and eleven inches, but with the loss of his foot and leg he was five foot five inches. He had lost a lot of weight from losing his leg and foot along with losing weight from being sick. Now, he was a helpless stump of a man who couldn't clean himself.

Andy tried to cover up his embarrassment by talking about the dream he had when his dinner came up all over him. He was surprised by how well he remembered the dream. "So then the forty trout I had caught were flying off everywhere and I couldn't get them back . . . " Said Andy.

"Why did you let em get away like that?" Sundance said with a smile. "I know I wouldn't let forty fish get away from me like that."

"You try puking your guts out and try keeping those fish from flying away from you," Andy replied with a slight grin.

Sundance was helping Andy get back into a freshly made bed when Andy said, "Thanks Sundance, for being cool about all this."

"It was all worth it to hear that fishing story of yours."

"It's too bad it was just a dream."

"Be glad you had the dream at all. So many guys in here only have nightmares about their war experiences. Think about it. Now you have the memory of that dream to compete with the nightmares of war and to compete against all those bad memories. Know what I'm saying?"

"That's an interesting way of thinking about it." Andy was feeling a wave of nausea come over him and he looked frantically for the kidney dish to throw up in. That was just the beginning of a long night of violent sickness for Andy. The last twelve attempts to throw up were dry heaves. Sundance called the doctor and they tried all the medicine they could, as soon as they could, to stop his vomiting. Nothing would work. The night seemed like it would go on forever.

Chapter Fifteen: A Day Of Hope

As a man thinketh in his heart, so is he. Proverbs

July 2012
Lake Shaft City, Wyoming

As Parley suffered, the minutes seemed like hours, the hours seemed like days, and the days seemed like months. In Parleys' more lucid moments he was amazed at how long a year would take to live in the midst of raging agony, yet that same year went by so much faster when he was healthy. Yet a day was still a day and a year was still a year.

As Parley was going through endless years of agony, the sleepless nights increased. The chronic fatigue never went away and the disabling pain would not let up. There were times when he didn't know the difference between night and day. *I can't do this . . . I cannot do this! Why can't I edit a single video all the way through? I've done it a million times. Why is this happening to me? I'm better than this, stronger than this. I can't lose my life's work. I can't do this. I can't fight this pain anymore. I'm so tired, why can't I think clearly? Why is this happening to me? Heaven help me. I can't live like this.*

Hank Standing Elk had left for Salt Lake City for a pain seminar at the University of Utah School of Medicine. He was not due back for eight more days. Miranda had been fighting a cold and sore throat for three days and had not gone to the doctor because Hank was gone and in her opinion, 'every doctor in Lake Shaft City was worthless.' None of them could help Parley and only a few even tried.

Finally, with a fever of one-hundred and one, Betty took her to the clinic. Having Betty take Miranda to the clinic added to Parleys' growing pile of failures. It was one more thing that Parley couldn't do. Miranda had picked up that slack with the kids, but now

Betty was picking up the slack by helping with Miranda. When they got to the doctor's office, he swabbed her throat. They diagnoses her with a strep infection. They gave her antibiotics. Walking out of the clinic, Miranda was beside herself. The very same doctor that helped her with her throat had seen Parley three times previously and did nothing for him. She could tell he recognized her, but he didn't ask how Parley was doing. With Miranda, he was friendly and helpful. She was glad for the help, yet she was still upset with the doctor and had virtually no respect for him.

While Betty was taking Miranda to the doctor, Bert kept Parley company. Parley was complaining to his dad about his lack of sleep. "I never get more than just a few minutes of sleep here or there. Sometimes I don't know if it's night or day unless I look outside the window. It's like I'm in a constant daze with no energy. I'm never fully awake and I'm never fully asleep."

"It's been a long, long time, but I think I understand. Back during my days in 'Nam when I was a POW I didn't sleep much. When we were first brought to our prison camp there were twenty-four of us POWS'. We were all scared, even the biggest and meanest of us were terrified. We had a hard time sleeping. Then, within just three or four weeks, six had died from their injuries. They never gave us any medical treatment treating us worse than pigs. That shook us up a lot."

"Then a little later they started taking us all in for torture and interrogation." Bert noticed the look of surprise and shock on Parleys' weary face.

"They took us in to ask questions. When we refused to answer they tortured us."

"How . . . What did they do to you guys?"

"That may take another forty years before I can talk about that."

Parley was interested and anxious to hear it. "Go on." Parley decided to just shut up and let his dad talk.

The mood was thick and Bert's voice was strong and powerful, but as he recalled these memories, he seemed distant and disconnected.

They would take five or six of us in each day and work us over. That gave us about three days to recuperate before they did it again and again and again. . . Well, that frayed our already raw nerves even more. With all that stress, sleep was hard or impossible to come by. It felt like what you said, always in a daze with no energy, never fully awake and never able to really fully sleep."

For a few brief moments Parley wasn't feeling the pain and his mind was remarkably clear as he processed this new information about his dad. Information he had never known. He felt like his suffering was trivial compared to what his dad went through.

"My gosh dad, I never knew. . .Does Mom know, does Nick know?"

"It was a long time before I told your Mom. Nick doesn't know. It's not a secret, it was just something I wasn't ready to talk about, I guess until now. It's hard finding the words. The way you described that dazed sleepless feeling brought that memory back to mind."

"I'm sorry about that. I didn't mean to dredge up those bad memories." Parleys' exhaustion and agony came roaring back and he looked like he was two or three seconds from falling asleep.

"You look like you're about to drift off Son, don't worry about it. Just relax. If you fall asleep great. Don't worry about me."

Just as Parley let himself relax, his eyes popped wide open and he wasn't the least bit sleepy.

Parley was often confused by his never ending and sadistic pain, constant lethargy and restless nights. Each symptom, a serious issue with its own problems. They all demanded attention and were never satisfied leaving Parley burned out on every level.

He didn't have the capacity to deal with all the demands that his body made. He was always in a quandary wondering how to satisfy the need to ease the pain and get the sleep and have the energy his body insisted on. Now he betrayed himself by not being able to give into the demands of his body and get some much needed sleep. He wondered when his next chance at sleep would come. A minute from now, days? Weeks? Months?

Long seconds turned into minutes and long minutes slowly turned into hours and hours slowly turned into more never ending days. Many more of these listless and painful days came and went. Parleys' dazed mind wondered how all of this suffering was possible without dying. Surely the human body could only endure so much.

Miranda was keeping her fingers crossed as she counted down the days for Hank Standing Elks return. She prayed and yearned for Hank to come back with some new knowledge, some new medical breakthrough that would cure Parley.

They were both frustrated because, according to all the doctors' Parley had been to, there was nothing wrong with Parley that would explain his chronic pain. They were all baffled that the traditional medicines for insomnia didn't work for him. Some of the doctors took a defensive posture toward Parley using extreme medical terminology to try and explain away what was happening or not happening to Parley. Hank wasn't much better. Really the only difference was he cared about Parley and was honest with Parley and Miranda.

The day for Hank to return finally arrived and they both tried to downplay his arrival. They let their thoughts air on the side of pessimism. They were afraid of hoping for anything out of fear that he wouldn't come back empty handed. But on the other hand, Hank was all they had to hope for if Parley was to ever get well again.

Miranda knew Parley was on the verge of letting go of any hope, giving way to the anger that was welling up in his heart. Anger at life and circumstances that let him be in constant agony. *It's time to bite the bullet and call White Flower for an appointment. I should have called earlier, maybe we could have gotten in later this afternoon.*

Every aspect of his life was affected by his never-ending agony and fatigue. Every now and again Parley thought back at his 'near miss'. He wondered if he had made the right choice, the choice to live. Since the 'near miss', he had come to learn that there were worse things in life than death. Even though he was glad he chose to live, he was still sometimes tempted to wonder if life was worth the suffering? Underneath the overwhelming afflictions he was going through, was it all worth it? Those recurring thoughts frustrated him.

The pain would wax and wane and when his pain was waning, he would hold out hope only to have his hope dashed when his pain increased. He got frustrated at his frustration.

His life had been going so well, he was achieving his dreams and he was happy. Now the agony of his life was spiraling out of control. He wondered how his life would end up? In spite of all this he had nagging thoughts and feelings telling him there was still something for him to do in life. Those nagging thoughts and feeling told him to hang on just a little longer.

As Parley was absently watching TV, he heard a car door slam shut. Then he heard the doorbell ring. He heard Miranda walking to the front door. He tried to understand what the muffled voices were saying. Then he heard the stairs creak as two people were climbing upstairs.

"Parley! Buddy! Boy am I glad to see you" With effort. Parley looked up and turned his head slowly to see Hank with a big expressive smile on his face. He didn't know exactly why, but he sensed they were on the verge of something big.

"I just got back from my seminar and, I think, at least I'm quite sure, I finally have some answers. It all made so much sense at the seminar. . . Well stand up my friend. I need to examine you again. Come on," said Hank as he reached his hand out to help Parley get on his feet. Slowly, stiffly and painfully Parley got to his feet. It took a few moments to get his breath. When he did, he let out a few pent up curse words. "Parley watch your mouth," Miranda said sternly.

"Oh, don't worry about his language, this poor boy is suffering."

"What's going on?" demanded Parley, annoyed at Hanks high energy.

"Just bare with me buddy. I am going to do an eighteen point trigger test."

"Is it going to hurt?"

"I sure hope so. The more it hurts the better. Just cooperate and I'll tell you as I go."

Starting with the back of Parleys' neck, Hank pressed tender points all the way down to his knees. Every single pressure point hurt badly except the two on his elbows.

"Very good, you have sixteen out of eighteen tender points. Knowing your medical history I can diagnose you with fibromyalgia. Normally I would have to run a series of tests to rule out the many other possibilities, but since all the tests have been done, I can be confident saying that your pain and all of your symptoms are real and they tell us you have fibromyalgia."

Parley had no idea what Hank was talking about since he was talking a mile a minute, but he was feeling hopeful with the enthusiasm in Hanks voice. "Does this mean I really am sick and it isn't all in my head like so many doctors said?"

"Yes," Hanks voice was brimming with excitement. And now I know what you have and with all the news information I've learned, I can treat you more accurately and with more confidence."

"How long will it take until I am better, until I'm cured?" Parley asked with excitement.

"Well," Hanks voice lost some of its excitement. "There is a down side to all of this. . .There's no known cure for fibromyalgia, at least for right now. But keep in mind, there are treatments to help manage the symptoms. Knowing you have fibromyalgia allows me to treat each of your symptoms, even though we will be masking the symptoms we won't be covering up some mysterious illness that could continue to get worse."

In an instant Parleys' hopes soared through the sky only to be shot down with the last bit of news. Now Parley didn't know how to feel. He was happy, disappointed and mad. For years, Parley had been waiting to hear a doctor say they could help him, treat him, and then cure him. Now he was being told he had a chronic illness with no cure. What kind of answer was that? What kind of life would he have, knowing he would always be sick with pain? The anger in Parleys' mind was edging out the short-lived hope Hank had given him.

Hank could see the glimmer of hope Parley had drain away into a lake of despair.

"I know a diagnosis with an incurable illness isn't what you wanted to hear, but remember, we can now really start treating and managing your symptoms. We can improve your quality of life. We won't get rid of all your pain, but we can reduce it."

Giving Parley and Miranda a few minutes to diagnose all that he had just told them, he wrote out a few prescriptions for Parley. Then he said, "We're going to be more aggressive with muscle relaxers, adding a pain pill to the mix and start looking at a few different anxiety pills. It might take a few months of tweaking your medication until we find the sweet spot, but we'll get there."

Hank handed Miranda a handful of prescriptions. "If you go get these filled now, Parley might start feeling less pain by later this afternoon." Miranda took the prescriptions and left for the pharmacy.

While Miranda was at the pharmacy Hank called up Rita to tell her that he was home safe and he told her what was going on. After talking to her he raided the Burnrise refrigerator and warmed up a hamburger casserole for Parley and him. They were almost done eating, when Miranda returned home, pills in hand.

Hank had Parley take one pill from each of the four bottles right away. He then wrote down on a sheet of paper detailed instruction on how to take these new medicines along with the prescriptions he was already on. He then went on to explain more about fibromyalgia.

"Before the seminar I spent a lot of time researching out different illness on the internet and I ran across fibromyalgia. When I read that eighty-five to ninety percent of all those who suffered from the illness were women, I dismissed it. What's the chance of you having something like that? Then I learned a lot more about fibro and several other pain related illnesses at the conference. The two doctors presenting the lecture on fibromyalgia talked in great detail about the illness and said that it was very possible that more men suffered from fibromyalgia than the statistics indicated. They either haven't been correctly diagnosed or the men haven't gone to the doctor yet. Some of the audience suggested the men might also be self medicating with booze or drugs."

"So what exactly is fibromyalgia?" Asked Miranda.

"It's an illness that causes chronic widespread pain throughout the body. It can cause pain in the joints, muscles, and other soft tissues. Pain isn't the only symptom, things like IBS, chronic fatigue, sleep problems, painful pressure points, concentration problems, and frequent headaches when considered altogether indicate fibromyalgia. If that's not enough to consider, there are still more issues with fibro like light, chemical and noise sensitivities, anxiety, and depression all fit into the symptomology. A lot of the medical community thinks fibromyalgia is a problem with the central nervous system and hyperactive nerves. Originally Rheumatologists treated fibro and they still do, but some think neurologists should treat it. Still others say we know enough about it that family doctors can handle it."

"So now what? Will this new medicine get me back to normal and keep me there as long as I take it?" asked Parley.

"Fibromyalgia is very complex. I know more than I'm telling you only because there is so much to digest. Feel free to research it as you like. As we work through this, I'll tell you all I know about it. To really answer your question. . .The fibromyalgia won't get any better because no one knows how to cure a disease that they don't fully understand. All we can do right now is manage the symptoms and try to reduce the pain you feel and improve on the other symptoms. We can't know exactly how well you'll be until you have taken the medicine for a while. The hope is to give you back as much of your old life as possible."

"What about the fatigue and sleep problems?"

"Now we have found a muscle relaxer that works during the day without making you drowsy we'll stay with that during the day time and have you try one of the other muscle relaxers that make you drowsy at night. Hopefully that will help with your sleep. Also, if we can lessen the severity of the symptoms, it could help the sleep problems, hopefully."

"Sounds complicated," said Parley. "Complicated, but a little hopeful."

"A lot hopeful. You'll come around as you see the medicine starts to work. The pain you're going through could be masking other symptoms that we may have to deal with down the road. But now we know what we're dealing with so feel free to enjoy some hope buddy, you deserve it."

"This is overwhelming," added Miranda.

"It is. If I didn't have a personal stake in this with you and several of my patients on the reservation, I probably wouldn't know this much this soon. I have a stack of reference materials to review. I spent a lot of money taking those two doctors to dinner to pick their brains. Oh yeah, I also gave them both a free family pass for a week." "Was it the Cabin special?"

"It was. Two cabins, all the meals and a boat for a week."

"Good, that's good thinking. Did it seem to help?"

"It did, especially after I showed them your blog and they read up on it. One is an avid trout fisherman and the other one is into water skiing. A score in both cases. Also, I told them if you were up to it, you would take them on a private fishing trip. If you can't go, I can take them. I know all your spots."

"Yes, but you're no where as good as I am." Parley said with a smile. Noticing the smile, Miranda asked him if the pain pill was kicking in. "Yes," Parley answered with a startled voice. Parley stopped talking and started to mentally scan his body starting with his toes all the way up to his head. "Hank, help me up." Hank bent over and grabbed one of Parleys' hands and placed his other hand behind Parleys' shoulder and helped him get up.

"Ouch," Parley groaned as he got up. He swayed a little until he had his footing. "Oh man. I'm stiff as a board."

Hank and Miranda were silent as they looked at Parley wondering what was going on inside his head. Parley stood in place for a long few seconds.

"What are you doing?" asked Miranda.

"Just wanted to see how I feel standing up."

"What level is your pain right now?"

"Mmm, seven, maybe. Well no. . .Wait a minute. . .Maybe a

six, a six, or a seven. That sucks. I was hoping for more." Parleys' voice had a hint of optimism laced with a little disappointment.

"Things aren't going to change overnight and I have more in store for you. We're, just beginning. I'll write down all the instructions with your new medication. We need to give them all a chance. As time goes on, you should feel even more relief. Just remember, we can't fix your fibro, only treat it."

Chapter Sixteen: Fight The Good Fight

I know the plans I have for you. . .plans to prosper you and not to harm you, plans to give you hope and a future. (Jeremiah)

August To September 2012
Walter Reed National Military Medical Center, Maryland

Over the past two months Andy had gone through weekly life altering chemotherapy treatments. The suffering was overwhelming and the nausea was gut retching. The side effects of the chemo made Andy feel like death's door was just around the corner. Wondering how others could face deaths door week after week, Andy wasn't sure he could. He had no choice, but to try.

Andy would start each week with a chemo treatment. By that evening his world was turned upside down with more agony and suffering than he could have previously imagined. He spent the rest of the week recuperating from the insane ordeal. When he was lucky, he had one or two days at the end of the week where he would feel almost human only to start the torturous process over again.

He was advised by one of the chemo nurses to 'take it one day at a time.' He wondered what that meant? After a few weeks of treatments he started to get a sense of what it meant and how wise that advice was. Concentrate on the moment you're in and keep your focus on today, not worrying about tomorrow. Each day he felt he was battling for his life. Learning to embrace the natural instinct to survive the day he wondered if he would have the energy to keep up the fight. Starting to understand what trusting in the Lord really meant he knew that he would only get through this torture with the help of the Lord.

There were many days where he didn't know which was worse, getting his leg and foot blown off or dealing with the daily trials of chemotherapy treatments. Sometimes he wondered if his cancer was payback for all the killing he was forced to do on the battlefield. During the occasional moments of peace during all the agony, he realized the cancer was unrelated to his war efforts. In the few moments of calm he was reminded he would make it through the treatments, but in the end, his life was in God's hands.

From time to time he was reminded during his suffering he still had a purpose in life, even without a leg and a foot.

He had determined when he was in college he had been called by the Lord to live a life of service. He knew it wasn't a call to be a preacher, but it was a call to serve just the same. After the terrorist attacks of September 11 occurred, he had an overwhelming feeling he should serve his countrymen by serving in the military. Even with all that had happened to him, like losing his foot and leg only to be followed by cancer, he still felt like there was someone out there to serve.

In the middle of his treatments the brass organized a ceremony at the Medical Center to award him the Navy Cross. A representative from SECNAV was in attendance, along with his Congressional Representative from his home state of Georgia. Andy was in his dress uniform that was now three sizes too big. He had lost a great deal of weight from all the surgeries and chemotherapy. As a result, his dress uniform was particularly baggy.

They did everything they could to make the event as memorable as possible for Andy. The ceremony was two hours before his next chemo treatment. They did this in an effort to ensure that he would be at his best physically. Andy prayed he would be able to make it through the ceremony without being sick. There was no controlling when a wave of nausea could hit. In the end he made it through the ceremony.

One of the things that pleased him the most about the award ceremony was several of his chemo buddies were in attendance to support him getting the Navy Cross. They made a big deal of it during their treatments two hours later.

When Andy was in college, he came across an outdoor blog that focused on camping, hunting, fishing, boating and everything related to the great outdoors. Now with nothing but sickness and time on his hands, he started visiting the site once again. There were more than a thousand videos and entertaining articles. Besides his frequent bible reading, he turned to OutdoorParley.com for something to occupy his mind. It was so much better than watching TV.

One of the first video's he watched when he went back to OutdoorParley.com was when Parley Burnrise was fishing and managed to film the golden eagle catching a trout on Lake Shaft. He had watched that video several times over the last couple of days and he even brought his laptop to chemo with him so he and his chemo buddies could watch it together.

They watched the mighty golden eagle with his brown plumed body pumping his powerful white feathered wings onward and downward, toward his next meal. The raw power of this golden predator flew steadily toward his prey. He flew so close to the surface of the lake that the tip of his left wing broke the surface of the water. Fully in control with his wings extended and his body pushing onward, the eagle's legs swung forward talons extended. He lowered himself just enough so his outstretched claws dipped into the water snatching a large trout. The golden eagle flapped his mighty wings soaring upward and onward to its nest in the nearby forest.

The collective oohs and aahs among Andy's friends were heard by the rest of the chemo group. So, by popular demand, Andy passed his laptop around for a few of the other guys to watch.

Suddenly Andy grabbed at his chest with a frightened look on his face. "Nurse. My heart is on fire! What's going on? Am I having a heart attack?"

The nurse who was nearest to him was sitting on a wheeled stool. When she heard Andy cry out, she pushed herself over to him as she readied her stethoscope. She immediately listened to his heart and took his pulse telling him, "your heart is okay. It's burning because the chemotherapy is pumped directly into your heart so the medicine can be pushed throughout your body. Frankly, I'm a little surprised you haven't complained about it sooner?"

"That's good, man that's a relief. I've had heartburn several times, but not like this." Captain Gerald Green across the semi circle from Andy said, "it's crazy they practically kill us to make us better."

"Ain't that the truth. It seems so barbaric to send poison into our bodies to kill the cancer cells along with so many healthy cells to make us better. It's a wonder we ever recover. I guess it beats the heck out of dying soon," said Captain Greely.

Andy was listening to them talk and wondered about their diagnosis'. They all spoke like they would be all right once their treatments were over. He knew all he was doing was buying time. There were many times he wondered if the living hell he was going through was worth an extra year or two, but the same overwhelming feeling come over him for some reason the Lord wanted him to live a while longer even without the use of a foot and leg. Selfishly, Andy would sometimes think, "it better be worth it." Then after thinking those thoughts, he would feel bad and apologize to the Lord. During one of his chemo treatments he came across an old familiar passage in Jeremiah and it caught his attention. He thought about it a little and reread it, "I know the plans I have for you," declares the LORD, "plans to prosper you and not to harm you, plans to give you hope and a future."

It's comforting to know that I am part of God's plan, but I sure would like to know my future. Why am I doing this? He read the verse one more time. He felt good about three parts; prosperity, hope and a future, but the harm part nagged at him. *I'm in harms way right now. How's that part of the plan?*

~

Lake Shaft City, Wyoming
October 2012

At first Parley was happy for the diagnosis of fibromyalgia.

With it came a degree of validation, but not a medical solution. He had to admit he was in less pain since Hank had prescribed new pain medications. Yet he found himself growing angry for having been sick for so long. He didn't want to have his symptoms managed, he wanted them healed.

Now days with all the miracles of modern medicine, he should be back to normal. When he broke his arms and ribs they hurt, but over time as they healed the pain went away. *Why isn't this suffering going away?* The more he thought about his condition the more upset he became. As he grew more angry, he grew more cross toward those around him.

Over the past four or five months since Parley had been diagnosed with fibromyalgia he had been living the life of an onion.

They finally started peeling the onion down with a diagnosis of fibromyalgia. The next layer was getting pain medicine. Other medications were prescribed and other layers were pulled back. The tears started to flow. While the layers of the onion were coming off, they were discovering other symptoms of fibromyalgia. They would have to peel those symptoms off, one at a time. More tears. As the intensity of the pain was reduced the anguish was replaced with more symptoms. The layers of the onion were being replaced as fast as they were being peeled off. Just when progress seemed to be noticeable, the onion grew more layers.

Parley was in a new and unfamiliar world where anger replaced gratitude. He knew he should be grateful the degree or intensity of his pain was improving. He was getting used to referencing the pain scale doctors offices and hospitals used. It made communicating his level of pain easier. He could say since he started seeing Hank his pain had gone from a ten to an eight and then to a seven and down to where it was now at a six. For a really good day his pain level might be a four or five. In spite of all he was feeling anger toward fibromyalgia or toward life for letting him experience fibro. It was an interesting, strange thing to be mad at life. He wondered if he was mad at God? Parley believed in a kind, caring, and loving God. God wouldn't make him go through such a terrible illness. Life, on the other hand wasn't so kind or merciful.

Life doesn't care who is suffering and who is not. He had always considered himself a devoted disciple of the Lord. Now he would need to lean on his Savior more than ever before.

Parley had an appointment with Hank at the end of August. Parley expressed his concern about getting addicted to narcotic pain relievers. He asked Hank if there were any other medicine could possibly ease his pain besides Lortab.

"There are a couple of medicines that treat the nerves rather than just mask the pain sensors in the brain like narcotics. Supposedly, they are better suited to treat fibromyalgia pain than narcotics. However, when it comes to managing pain, I find narcotics work for more people most of the time than these other medicines do. Now we know you are responding to Lortab, we will have something to fall back on if neither of these pills work."

"This sounds complicated. I'm glad you know all about this stuff. I could never keep track of it all," remarked Parley.

"So what we will do is begin with this pill," Hank said, holding up a sample pack. "We will start at a low dose and work it up to a therapeutic level. We won't know until you're at that level for a while if it will work. We will take you off the narcotic and see how things feel for you. If they work, great, if not, then we'll put you back on your normal pain pill and slowly take you off the nerve pill. There is a second similar medication we can try if the first one doesn't work."

"How long will it take until we know if it will work?"

"They way I'm dosing you, it will take seven weeks to ramp you up to a therapeutic level and a week of tapering you off the narcotic. The makes eight weeks, but we'll want to give it a full week without any Lortab to be sure of how it affects you. So we're talking about nine weeks."

"Why so long and why does it sound so complicated?" Asked Miranda.

"I will write this all down in detail so it won't really be complicated. It takes time to build this drug up in your system. It's not a type of medicine you can start at full strength like you could with narcotics."

"So, after all this it might not even work?" Parley said it with a doubtful tone.

"That's right. It might not even work, but if it does its better than being on narcotics."

Parley took a deep breath and mournfully said, "all right then, let's do it."

Chapter Seventeen: The Next Step

May you see God's light on the path ahead when the road you walk is dark.
May you always hear, even in your hour of sorrow, the gentle singing of the lark.
When times are hard may hardness never turn your heart to stone,
May you always remember when the shadows fall—You do not walk alone.
Old Irish Blessing

March 2013
Atlanta, Georgia

As Andy was waking up, the first thing he noticed was the scent of fresh bed sheets. With effort he rolled over noticing the crisp newness of those brand-new linens. There was a faint smell of dust in the air. His foggy eyes started to clear as he focused on his new surroundings. He noticed a different color on the bare walls. Something was different. The air was a little more humid than usual. He noticed the pillow case was also crisp and new.

Everything was pleasant, as pleasant as it could for a double amputee. What started out as a pleasant surprise turned into concern. Andy looked around. Nothing was familiar. Nothing was as it should be. Where am I? He rolled over to his right side with some effort. There was his wheelchair that was good. His crutches were propped against the wall at the foot of his bed. That's good, but where am I?

He was not in the Walter Reed Medical Center anymore. He was sure of that. His heart began beating heavy and quick. Holding himself up with one hand, he wiped sweat from his forehead. He had a feeling he should know where he was, yet he didn't. There was a lump in his throat. He couldn't breathe fast or deep enough to satisfy his wildly racing heart. Where am I? Wheelchair, good.

Where's the nurse call button? I'm not in the hospital anymore.

At the sudden loud ringing of his cell phone, he jumped out of his skin. At first he didn't recognize the ringtone of his cell phone. Like a flash everything suddenly made sense. His new reality came flooding back. He realized he was in his newly rented apartment in Atlanta Georgia. His cell phone was ringing. Where is my phone? He looked all around him. No phone. The ringing stopped.

He scooted himself against the wall on the left side of his bed. He was in a strange sitting position. Since he had gone through physical and occupational therapy at Walter Reed, he was starting to adjust to his stump of a body that was missing a foot and a leg. Am I going to make it? Is this what life is now?

He looked at an empty, cold despairing wheelchair. He knew he had to get into it. He didn't want to, but he had to. The only thing standing between him and the bathroom, was a cold, lifeless wheelchair. Motivated by the morning call of nature and his desire to eat, he made a temporary truce with his bad attitude and scooted to the edge of the bed.

He went through his mental checklist. Are the breaks on? He checked. Am I positioned right? He checked. They said this would be second nature. I wonder when? In a fluid motion, he was able to gain enough momentum to swing his body onto the wheelchair. He wore a necklace with a pendant that had a button he could press if he found himself on the floor and unable to get up. He could press it to get help with the local fire and rescue. His goal was to never use it. Ever.

Cool, I'm off to a good start. Within twenty-five minutes he had a bowl of oatmeal, a cup of coffee and two pieces of buttered toast in front of him. He was sitting in his wheelchair at the kitchen table with his laptop open. He was amazed at how good his simple meal tasted. It was far better than the hospital food he had lived on. Everything smelled better and everything tasted better. He was sipping his black coffee and watching some fun outdoor videos from OutdoorParley.com. What a life Parley Burnrise has, hunting and fishing all day, every day. I sure would like to be in his shoes– yeah right. Shoes. That would be a nice trick.

Andy had been discharged from Walter Reed and he had been retired from the United State Marine Corp with full benefits. He had no place to go since he was not married and since he had no family. He was from southern Georgia. One was usually discharged from active duty to the place they were from. In his case he had a strong feeling he wouldn't be in Georgia for long, so he decided to muster out in Atlanta. With the help of several nonprofit groups designed to help veterans, especially disabled veterans, he was hooked up with a nice studio apartment.

A studio apartment was good for him since he was in a wheelchair. It was one very big room with a large handicap friendly bathroom. Jeff Bellows, his social worker with the help of Father Friday who had connections in Atlanta, were able to reach out to some great groups came to Andy's aid. There was a VA Hospital in Atlanta and many programs to help the handicapped.

Andy had many reservations about facing life on his own with no foot or leg, yet he was chomping at the bit to get out of Walter Reed. Today was Andy's first full day on his own. He had some prepared meals in the fridge and freezer that only needed thawing and warming up. He had three weeks scheduled out with visits from a social worker, occupational therapist, benefit's counselor, a preacher from a local Christian congregation, someone to help him understand how to take advantage of the many different transit options including several VA transportation services. The list was long and written down so he wouldn't forget.

Some of those visitors were there to help Andy take advantage of volunteer organizations design to help disabled vets. One of those was scheduled at one in the afternoon. He had long since finished his breakfast and was still sitting at the table watching videos from OutdoorParley.com. He had stopped watching the hunting videos because it made him want to hunt. He didn't see how he could hunt, but he knew he could fish so he confined himself to the fishing videos. Two hours later his eyes were blurry and tired. They were strained from too much time in front of a computer monitor. His sixteen story apartment had a great view over the southern part of Atlanta. He wheeled his way over to the big window and put on his brakes and looked out the window. His cell phone rang again. He was easily startled. Not as much as he was earlier, but enough to cause his heart to start pounding again. Why am I so jumpy?   "Hello?"

"Gunny, How are you?" the voice said excitedly. "This is Jeff Bellows."

"Oh, hey. Hi. I'm doing all right."

"That's good to hear. I was just calling to see how things are going on your first day back in the real world. It's hard enough for battle hardened warriors to adjust back to civilian life, let alone being a disabled vet with a recent battle with cancer."

"Hmm, since you put it that way, I guess I'm doing really well, all things considered." They talked for a while.

"To tell you the truth Andy, I didn't know what to expect when I called you this morning, but what I'm hearing sounds really good. Gotta run to my new case. Another leatherneck from Iraq."

"Thanks for calling Jeff. I appreciate it. It was good to hear from you." After talking to Jeff, Andy continued looking out his window at the nice view. He got lost in his thoughts. He was jarred back to reality by the doorbell ringing. He had been deep in thought thinking of many of the events from the past eleven months. He had lived a lifetime in the past year. He had experienced unspeakable pain and agony and he had been more sick than ever before in his life. But now, he was feeling better. They still couldn't tell him how much time he had before the cancer would kill him. However, they had greatly reduced the size of the tumor.

He was making his way to the door. It was unlocked and he could have yelled out for them to come in. He was instructed not to get in the habit of inviting people into is home without visually verifying who it was. People in wheelchairs were so much more vulnerable than traditional society. He needed to be ever vigilant.

Chapter Eighteen: Panic

God's help is nearer than the door. Irish Proverb

March 2013
Lake Shaft City, Wyoming
Nine months had passed since the diagnosis of fibromyalgia. Over that time period Hank had prescribed two different medicines on Parley hoping they would help manage Parleys' pain well enough to take him off of narcotic pain relievers. The ordeal was a long and frustrating trial for Parley. While both of these nerve related prescriptions were promoted to help manage fibromyalgia and muscle pain, they didn't work for Parley. The only thing they did for him was making him so groggy he couldn't function on either of them.

For Parley, it was an unpleasant ordeal trying each of those two medications. At least he could keep taking his Lortab. Parley was, as usual, conflicted. His pain was less severe, but he still hurt. He still had all the other symptoms, but some of the symptoms weren't as bad with medication. He just wanted to take a pill or two and be back to normal. He felt a little guilty for not appreciating the fact that his insomnia was steadily improving.

Most of the time, when he thought about his near miss with death, he was glad he chose to live even though he felt like life still had little to offer him. He seemed to be feeling less hope with each passing day. That hopelessness was wearing him down.

Despair was an unwelcome visitor in Parley's mind, but as it persisted, he became more accepting of it. He was in his recliner with the TV providing background noise with his laptop resting on his lap as he browsed the internet. He was looking for ideas on how to deal with his fibro.

As he was browsing, he started to notice something strange was happening to him. It felt like it might be muscle spasms. The muscles between his shoulder blades seemed to contract and convulse. The painful sensation began spreading to other parts of his back. He closed his laptop and put it on the end table in jerky moves. He quickly opened his bottle of muscle relaxers and dry swallowed a soft pink tablet. The frenzied pangs were spreading around his ribs and painful taking up residence in his chest. He tried to relax his back muscles which were impossible to do. The spasms or pain, whatever it was, was increasing in intensity as they settled into his chest. He quickly took a pain pill knowing that it would take almost an hour for either pill to kick in.

Quickly, everything seemed to take a turn for the worse and got scary as he clutched his chest in response to a sudden dull throbbing ache. Those throbbing aches seemed to feel like they were also burning. With every heartbeat that fiery, dull ache got worse. He had experienced all kinds of aches and pains over the years, but never anything like this. *Am I having a heart attack? I'm having a heart attack!*

His chest gripped tighter and tighter and burned more and more. "Miranda." Parley tried to call out for his wife, but his voice just whispered with a rasping painful tone. She couldn't hear him and if she couldn't hear him, she couldn't help him. It was getting hard to breathe. He was gasping for air. He tried calling Miranda again. The only sound that came out of his mouth was a raspy, wheezy sound barely audible. There was no shout in his voice. He simply didn't have the power to break through the pain gripping his chest.

The last time this happened, it wasn't a heart attack. He tried to relax knowing he would be fine when the pain eased up. *Give it a few minutes, breathe, just relax.* He tried to push his legs down while scooting back into the recliner. He was trying to get up on his feet. A sense of panic overtook him. He felt like he was dying. It occurred to him just how much he wanted to live.

He saw his cell phone out of the corner of his eye resting on the side table. He tried to reach it, but the gripping ache in his chest caused him to come up short. *Push through the pain, push!* He coached himself. *Grab the phone!* He tried again and reached his phone, grabbing it tightly and brought his arm back to his side.

The chest pain was radiating to his arms and his hands

were feeling numb. He had read somewhere that people having a heart attack often felt pain or tingling in their arms and extremities. He was sinking fast. He could feel his life ebbing away. He dialed 9-1-1 and pressed the call button.

"9-1-1, what is your emergency?"

"I'm. . .Having," he slowly drawled, "A, heart. . .Attack" Parley gasped between each word.

"Sir, what is your address?"

"1-2-1-9-Lava-Rock-Road. . .Lake-Shaft– " The pain clipped his voice.

"Sir, are you there?"

Parley was trying to talk. He was breathing hard and irregularly, but loud enough for the operator to hear.

"Sir, I hear you breathing. An Ambulance is on its way. It should arrive in two minutes. I will stay with you. If you can talk say something."

The operator listened for a response that wasn't coming. The pain started to recede as the muscle spasms lessened. "I'm still here," Parley gasped. As the muscles started to relax, Parley was able to breathe a little easier. "I think, I can talk now," Parley managed to say as he gasped for breath.

"The ambulance should be there in less than a minute," the operator said. The pressure in his chest was slowly starting to ease up. His lightheadedness slowly lessened. Parley was still frightened.

Suddenly there was a loud knock on the downstairs door, followed by the doorbell ringing several times quickly followed by the sound of someone banging on the front door. He heard Miranda open the door. She saw two paramedics laden with emergency equipment.

"What's going on?" Miranda said frantically.

"We received a 9-1-1 call from this address."

Miranda was stunned as she tried to make sense of what was happening. She pieced together the fact her children were gone and the only ones at home were Parley and her. "Parley!" She shouted as she turned and raced up the stairs with the Paramedics in step behind her.

"Parley, Parley," Miranda was screaming as she ran up the half flight of stairs and down the hall to Parleys den. She saw Parley sitting on his recliner with his cell phone laying on his chest.

"What's going on?" She screamed.

"Step aside ma'am," said the first paramedic as they both slid into the room between Miranda and the doorway.

"What's wrong, sir?" asked Ralph, the first paramedic in the room.

"I think I'm having a heart attack. My chest hurts."

The second paramedic picked up his phone and told the operator they were on the scene and hung up, handing the phone to Miranda who was beside herself with worry. She was holding her hands over her mouth with her eyes big with worry.

Parleys' voice improved enough for him to tell Miranda, "I tried to call you honey, but I could hardly get a breath out to yell."

As he was talking, the paramedics went to work removing his shirt as they lifted him out of the recliner to lay flat on the floor. One paramedic started to get an EKG ready while the other took his vitals. A police officer showed up in the bedroom.

"Can I help with anything?" the officer asked.

"Yes, would you bring up the stretcher from the ambulance?"

"On it," answered the officer as he quickly stepped out of the room.

"Hold on guys, I'm feeling a lot better," declared Parley. The pain had suddenly let up enough to change Parleys' mind.

"What is your name, sir?"

"Parley Burnrise."

"Mr. Burnrise, we can't take any chances with a possible heart attack. We have a procedure to follow."

Parley saw a look of horror in Miranda's eyes. He felt sick inside. Within five minutes he was speeding safely to the Emergency Room in the back of the ambulance.

While racing to the hospital Miranda called Hank to tell him Parley had a heart attack and was on the way to the hospital. Hank told Miranda he would leave immediately and go straight to the hospital.

He had White Flower reschedule his appointments. To help Miranda he called Bert. Both Nick and Bert were in the back room at the store when he called. Bert, Betty and Nick made a beeline for the hospital, arriving only five minutes after the ambulance.

Miranda admired the efficiency of the medical center with their speed and organization in treating a heart attack and being that this was a small town hospital. Actually, it was a regional hospital for many rural communities in that part of Wyoming so they had a much better hospital than they ordinarily would. I'm glad they're so efficient. *If they can do all of this so well, why can't they help Parley with his pain?*

Miranda was also surprised at how fast Hank showed up. He spoke with Miranda to get the full story before going back into the ER. He had privileges at the hospital and so he worked with the ER doc and the cardiologist was called in. They paced him through a series of tests that in the end said his heart was healthy with no signs of a heart attack. His blood pressure was slightly elevated. They surmised that it was due to the stress of Parley being rushed to the hospital. The cardiologist acted bothered by the false alarm and left without seeing Parley. Hank went in to see Parley and tell him the good news.

"Hey Parley, good news, your heart is just fine."

"I thought it would be. The pain started to subside when the paramedics were there. The pain seemed to steadily decrease through all the tests."

"I know you said all that, but we have protocols, it's in your best interest to get the old ticker checked."

"Well, it's kind of embarrassing to go through all that for nothing and to do it for the second time."

"How is your pain level right now?"

"My chest is sore, kind of achy, but it's not flaring like it was. Everything else is like the new normal."

"On a scale of one to ten, how is your overall pain?"

Parley thought about it for a moment, "I guess it's around a six."

"All things considered, that's not too bad."

Hank asked Parley a few questions and did some poking and prodding, he came to the conclusion Parley had a condition called Costosternal Chondrodynia. That illness was otherwise known as chest wall pain that is often mistaken as heart attack pain. It is inflammation of the costal cartilage, which connects the ribs to the sternum. It can be a temporary inflammation or a chronic condition.

After hearing this explanation Parley asked, "So is this what I have and not fibromyalgia?"

"No. You still have fibromyalgia. This is different. It's in addition to your fibro. It could be inflammation, like the traditional diagnosis or it could be related to fibromyalgia. Fibro is a wide spread painful condition of the muscles and other soft tissue of the body. Cartilage is a soft tissue. It's hard to know if this is a stand-alone condition or related to your fibro, but we treat it the same."

Parley sighed as more was heaped upon him and his lousy health. "So what do we do about it? Will it come back?" asked Miranda.

"It very well could come back. It could also be a one time deal. I'm going to give Parley an anti-inflammatory. If this pain comes back try this pill. It will likely take away the pain. Just remember though, when in doubt about chest pain, come to the hospital, call an ambulance or whatever, but come to the hospital. It's better to be safe than sorry."

"Sorry to drag you all the way out here. Thanks though, for coming," Parley said.

"No problem, glad to do it."

Chapter Nineteen: Purpose

Do all the good you can, by all the means you can, in all the ways you can, in all the places you can, at all the times you can, to all the people you can, as long as ever you can.
John Wesley

March 2013
Atlanta, Georgia

Between a series of firsts and a lot of boredom, Andy's first week living in Atlanta had been the longest week of his life. Limited to his wheelchair, he was nervous leaving his apartment. He had several appointments, but after his visitors left, he was lonely. In the hospital, he was surrounded by people and had to make an effort to be alone.

One way Andy fought, the boredom was OutdoorParley.com. Without it, he would have gone crazy. He also wondered if he was using it as a crutch, living his life through the adventures of Parley Burnrise. He had recently discovered the few episodes of the reality show From Catch To Plate, that Parley and Miranda did some years back. He also had been reading his Bible a lot. He always considered himself a devout Christian, but reading from the Bible for more than an hour was asking a lot. Andy was grateful that Parley Burnrise, whoever he was, had dedicated his life to blogging about the outdoors. He had only been outside of his apartment twice in the past week. One was to go to the convenience store for some food. Feeling excited and confident about getting out of his apartment building and going to the mini mart, he ran into several kids there. He avoided them, because their presence triggered his PTSD. His trip was productive, on the one hand, but ended on a bad note. All in all, he felt he was adjusting fairly well to his new environment other than being bored out of his mind.

Even though it had only been a few weeks since being

discharged, Andy had been stuck with a persistent feeling he was floating, not going anywhere, stagnating. Ever since graduating from college, he had dedicated his life to serving America. He joined the Marine Corp to serve his countrymen. His whole adult life was committed to serving. It was his calling and made him feel good giving him a meaningful purpose. Not only was he a man without a job, he was a man without a purpose.

Now, here he was with maybe enough time to do one good last act of service and he was coming up dry. He didn't know what to do. He had been praying about it off and on for a long time. Unaccustomed to a lack of purpose in his life, he was growing impatient.

He was, feeling quite good, reasonably healthy and feeling more energetic every day with nothing meaningful to do. He wanted something rewarding to set his sights on. He couldn't be a Marine anymore. He had some time left, not enough time to go back to school and get new training or additional education, but he had time to serve and he wanted to make the most of it.

There was a double ding on his doorbell. He wondered, as he wheeled himself to the peephole in the front door, who it might be. Whoever it was, Andy could see a man through the peep hole. He didn't recognize him, but he didn't look threatening. He opened the door.

"Hello?"

"Hi, my name is Staff Sargent, Jackson Miller. I'm from the local chapter of the VFW. I got your name from Jeff Bellows, your social worker. I'm wondering Gunney, if I could come in for a visit?"

Andy gave him a good look up and down. "Could I see some identification Staff Sargent?"

"Yes," said Jackson as he pulled out his wallet and presented his military ID card. "That's a good idea to check ID."

Parley looked at the ID card and was satisfied. "Come on in and have a seat on the couch."

"Thanks. You can call me Jack. I'm from the Army. I did two tours in Iraq. I'm a disabled Vet as well."

"What's your disability?" asked Andy.

Before sitting down, Jack pulled up his pant leg enough to show a prosthetic leg. "Also, I have a bad case of PTSD."

Andy reached his hand out to shake Jack's hand before letting him sit down. "Can I get you something to drink? Water, soda, coffee, milk?"

"Got a Seven Up?"

"No, just Coke for soda pop."

"That'll do."

Andy brought him a can of coke. "So what brings you here?"

"Like I said, I'm from the VFW, I got a letter from Jeff Bellows telling us about you coming from Walter Reed and being newly retired. I know it's only been what, a week or two since you arrived, but I thought what the heck, why come and visit you and say hi."

"Well, hey. It's always nice to meet a vet such as yourself," said Andy.

"I agree. There seems to be an easy bond between us soldiers that have been wounded in action. I understand you received the Navy Cross?"

"That letter that Jeff Bellows sent, he mentioned that you were a recipient of the Bronze Star, Silver Star and three Purple Hearts in addition to the Navy Cross."

Of course he did.

Two hours passed by quickly. Jack looked at his watch and a surprised look came over his face. "I had no idea that I've been here for two hours."

Andy looked at his watch in surprise. "I have to say, this might be the most fun I have had since before I got blown up."

Jack had a look of understanding to the unique remark from Andy. "I guess I had ought to be on my way."

"Got a wife to get home to?"

"No. She left me a few months after I got home. The PTSD was a little too much for her."

"I'm sorry to hear that. Are you in a hurry to get somewhere?"

"No. Just don't want to overstay my welcome."

"I'd invite you to stay for dinner, but I don't have anything to eat. I could order us a pizza?"

"That sounds good. Do you prefer to stay in?"

"I can take it or leave it."

"I got a truck. We could go out to dinner. We can throw your chair in the back of the truck. I'm a big guy. I can help you get in and out. I don't know, but it might do you some good to get out of the apartment."

Andy surprised himself by agreeing to the invitation without evening thinking about it. That was the beginning of what would become a nice new friendship.

Andy's third week of civilian life flew by as they became friends. They went fishing at a local lake just twenty miles out in the woods. They were catching fish and having a good time. They got to know each other better. Besides the obvious, they had a lot in common.

"There are several guys at the VFW going on a camping trip next week. Most of them are disabled so they understand guys like us and our situation. There is a guy named Brick who is in a chair as well. I think he's going. Want to come with us?"

"Ya, probably. I think I'd like to meet them before hand."

"You haven't come to the VFW yet. Why don't I come and get you tomorrow night around seven and bring you over? There should be at least a few of the guys there you could meet, you could fill out a few papers and join up with us officially."

"Okay. . .All right," Andy was shaking his head in agreement. "I'll do it." He pulled out a pill box from his shirt pocket. He opened it up and threw a pill into the back of his throat and swallowed.

The next day Andy slept in. He was a little worn out from spending the previous day fishing. He thought it strange that a day of fishing could wear him down. It was Saturday which meant Jack would be picking him up for the VFW. While he was in the shower, Jack called Andy's cell phone and left a message reminding him of the VFW later that day.

It was half past seven when he stopped reading his book

long enough to notice Jack was late. He decided he would give him a call. As he picked up his phone, he noticed there was a message. It turned out to be the message Jack left a few hours ago reminding Andy of the VFW. *I guess he hasn't forgotten me. . .Must be running late.*

He put his phone down and picked up his book. He was so engrossed in his book. He didn't notice the passage of time. The only reason he put his book down and noticed the time was because it was getting too dark to read. He looked at his watch to see it was almost nine. No Jack. That's strange. He called him up on his cell phone and there was no answer. It rang five times before going to his voice mail.

"Jack, buddy, where are you? Weren't we going to the VFW tonight? Call me. This is Andy by the way."

He found some leftovers he warmed up and picked up his book. He read while he ate. He enjoyed reading. It was nice to read. During chemo he was generally too sick to read. He looked at the clock on the kitchen wall while putting dishes in the dishwasher. Ten o-clock and no Jackson. He didn't know Jack really well, but they had spent many an hour talking and getting to know each other. They even started swapping some war stories, but he didn't know where he lived. All he knew, for the most part was his full name and phone number.

There was nothing he could do but wait. Andy decided to call him again, just in case. He left another message and fell asleep on the couch.

Andy woke up with a start. He was rubbing his eyes wondering if he had heard something and then heard another loud bang on his door. He looked around to see he had fallen asleep on the couch. It was morning. He turned his wrist to look at his watch. Seven in the morning. *I wonder if it is Jackson?* He swung himself onto his wheelchair and started for the door. The doorbell rang. *I wonder when I am going to get that new foot?* His first prosthetic foot was too sore to wear so he couldn't use crutches. He was confined to his wheelchair. *I hope it comes soon.*

He looked through the peep hole and saw a police officer

standing at his door. Andy rolled backward enough to open the door. "Can I help you officer?"

"Are you Andy Zimmerman?"

"Yes, sir. I am."

"I'm Officer Kowalski. Do you know Jackson Miller?"

Hearing Jack's name caused his stomach to flip as a fearful wave of emotion swept over him. His face drained leaving it pasty white. His head was swimming as he assumed the worst.

"What– what's wrong," Andy's voice choked. "Something happen to Jack?" his voice cracked.

"I'm sorry. Jackson Miller is dead. Could I come in and talk to you?"

Andy's throat was as dry as sand paper. He reached for the rims of his wheels to pull his chair back and out of the way of the officer. The officer came inside and shut the door. Andy motioned with his head to the kitchen table where the officer sat in a chair across from Andy.

Officer Kowalski started from the beginning. "We received a call from one of his buddies at the VFW. They had been expecting him earlier that evening. He was supposed to be bringing a new friend to meet his buddies."

Andy raised his hand and pointed to himself.

"So you were that friend?"

Andy squeaked out a "yes."

"His buddy told the dispatcher Jackson had PTSD and asked for a welfare check be made. It was a busy night. I finally got to Jackson's home about five in the morning. His door wasn't locked. I went in and found him lying on his couch. He was pale. There was no discernable heart beat. I called it in and pulled him to the floor and started chest compressions. The Paramedics called it a few minutes after they arrived. They guessed he had been dead for a few hours. I found a few empty bottles of pills. They will be doing an autopsy." Officer Kowalski cleared his throat a little before continuing. "I found his phone and the only two phone numbers he had recently talked to were you and his friend from the VFW."

"Are they calling it suicide?"

"Not officially, but I've seen enough of these to tell you, unofficially of course, that it really does looks that way. I'm sorry to have to tell you this."

Andy's eyes were open wide in disbelief. His fearful premonitions verified.

"Did you guys meet in the service?"

"No. We met through the VFW. He looked me up and we were well on our way to becoming good friends. He was going to bring me to the VFW and meet some guys who were going camping next week. I was thinking about going with them. I've only known him for a few weeks."

Andy's face was still ghostly white, but his voice was coming back. "Why would he kill himself? He seemed like he had it together." Asked a bewildered Andy.

"Sadly, I've seen this a lot over the last eight or nine years. The military trains peaceful men to be killers and then when their time is up, the military sends them home to unlearn how to be killers without anyone unteaching them. It's tough," responded a thoughtful Officer Kowalski. He asked Andy a few more questions and then gave him his card and left.

Andy was dumbstruck. He knew this sort of thing happened all the time. He was shocked at how hard he was taking it. He had been thinking maybe Jack was meant to be his last act of service. They had become good friends in a short time. Andy was wondering if maybe he was meant to help Jack with his PTSD or something else he didn't yet know, now Jack was dead.

Why would Jackson kill himself? It's so sad, he seemed to have it altogether. As Andy was eating breakfast, he wondered if there had been any clues to Jackson's behavior, he should have picked up on them but, he couldn't think of any. Andy was heart broken for his new friend. He remembered an article he read somewhere that said the suicide rate for the Military was twice the national average of civilians. Now he knew someone personally that added to that sad statistic. A while late he called the VFW and introduced himself and asked about Jackson. They were helping the authorities find family for Jack. They said they would call him back when a funeral was announced.

The evening darkness was rolling in along with mournful feelings. Andy had done a lot of thinking. He wondered why he had gone through this experience with Jackson without having the chance of helping him. His new life outside of the Marines got off to a slow start until Jack came along. With Jack's help he had gotten out of the apartment many times in the past week and a half. Maybe Jack was sent to help Andy. Andy's mind set was that he was out to help the world.

That thought danced around his head many times that evening. He turned the TV on. Andy needed some passive entertainment. His mind was numb and worn out.

When the 11:00 p.m. news came on, he turned the TV off so he could go to bed.   He woke up the next morning with a hole in his heart left by Jackson. If Jack wasn't the one for him to help, then who was? As Andy was thinking about finding his one last act of service, the thought came to him he should go look for that person.

Chapter Twenty: On The Road

True, you only crossed my path for a brief moment, but in that moment was a lifetime of memories and experiences. Thank you. CallahanWriter

April Fools Day, 2013
Bus Stop, Atlanta, Georgia

It was April first, when Benny Blackwell from the VFW called Andy Zimmerman. The phone rang several times. Andy looked at his phone. It said Unknown Number. He didn't answer. Benny left a message updating him on Jackson and told him about the funeral arrangements. Andy called right back.

"I didn't know Jack as well as I would have liked. I'm racking my brain to know if I could have spotted a sign that could have clued me in knowing he was suicidal."

"You know the statistics about vets and suicide. But that doesn't make it any easier when it is someone you know. I thought Jack was doing well, I guess we all missed it," said Benny. They talked for a few more minutes before they said "goodbye."

Andy was still thinking about getting out of Atlanta and searching for someone to help. Jackson helped Andy be comfortable with being outside of his apartment. He hadn't found his next service project as of yet and he felt like if it wasn't going to come to him, then he would go out and look for it. He felt like being proactive but didn't have much time. He had also been intrigued with the idea of actually going to Wyoming and checking out Lake Shaft. He would go fishing there and take a good look around. If he was lucky, maybe he would run into Parley Burnrise and some of his family. Along the way he would keep his eyes open for the opportunity for a good service project.

On the surface the whole idea of taking the bus to Lake Shaft seemed strange, but Andy thought "why not?" His time on earth was limited. He could sit around his apartment and watch the sunset on his life or he could get out into life, have some fun and maybe find his next opportunity. Andy was ready with everything. All he needed to do was wait for his new prosthesis to arrive.

His foot was due anytime within the next three days. Jackson's memorial service was scheduled for April third. He had decided he would go to the service if his foot hadn't arrived by then. He hoped it would. Even though it seemed like the right thing to do, he wasn't all that anxious to go to a memorial service. He felt the need to support his new friend, even in death, but the reality made Andy hesitant for some reason.

It was Wednesday morning and while Andy was finishing his breakfast, he was looking on OutdoorParley to see if there were any new posts. There weren't. Andy wondered why. He shut his laptop and decided he would need to get dressed for the memorial. He had made plans for transportation the day before. He was wheeling his chair out from under the kitchen table when he heard a knock on his door. By the time he got to his door and looked through the peep hole, there was no one there. He was frustrated. This wasn't the first time someone had knocked on his door and left because he was too slow getting to the door. On a hunch he opened the door. *Maybe it's my foot.* To Andy's surprise, there was a package on the floor. He was able to reach it and place it on his lap.

He closed the door and made his way back to the kitchen table. He opened the package and, sure enough, it was his prosthetic foot. He was excited. He tried it on. It fit nicely. Now with his crutches he would be able to get around quicker and in an upright fashion. He had forgotten for a few moments about the memorial service. He looked at his watch and realized he had missed his ride. He was more excited about leaving Atlanta than sad he would miss the memorial service.

He wasn't sure how to feel about it. He knew there was a bus leaving in the afternoon for Wyoming. He didn't have much to pack. Since he was now on crutches, he could move faster. He decided he could make the bus in time if he hurried.

On his way out the door, he had a good feeling come to him. It felt like Jackson was okay with him not showing up for the service. He was excited to be on his adventure. He felt like things were finally falling in place in this chapter of his life. While Andy was on the metro bus on the way to the bus station, he was thinking about the past few weeks. They had been filled with good memories. Jackson's death was the only bad memory. *Maybe things will be better for Jackson on the other side. I hope so.*

Andy was happy with the ease of movement the crutches gave him. He made much better time than he did with the wheelchair. He easily got to the station on time. It wasn't too difficult to get on the second bus. He didn't even use the handicapped assistance. The stairs were steep, but it wasn't a big deal. He was getting excited with his new found freedom. He found a seat and settled in. He looked out the window feeling like this might well be the last time he would ever be in Georgia. He knew he wouldn't miss the humidity.

He turned his mind to Wyoming. He was excited, not just because he was now on crutches, but he was feeling good about his decision of going to Wyoming. *Will I find someone to serve? Who knows, at least I'm being proactive.*

The sound of the bus driver releasing the brakes and the faint smell of diesel fuel brought memories back to Andy. Memories he hadn't had in a long time. The first memory flashing into his mind was a nightmare memory of him shooting two kids with grenades in their hands as they were trying to ambush his guys down below. He managed to shut the memory down before he pulled the trigger. He was breathing heavily when he came back to reality. He was feeling a little squeamish and lightheaded from the diesel fumes.

Luckily he had packed several cans of coke in his bag to calm his stomach if the diesel fumes made him queasy. Two hours and several stops later they were out on the interstate making good time. He was on a seven-state quest to reach Wyoming. Once he got to Cheyenne, he would look for a smaller bus line or see about a train going the rest of the way to Lake Shaft City. He had never been to Wyoming and didn't fully realize the sparse population and lack of services bigger states provided.

He was planning on two overnight stops if needed. He didn't know what he had as far as energy was concerned, and this was the biggest adventure since before the IED. He didn't want to over do it. They crossed the state line into Indiana. By the end of the day they crossed into Illinois. He planned on an overnight stay in Mount Vernon, Illinois. He was happy with the choices for hotels. Everything went well for him. He was able to catch a bus mid morning the next day. Soon they were in Missouri. They spent a long time driving through. There were several stops in Missouri. On the last stop before a long stretch on the interstate, a mother and three young children boarded the bus.

Andy had been lucky to not run into too many children since he'd been discharged. He had seen a lot of them, just not close up. These four new arrivals had to sit in the two rows in front of him. The closer they got to him the harder Andy's heart beat. There was a big lump in Gunnery Sargent, Andy Zimmerman's throat. Sweat started to bead up on his forehead and upper lip. He wiped the sweat from his eyebrows with his shirt sleeve. He checked his rifle. His magazine was fine. His rifle was on automatic. He could smell the dry sand as it drifted through the air.

His old friend, Master Sargent Todd Buckingham was on point. They were on patrol. They had to make sure no one got to the busy intersection. There were five large convoys going through the area that day so they beefed up patrols to guard against insurgents planting IEDs in the open intersection. Standing orders were one warning shot and then if disregarded, neutralize the enemy.

Todd yelled out at a small group of people making their way to the intersection to stop and turn around and go back. They interpreter relayed the message by yelling the translated command. The people stopped long enough to process what was being shouted. Then they bunched up closer together and scurried faster toward the intersection. As they did, they brought out rifles and a rocket launcher from under their flowing robes. Major red flag. Normally Bud and Andy tried several warnings before opening fire, but never in these kind of circumstances. "Fire!" shouted Master Sargent Todd Buckingham. "Fire at three o'clock!" they dropped to the ground, taking up prearranged firing positions. The rapid sound of automatic fire filled the air. The small group of people were sprawled out on the dirt sixty yards in front of them.

The target was neutralized in seconds, ending the skirmish. There was a woman in her late thirties with a young teenage son and two girls around ten or twelve. There were also two older men, likely in their sixties with long gray beards. No military uniforms and no military markings, but there was an RPG launcher, and three AK-47's and two grenades lying in their midst. It was a good kill, but to Bud and Andy, killing kids was never a good kill.

The pain in Andy's knuckles brought him back to the present. He had been gripping the arm rests so tight his fingers were white and sore. Andy wiped the sweat away with his shirt sleeve. He had been staring at the two girls in the seats in front of him. They were around ten or twelve years old, he guessed. He quickly looked away. Andy was breathing hard. He let go of the arms rests and rubbed his hands together, trying to rub the numbness out of them. *That was a strange trigger. I hope that doesn't happen again. Don't look at those kids. Take a deep breath. Keep breathing. It will be all right. You're safe now.* He was remembering back to one of the group therapy sessions he had gone too in the hospital. Several of the guys had talked about what events had triggered PTSD events. He was glad for the awareness.

He finally got his breathing back to normal. *Don't look at those kids, just ignore them.*

He pulled out a book to read. He was feeling queasy again from the diesel fumes and from reading. He put the book down and sipped on some coke that was no longer cold.

He caught himself staring at the kids again. He forced himself to look away. *Why do kids irritate me so much?* A few minutes later Andy was starring at the kids again. He was a little light headed. He couldn't read and he couldn't look outside. He was trying to relax and maybe doze off. He caught himself looking at the girls again. He couldn't keep his eyes off of them. It made no sense to Andy, but those kids made him hyper vigilant and nervous. These were good old American freckled face kids.

Now he was half a world away, in the relative safety America, why would these kids spook him? He wasn't afraid of kids. When he was in Iraq and Afghanistan, he and his buddies went out of their way to be friendly to them. Now he avoided kids. They annoyed him. They even scared him. He sat back in his seat and kept watching them. They laughed and giggled with each other. They read their books and listened to their music. They presented no danger to anyone. Anyone except Andy, Andy, the killer of women and children.

He couldn't wait to get to Topeka. He was getting off there for the night. He gathered his stuff together, trying to be one of the first ones off the bus. He wanted to put as much distance as was possible between him and those sweet looking kids. Getting off the bus wasn't easy on crutches. He ended up being the last one off.

Chapter Twenty-One: Together At Last

Having a positive attitude is about making the best out of whatever situation life gives you. CallahanWriter

Spring 2013
Burnrise Family Resort, Wyoming

At the end of each day during his bus trip Andy got car sick from the diesel fumes. By the time he checked in at the Burnrise hotel he was queasy, exhausted, had no appetite, and went straight to bed. He had been in countless diesel fuel vehicles in his career as a Marine. The exhaust was never a problem. He was surprised the fumes bothered him now. He slept with the window opened and found that not only did the fresh air clear his head, it acted as a natural sedative. He slept for eleven hours, waking up at 10:00 a.m.

Andy crutched himself down the hall to the elevator, from there to the main level, and then to Betty's Café. He noticed his appetite was back and he felt his stomach growl as he detected something heavenly in the air. He recognized the familiar scent of coffee, but there was also a fragrant sweet smell of maybe hot cocoa, he wasn't sure. Whatever it was, he was going to have a cup of it.

"What can I get for you today sir?" asked the waitress.

"I smell something awesome in the air besides the coffee. What is it?"

Sniffing the air, the waitress said. "That's Betty's hot chocolate. It's awesome."

"I want to try that hot chocolate. I'll also have the Denver omelet."

As he was eating his breakfast, he was pondering over what to do. He was typically a methodical person living according to a well-thought out plan. His attention to detail served him well in life and on the battlefield. Now he was in Wyoming looking to have a little fun all the while looking for his last act of service. Who was he supposed to serve now?

The Burnrise Family Resort was made up of Betty's Café, the retail space of Bert's Outfitter shop and the small Burnrise Hotel. They were all connected to each other with a grand lobby. The grand lobby featured several fresh water aquariums with fish from Lake Shaft. Two of the aquariums were five thousand gallon tanks built into walls. One tank was a two thousand-gallon circular tank you could walk around and see it from all angles. For a delightful contrast, they also featured an eight hundred-gallon fresh water tropical tank to compare with the local freshwater game fish. There was a two-sided fireplace, big enough to make a small bonfire in.

The grand foyer was opulent with a rustic outdoor feel. Part of the foyer served as a small museum with pictures of state record fish caught from the lake along with relics from five generations of the family business and other historical items. Andy had noticed a large and distinguished plaque on display commemorating Parleys rescue mission for the people at Willow Creek.

As Andy was eating, he thought he spotted Bert and Betty Burnrise. He was sure he would recognize the Burnrise family from all the videos and pictures he had seen from Parleys website. Yet, as the elderly couple went past the café and into a hall adjacent to the shop he wasn't positive it was them. They hadn't been in a video for OutdoorParley for a few years.

Andy was taken by surprise at how the resort had such a peaceful and relaxing atmosphere. The videos he had seen were mostly of the lake and nearby forest. The few that showed the interior of the resort didn't do the place justice. Andy knew he needed to actively look for that certain someone to serve but for the first time ever, he was tempted to just relax and enjoy the atmosphere. *Would it be wrong to just relax for a few days?*

After breakfast and three cups of Betty's world famous hot chocolate Andy found the perfect overstuffed chair to sit in. The chair was angled just right to see two of the biggest fish tanks. He was enthralled with watching the fish swim aimlessly around the tanks.

~

When he was first diagnosed with fibromyalgia, Parley was happy. He was relieved to know he wasn't crazy and that there really was something wrong with him. It made him feel like giving all his previous doctors the finger for ignoring him and not diagnosing him and letting him suffer so badly. It was a validating moment. Since then he had been on a roller coaster of emotions and misery. He thought that once they knew what was wrong, they could fix it. Hank said to Parley "Remember, I told you there is no known cure for your illness. The best we can do right now is to treat your symptoms."

With a year of dealing with his diagnosis Parley was coming to terms with the concept of treating the symptoms. Most of the problems showed improvement, but none of them went away. Then he had the heart attack scare and Hank reminded him of the importance of dealing with any new symptoms or pain. A common problem for those with fibromyalgia was to assume any new pains or ailments were just a part of the diagnosis and they might be, but Hank had told Parley not to make that assumption. Get the problems checked out before thinking they are just part of the illness.

Going to see Hank every time he felt something bad might be happening was frustrating for Parley, but he was grateful for Hanks support and the treatments he tried on him.

Parley had slept with the window open. It was still spring and too early to turn on the air conditioner and too cold to turn off the heater. The night before was a perfect time to open the window. Parley enjoyed his sleep. In the last year one of his improvements was getting on top of his insomnia. He now experienced more good nights than bad.

He woke up from that fresh air deep sleep and felt surprisingly good. Typically mornings were the worst time of the day for pain and morning stiffness. He took his first pain pill of the day along with a muscle relaxer. He got dressed and started for the den, but decided to brave the stairs and go down to the kitchen since he could hear Miranda knocking around down there.

He had six steps to take. In the old days before the chronic pain he could scale the stairs in two steps. With each step he could feel a sensation of bone scraping bone and muscle scraping muscle.

By the time he hobbled into the kitchen, his face was pale and he was exhausted. He went straight to the kitchen table and sat down.

"Hey sweetie, hot chocolate or coffee?"

"Coffee." The familiar feeling of fatigue was washing over him and he was hoping for a little pick me up with the caffeine.

"How are you feeling today?" Asked Miranda.

That simple question would have taken one word to answer four years ago. Now it required a series of evaluations. There were so many things to consider when searching for the right answer. In reality, he was almost never completely fine.

"It looks like it might be a better day than yesterday," Parley answered.

Another problem Parley faced was how often things could change in the space of one day. He could wake up and feel horrible, he usually did. Then after his morning medicine he could start to feel better. A few hours later, regardless of whatever he did or didn't do, he could be having a pain flare only to see it subside for the rest of the day. He couldn't know from one hour to the next how he would feel.

"I don't have all that much on my plate today. Want to try and do something fun?" Miranda had a hopeful look on her face.

"Maybe," Parley sighed. "I just hate to plan on something only to let you down again."

"I've told you repeatedly that I understand. I'm willing to give it a try. I know what I'm getting into when I suggest something fun." The problem was that Parley would agree to do something and then when the time came to do it, he might have a major pain flare up causing him to stay home. This was hard on everyone. The kids were always skeptical when they made plans. Miranda was more supportive, but it wore on her as well and Parley knew it.

"How about I eat breakfast and then rest for an hour and see how I feel?"

"Okay. Good, let's hope you feel better."

They enjoyed their rare breakfast together at the kitchen table. Parley took most of his meals in his den while resting on his recliner. He got lost in his thoughts as he made that long trek up the stairs. He might as well be climbing Pikes Peak for the amount of time it took to hike those steps.

As he was making that six-step hike, he reflected on the last time he posted anything to his website. Even though he had lost all of his advertisers, he still felt compelled to post to his blog. He wasn't sure why it was so difficult to write an article or to edit a video from his archives. He had done it a thousand times. It didn't require physical effort, just a little mental work and the use of his hands and eyes. He wondered if he wasn't motivated anymore, but then he realized he still felt an urge to post. As usual, most of his thoughts ended in a stalemate, and this was no exception.

If only I could concentrate better! He was trying hard not to be angry.

As Parley sat in his recliner, he realized he didn't feel like watching TV. He didn't feel like reading. He felt the urge to get outside and feel the sun and smell fresh air. He started to contemplate going outside, one thought led to another and before long he was mentally watching himself catch a fish. His mind wandered a lot.

Hmm. What could it hurt to try and go fishing off the dock? I could take my pills with me and if worse comes to worse, I could lounge in the back room. Just thinking about something normal was a little frightening. He feared being stuck away from the comforts of home when the pain flared up or when he lost all energy.

~

While resting and watching the trout and bass swim around

in the aquariums, Andy had drifted off to sleep. His belly was full and his body relaxed. The perfect recipe for a nap. Bert was walking through the foyer and noticed a man with a military style haircut on the couch. He could see his crutches propped against the arm rest. He noticed the better part of Andy's right leg was missing and he could see that he had a prosthetic left foot. Immediately Bert knew Andy was a veteran, a disabled veteran. *This young soldier looks older than he probably is. He looks like he's been through a lot in his young life.*

Bert was a little concerned. He didn't want to worry over this stranger, but he felt drawn to him. He had gone through a terrible trauma being a double amputee. Bert could see that this war hero was stirring. He didn't want this man to wake up and see him staring. He was standing near a chair so he quickly sat down and acted like he was watching the fish.

Andy stirred some more then slowly, his eyes fluttered a few times. He yawned and rubbed his eyes. In the chair to his right was a familiar looking man watching the fish. *Is that Bert Burnrise? Wavy, brownish-gray hair. Hmm. He combs it back like Bert did in the videos. I think it might be him.*

He arched his back and stretched and yawned some more. He caught the mans eyes. He nodded his head. Bert nodded back.

Andy caught Bert looking at him. Bert asked, "is that a war wound?" he nodded toward Andy's legs.

"Yes, sir, IED explosion."

"Sorry to hear that. What branch of the service were you in?"

"Marines." *I thought he was a Marine.*

"I was a Marine in Vietnam."

"I'm Andy Zimmerman. It's nice to meet a fellow Marine."

Bert got up and walked over to Andy and held out his hand. "I'm Gunnery Sargent, Bert Burnrise retired, I own this place. Well, most of it."

Andy shook his hand. "It's good to meet you. I was a Gunnery Sargent before the Marines kicked me out."

Since they were both Marines, they had an instant

connection. The fact that they both served in a war deepened that connection. Bert sat back down. This time it was on the same couch as Andy. Hey started chatting and two hours passed as quickly as a three minute egg timer. Out of no where Bert's stomach growled loud enough to draw a look from Andy. Bert looked at his watch. "Son of a gun, its past lunch time. Want to go eat some lunch? It's on me."

"Come to think of it, I'm hungry as well. I'd be glad to join you. This morning I ordered Betty's world famous hot chocolate. I couldn't believe just how good it was. It tasted even better than it smelled."

Extending his hand, Bert asked, "can I give you a hand?" it was a question that sounded like an order.

Taking Bert's hand, Andy pushed up on his left leg and the prosthetic foot as he tried to keep his balance. He half felt and half heard a snap. Then he felt a deep wrenching pressure on his left leg where his prosthetic ankle connected to his leg. He let go of Bert's hand and sat right back down. He was more scared than hurt. The foot-ankle assembly that connected his foot to the liner on his left leg broke. *Judas Priest, this isn't supposed to happen!* His defective foot looked as though it was pointed unnaturally to the left. It looked like something had twisted his ankle bad enough that his foot was almost at a forty-five-degree angle of normal. He was mad and irritated.

"Are you all right?" asked Bert. "I think I heard a snap."

"So did I." Andy stared at his foot shaking his head. They both starred at the foot with disbelief and shock.

"I think my prosthetic foot is broken unless there is a way I can twist it back in place?"

People were staring as they walked by. The look on their faces, seeing a foot jutting out at such an unnatural position, was a little comical.

"Why don't I go get a wheelchair and I'll bring you to the back room and we can look at your foot in private?"

"I appreciate that. I can't use my crutches without my foot to bounce off of. I guess I'm in a bit of a bind."

"You're among friends. We'll get you taken care of. Give me a minute and I'll be right back with a wheelchair."

~

Miranda pulled into the small parking lot on the east side of the building. They maintained reserve parking. There was a private entrance that lead into the back room. That was also the side where the docks were and where they kept their private boats. Further down the line were all the various boats, canoes, jet ski's, row boats, paddle boats and houseboats they rented out. If it floated, they rented it.

She parked in the closest spot near the east entrance. Parley opened his door and took a breath. Whenever he was sitting in a spot for more than a few minutes, he became as stiff as a statue. He groaned as he started stretching to a fully upright position. He swallowed a couple of deep breaths before continuing. After a couple of minutes he started shuffling toward the door.

"I have an idea sweetie," said Miranda. "Sit here and I'll go get you a wheelchair. It will be much easier for you and help preserve your energy." They were both still trying to come to grips with his dramatic lack of energy. Parley was struggling to come to terms with his new normal. He didn't argue the point as he sat down on a nearby bench.

Miranda went inside and found that Bert, for some unknown reason had taken the last wheel chair. *Why would Bert need a wheelchair?* She went to Parley to share the bad news. Parley was frustrated. He was steadily losing his old personality and replacing his natural optimism with anger. *I'm getting so sick of all this pain and stiffness. Will it ever end? Will I ever get my old life back?*

Parley hobbled his way to the door that Miranda was holding open for him. *I'm supposed to be opening the door for her. Crap.*

As they entered the back room, they saw Bert sitting at the table eating lunch with someone neither of them knew. That person sporting a military style haircut was sitting in a wheelchair. Parley hobbled to the nearest chair. The pain in his hip and lower back was on the verge of erupting.

"Parley! Miranda! Where did you kids come from? Hey guys! It's good to see you." Bert smiled. "Miranda come over here and sit down. I have someone to introduce to the two of you."

Miranda sat down and Parley decided to move to the recliner and get more comfortable, he had a feeling he would be sitting for a while.

"Gunnery Sargent, Andy Zimmerman, this is my son Parley and this is my daughter-in-law Miranda. Kids, this is Andy Zimmerman. He's a real American war hero." Bert emphasized the word 'hero.'

"It's good to meet you Andy." Miranda held out her hand.

Shaking her hand, Andy said, "It's good to meet you. I've watched a lot of you cooking videos on MirandasHomestyleGourmet."

"Really? Have you tried any of the recipes?"

"Sorry to say, I haven't. I saw them while I was in the hospital. Truthfully, I found links to your site from Parleys blog. But I still enjoyed a lot of those videos, especially the ones where you cook whatever Parley caught or killed. I used to cook trout, catfish, venison and boar in my younger days."

"Boar is one thing I would like to cook someday."

Parley was debating within his mind whether or not to try getting up against the agonizing stiffness of his lower back and hips. His body made the decision for him. "Excuse me for not getting up. It's nice to meet you." Parley extended his hand in a wave.

Andy returned the wave with an understanding smile. "No worries. I can't get up right now either. I've seen all of the videos on your blog. I also watched all the TAN episodes. It's very nice to meet you. I may well be your number one fan."

"Andy is a bonafide war hero. He won the Navy Cross, and both the Bronze and Silver Stars. He also earned three Purple Hearts. We are in the presence of a real war hero. I guess I said that already, but it's worth repeating," Bert declared emphatically.

"That is very impressive," Parley nodded his head. "I'm sorry

you were wounded three times. That's an incredible sacrifice."
Parleys' tone was thoughtful and respectful.

Chapter Twenty-Two: Getting To Know You

The power, grace and mercy of God are greater than anything we can do, think or feel. Father Friday.

Spring 2013
Burnrise Family Resort, Wyoming

Miranda was irritated with herself. She kept stealing glances at Andy's left foot. Looking at his right leg wasn't a big deal, but seeing a foot pointing unnaturally to the left at a ninety-degree angle and hanging lower than was normal was weird. It just seemed to dangle. It almost made her hurt just looking at it. Obviously it was a prosthesis, but with a sock and shoe covering it, it looked real at first glance. If her kids were staring, she would nudge them or give them the evil eye. She kept looking away awkwardly, hoping Andy wouldn't notice. *What is wrong with his foot? Poor guy.*

Andy noticed Miranda looking at his stump. "My prosthetic foot broke in the ankle area," Andy said as he pointed to his left foot.

"A fake foot can break? Really? I've never heard of that happening." Parley nodded his head.

"I was shocked when it snapped," Andy was chuckling.

"How long have you been wearing that . . . That foot?" asked Bert.

"This prosthesis? About a week. When I was at Walter Reed I trained on a different trainer prosthetic while I waited for a customized foot. I just got it in the mail a few days ago."

Everyone seemed a little unsettled talking about the prosthesis with a stranger, "do prosthetics come with a warranty?" asked Bert.

"Good question. There were several papers that came in the box. I think I have those papers in my room."

"What I'm thinking," Bert said, "is that we could call the

manufacturer and tell them what happened and maybe they would replace it. I don't know about these types of products so I am just guessing."

"That's a good thought. It's a start anyway. I'm pretty much stuck until I get a working foot. Traveling with crutches isn't a big deal, but I don't like the idea of traveling with a wheelchair."

"If you like I could go get the papers and help you deal with the whole red tape dance that the VA is so well known for. Being a veteran myself, I understand the red tape jungle that camouflages the Veterans Administration."

"That's a kind offer. I'd be glad to let you help. Truthfully, I don't know where the papers are, probably tucked away in my backpack or suitcase. I can go get them and bring them down here."

"That's fine. Need any help with the chair?" asked Bert.

"No, I'm fine. I could use the exercise. I should take my foot off before I go back out there. The way it looks now might freak some people out." Andy smiled.

Parley was feeling just a bit better having reclined his chair. "Hun, could you get me a heating pad please?"

"Sure."

Andy had been keeping an eye on Parley since he came into the room. This 'back room' was bigger than his studio apartment in Atlanta and a lot nicer. There was a hot tub near the sliding glass doors.

Pointing at Parleys' back, Andy asked, "Bad back or did you pull a muscle or something?"

"I wish. If I had wrenched my back, it would get better." Parley took a deep breath, "no. I have fibromyalgia."

"I've never heard of that. What is it, if you don't mind my asking?"

Parley had been struggling for a long time on how to quickly explain his condition to others. Hank suggested telling them it was like having arthritis of the muscles. When Andy made the 'pulled muscle' comment that registered a thought in Parleys head. Fibromyalgia was like having dozens of pulled muscles at the same time. No, no, scratch that. Imagine what a badly pulled muscle feels like? Then imagine all of your muscles or even just a major part of your muscles all feel that way? Add to that sensation what it feels like when you have the flu and feel achy all over? Mix those two feelings and that is at least partly what fibromyalgia feels like.

"There are other slightly less dramatic symptoms like insomnia or other kinds of sleep problems, fatigue, memory issues, stuff like that."

"That's all one illness? What causes all that?" asked Andy. "It sounds serious, even life threatening."

"I don't know. The doctors don't yet know. It's a relatively new illness, at least it's new as far as not every doctor knows about it yet or understands it. Funny thing, at least as of now the doctors are saying that no one dies from it and that once you have it, it won't get much worse."

"How long does it last?"

"Forever. Right now there is no known cure because no one knows what causes all the symptoms."

"If they have a name for it, why don't they know what causes it?"

"Good question. I don't know."

"That's unbelievable," Andy said with an understanding tone. "It sounds awful. Are you in pain all the time?"

Parley was impressed that someone believed him right from the start without suspicion. It was refreshing and validating.

"Yes, the degree of pain or the intensity varies, but it's constant."

"So you're saying you have pain all the time? Every minute of every day?"

"I guess it sounds hard to believe, but yes, it's every day, every minute of every day. The pain level is not the same, the intensity varies, but the ache is there always."

"That's hard to believe. I'm not arguing with you, but even when I had cancer or when I got shot or blown up and lost my leg and foot I had moments when I didn't feel pain. Most of the time I did, but there were times when I was feeling fine. All my serious pain eventually went away. Some people die from cancer and others heal from it. Either way there is a lot of pain. But it eventually goes away by dying or healing. I can't fathom a never ending, constant pain." Andy shook his head, "Amazing."

"I guess I would have a hard time accepting it, if I wasn't going through it myself,"

Parley responded as he thought about how hard it was for other people to understand the concept of his chronic pain. Parley and Andy went on talking about various videos from the outdoor website. Andy pulled up the Willow Creek rescue video on OutdoorParley. They watched it together and Andy asked him a few questions about different parts of the ride down the mountain. He asked how it felt getting caught in an avalanche. Parley brushed the question away much like Andy did when asked about some of his daring exploits. It bugged Andy until he realized he responded the same way. Soon Bert and Miranda left them alone since they didn't seem to notice there was anyone else in the room. They were covering a lot of ground as they swapped hunting and fishing stories. As long as they stayed on the neutral ground of hunting and fishing time went flying by. A few times they each had to dodge a question or two about heroic exploits. They didn't seem to want to talk about that.

Later that afternoon, Bert came back to ask Andy about his broken foot.

"Andy, it's 4:00 p.m., have you got the paper work for your prosthetic?"

"Shoot, no. I got carried away talking to Parley."

"I was just thinking that if you're in any kind of a hurry, we should try to make contact with the manufacturer. I guess, since it's getting late, we could wait until tomorrow. Either way, I just thought I would see if I can help you with it."

"I guess I better go get the papers." Andy asked, "Parley, are you going anywhere? I don't want to break up our conversation."

"I was going to ask you Parley what you wanted to do about dinner?" Miranda broke into the conversation, "If you guys want, we could eat dinner here and you two chatter boxes could keep your conversation going."

Parley glared at Miranda when she said "chatter boxes," he patted his pocket to make sure he had his bottle of pain pills. He did. "Dinner here sounds like a good idea, that is, unless you have any dinner plan's Andy?"

"My only dinner plan was to eat it." Andy smiled at his poor attempt at humor.

"Great. Let's eat here," responded Parley.

"I'll go get those papers and I'll meet you down here in a few minutes. Is that good with you Bert?"

"Sure. I can go with you if you want. It could speed things up?"

"Sure, I'll take your company."

As they were leaving the back room Andy heard Miranda tell Parley, "I'll call the kids and have them meet us here for dinner."

"Sounds good," Parley reached for his pain pills and took another one.

Andy was shocked at hearing that Parley and Miranda's kids would be joining them. He was worried about the kids pulling his PTSD trigger. Andy reflected back on the last time he saw the kids in a video clip. It had been quite a long time. They must be older now. As they were walking down the hall, Andy asked Bert, "How old are their kids?"

"They're seniors in high school. Eighteen. They're twins."

Andy was nervous about meeting the twins. He wondered if they would really trigger a reaction. *Maybe they're old enough that they won't scare me?*

Andy and Bert were able to get a hold of the manufacturer who referred them to the hospital. They called Walter Reed and explained the situation. The guy they needed was gone for the day.

"Well, we made some good progress in cutting through the initial red tape. I wonder how bad it will be tomorrow?" asked Andy.

"One thing I learned long ago," Bert said, "There is always red tape. There's red tape just for red tape. But you're right. We made good progress for today."

"Are you traveling on a schedule?" asked Bert. "Do you have somewhere you're supposed to be?"

"No. This was my first stop. I haven't decided where I want to go next."

"That sounds fun, traveling around like that. I admire you for doing this. I'm glad you're living your life," said Bert.

"I don't have much else to do."

"What made you want to make Lake Shaft your first destination?" Bert asked.

"OutdoorParley. I've been a fan for a long time. Thought it would be nice to check this place out."

They went to the back room and found Parley still there.

"Andy tells me that it was OutdoorParley that brought him here. What do you think about that?"

"I'm flattered. It's been a long time since I've met a blog fan."

Andy went on to tell them, "I've been a fan of your blog since I discovered it in college. After going overseas and back those several times I kind of lost track of it. Then when I was at Walter Reed dealing with my amputations, I got back into following your blog. I was so tired of TV and videos . . . You can only read so many pages in the Bible every day. Your blog came in really handy, helping me pass time."

"How long were you in the hospital?"

"Geez, how long was it? It was a long time. Less than a year. Maybe nine or ten months."

"I had no idea that amputation was so involved."

"It was more than that. While they were operating on me, finishing the amputation they discovered a tumor in my thigh. They had to remove additional tissue to get as much of the tumor as they possible could. Then I had chemotherapy treatments followed by radiation treatments followed by some physical and occupational rehab along with some training for the prosthetic. It was a long time."

Parley was stunned by that revelation and the word tumor. *He did mention cancer earlier.* Parley thought a few times that the cause of his pain might be cancer. A few doctors ran the tests they could, testing for the cancers they knew how to test for.

"My gosh. I can't imagine what that must have been like. I'm sorry to hear all that."

"Ah . . . Well . . . That's the way it goes, I guess. Anyway, I was glad for your blog. It brought back a lot of memories from my younger days when I went fishing every single day during summer break. All those hunting trips with my Dad. Those were some good times . . . Good memories."

Parley felt humbled by Andy's compliment. *Maybe that's why I always got that nagging feeling to keep posting.* Parley started feeling bad about all the times he felt the need to post but didn't.

Bert had been listening to their conversation on and off through the afternoon. He had also noticed how Andy and Parley had been getting along, and he felt a deep need to help this young Gunnery Sargent. He was a fellow Marine after all.

"Gunny," Bert's voice commanded attention. "I don't know how long you're planning on staying here and it doesn't matter. You'll be here a while at least. Who knows how long it will take to get your foot taken care of. You will be staying here as our guest. That means your money is no good here. We have a suite that will be open in two days. I'll move you there when the room is cleared and cleaned. Our mess hall is free. Whatever you need. It's on us. You can give the prosthetic guy our address for whatever they do with your foot."

Andy was surprised and took a deep breath. "I'm touched. Really, I appreciate the gesture, but I can't accept. I've got more than enough to pay my way. Really, I do. But– "

"Gunny," Bert used the power of his voice to put his point across. "I was a Gunnery Sargent and I am your senior by a lot of years, so that means I outrank you. You will not disregard someone who outranks you." Bert's face held the expression of 'just go along with what I'm saying.' "That's the way it will be. It's an honor to pay tribute for one our nations finest."

Andy was a friendly guy, but he had Marine Corp emotions. His voice betrayed him this time when he said "yes Gunnery

Sargent. I appreciate it." His voice choked ever so slightly. "I really appreciate it." Andy forced a cough to hide the quiver in his voice.

Andy's thoughts came rushing back about eating dinner with a couple of kids. *Be cool Marine. Be cool. They're teenagers, almost adults. Be cool. Take a deep breath.* The thought of sitting at the same table with a couple of kids stabbed him in the heart with a knife of fear. It wasn't logical, it wasn't rational, but the fear was real. As real as any battle he fought in. He could feel the anxiety and fear boiling up inside of him. Out of nowhere, deep inside his memory came an almost forgotten quote that his old Chaplin from the hospital, Father Friday had told him, "The power, grace and mercy of God are greater than anything we can do, think or feel." That quote hit him hard and brought overwhelming comfort to him. *Maybe I can make it through this dinner with those kids. Lord, please help me.*

Soon they were gathered around a big table in a far corner of the dinning room. He had wheeled himself into place when he saw a young looking boy and girl. They looked young, but they didn't look like kids. *Could they be the kids?* A moment later, after they were all seated Parley spoke up. "Andy, this is Emily and this is Ted," he pointed to each of them. "Kids, this is Gunnery Sargent, Andy Zimmerman, a true American hero." Andy felt his face flush which embarrassed him which made him blush even more. "Hello."

"Hi, good to meet you kids. I've seen you a few times on the Internet. You both look quite a bit older." They both smiled. *Good job Marine. You got this.*

Everyone at the table ordered without looking at the menu except Andy. He looked over the menu and saw Betty's World Famous Hot Chocolate. *I'm getting that for sure, but should I order it for dessert or with my meal?* This menu is huge. There were so many incredible dishes to choose from. Knowing that he was going to be there for a while, he decided to take away the anxiety of what to order and just start at the top on the left side and work his way down. There was not one thing on the menu that looked bad.

Soon the appetizers showed up. Before long there was nothing but food in the horizon. There was loud talk, a lot of eating, loud laughter and a lot to drink. He ordered Betty's World Famous Hot Chocolate. It was so wonderful that it almost deserved its own food group.

Dinner was almost over and then it dawned on Andy he had actually talked to both Ted and Emily, not very much, but there were a few small exchanges. *Wow! That's a borderline miracle. That's amazing. No triggers got pulled.* As he was wheeling himself to the back room, he realized that while he had enjoyed Betty's company, he hadn't had the chance to talk to her about the heavenly cocoa named after her.

Chapter Twenty-Three: Empathy

We should only spend as much time in the past as needed to learn from it, but not enough time to live in it. CallahanWriter

Spring 2013
Burnrise Family Resort, Wyoming

As a result of pain flares and chronic fatigue, by the end of the evening Parley felt wiped out and fully spent. He didn't have the energy to hurt, but he did.

Parley had somehow managed to get himself in the back room and stretched out on one of the recliners. He wasn't entirely sure how he had managed to move that far. As he tried to relax, he could feel a dull ache seep out from his core filling the rest of his body. It was one of those moments where he was beside himself in an agony that wouldn't let up. The sensation was unrelenting.

With the pain taking up most of his mind, he realized how narrow his focus was. All he could think about was what to do next. He considered how many steps it would take to go from his recliner to Miranda's car in the parking lot, or the number of steps from his garage to his bed at home.

Even if Miranda pulled the car to the curb it would take sixty-three steps from his chair to the passenger seat of her car. Then when he got home it would take forty-three steps to get to his own recliner in his den. The way his back was throbbing and his hips were aching, he would not be able to negotiate the last twelve steps to his bedroom. That was the best case scenario. All that pain and suffering to get where he was already at, resting uncomfortably in a recliner in the comfortable back room. The back room started off decades ago as a break room.

Over time and different generations running the family business, it went through many renovations and now served as a home away from home. It was almost like having a cabin as a break room. The back room was situated at the end of a hall between the café and retail space. The sliding glass doors opened to the Burnrise private dock. Inside the sliding glass doors was a six-person hot tub. Because of those renovations there, were two great rooms remodeled into one huge room sectioned off with fold out sofas and recliners. One part of the room had a pool table, ping pong table and a foosball table. There was also a banquet table for board games and other family activities. On the other side, a section was defined by sleeper sofas, recliners and a big screen TV. In the middle of the massive room there was a large kitchen table, a pair of refrigerators, two stoves and microwaves all reflecting on two gourmet chefs in the family, Betty and Miranda.

Another result of the remodeling over the years was a private bedroom for Bert and Betty, though they seldom used it. Additionally, there were two full bathrooms. It was a home away from home. The family held family holiday celebrations there. They also made it available to their Church for youth events. Over the years everyone in the extended family had spent many nights there for many different reasons. It was a reasonable thing for Parley to decide to spend the night there.

As he was taking another pain pill, he realized he had nothing to gain by going home. He had his pain pills and a comfortable recliner already. All the other comforts of home without the trouble and discomfort of going to his house. The only thing it didn't have was Miranda, but he seldom woke her up while she was asleep so that part didn't matter. Why have I never thought of this before? *It made sense in a strange sort of way.*

He explained his thoughts to Miranda and she conceded to the sound logic. She was just worried that something would happen and she wouldn't be there to help. She also knew not to take issue with Parley and his perceived logic. She set things up for him as best she could think to do. A large glass of ice water and a few snacks on the side table, the remote was within reach. She got him a blanket to use if needed and the heating pad was resting on the arm rest.

"Are you sure about this?"

"It's not like I'm going to kindergarten for the first time," Parley replied.

Andy was in the background watching events unfold and for the first time in his adult life he felt some regret for not pursuing a wife. Of course married life and being a Marine was tough, but possible, but difficult to do. He hadn't seen many marriages survive several deployments.

Parley also reminded Miranda that he could call whoever was working the front desk at the hotel to help him if he needed. He didn't know Bert was filling in at the front desk that night. As Miranda was leaving, Bert pulled her aside and told her he was working the front desk until 6:00 a.m., filling in for Chuck who called in sick. "I'll check on him a few times," he told Miranda.

Everyone was gone except Bert and Andy. "Andy, if you need anything you can call me at the front desk or you can feel free to come into the back room and raid the pantry or the refrigerator."

They both said good night to Parley. He kicked off his shoes and emptied his pockets. Painfully he reclined the chair and situated the heating pad on his lower back.

Andy slowly wheeled himself up to his room. It was interesting for Andy to realize how much better life was when you're standing up. He had quickly got out of the habit of using a wheelchair once he got his foot and was able to use crutches. Now he was back into a wheelchair. Not the best wheelchair in the world, but it was adequate. He was tired so he just locked his door, wheeled over to his bed and slowly and painfully climbed into bed. His occasional pain was flaring up. He was too tired to get a glass of water so he dry swallowed a pain pill.

He stayed upright for a short while to let the pill make its way down to his stomach. As he was doing so he thought back to the constant pain Parley was in. While Andy had a type of chronic pain, it wasn't constant. Out of nowhere a phantom ache would strike or he would knock his stump on something and irritate the nerves, sending agonizing explosions to his brain. He had a refillable bottle of pain pills to help manage the chronic on again and off again agony. He was glad it wasn't constant. *How can anyone be expected to live with the kind of pain Parley goes through?* He wondered if Parley exaggerated his so-called pain. But then he remembered the involuntary expressions he saw on Parleys' face. He knew how things hurt and he knew those facial expressions were real responses, to some sort of deep-seated suffering.

Sleep seemed hard to come by for Andy. He tried deep breathing exercises to relax, he prayed for sleep. He tossed and turned as he yearned for sleep to take over his exhaustion. He had just experienced his busiest day since the war and he was worn out yet sleep refused to relieve him of his fatigue.

Parley was sweating from the heating pad and the blanket. He took the blanket off and turned the heating pad off. After a while the cold made his muscles hurt. He decided sweating was better than the brittle ache that the cold caused his muscles. As he tossed and turned he realized he had made one serious mistake. He had forgotten about his night time muscle relaxers and other night time medication that helped him relax and sleep. *Oh crap!*

He wouldn't call and disturb Miranda and he didn't want to go talk to his Dad because the only chair behind the front desk was terribly uncomfortable. He was looking for the remote that Miranda had placed on the arm rest. He couldn't find it. *Now what am I going to do?* He tried to get up to turn on the light, but he was too stiff, too sore and too tired.

He was getting frustrated when he thought he heard something. He couldn't tell what it was, he wasn't positive he heard anything. Then he saw something shadowy glide by in the corner of his eye. He swung his head to see Andy in his wheel chair.

Hey there Andy. You surprised me. He couldn't admit that he was momentarily scared.

"Did I wake you up?"

"No. I couldn't sleep. I forgot about my night time medicine. Without it, I can't sleep much. I have insomnia."

"That sucks. I can't sleep either. I was hoping to find some of your Mom's crazy good hot chocolate to warm up."

"Turn on the light. It'll be easier to rummage through the

fridge."

He found some cocoa, warmed it up and they started a conversation.

A while later they discovered they had a similar taste in music. They had some 1970's arena rock music playing in the background and were easily able to talk over the music. They started off with more fish tales and then they swapped some adventure stories which led Parley to ask Andy about war experiences. Andy was the type that didn't care to talk about his war stories, but after a half hour Andy was surprised that he was enthralling Parley with some of his daring exploits. For some reason he felt comfortable talking about some of his war adventures. Parley was easy to talk to.

"How long have you had fibromyalgia?" asked Andy.

"I think it's been about four . . . Maybe five years. I should know how long I've been sick. I guess it's the fibro fog."

"That's interesting. There's a thing called chemo brain that a lot of people that go through chemotherapy have. It's where you forget things. I'm a journal keeper. I was reading entries back when I was going through chemo and I have no recollection of them happening. If I hadn't read about it, I wouldn't believe those things happened."

"Maybe I should consider keeping a journal. Maybe that would help me keep track of doctors visits and who says what. It's tough to keep track of it all," agreed Parley.

"I've noticed there haven't been many posts on your blog lately, is it because you can't go fishing?"

"Partly. I have a few hundred video segments saved on my hard drive that I could clean up and post, it's that with all the chronic pain and all, it messes my mind up. But I haven't been out on a boat in a long time."

"Does boating hurt your fibro pain issue?"

"Sometimes. My doctor or nurse practitioner person is Hank Standing Elk. We've been best friends since grade school. He's the one who discovered what's wrong with me. He lives on the other side of the lake on the Washakie Indian reservation. I have to take a boat to get there and it can get quite rough. Sometime's I just worry that it will hurt. Sometimes it does and sometimes it doesn't. Our big boat feels a little better than the smaller fishing boat I used to use. It doesn't get bounced around as much."

"What is it about the boat that hurts?"

Parley had to think a moment before answering. "It . . . Well . . . The pounding of the boat on the water can make my tail bone ache and then the pain radiates up to my hips and sometimes all the way up to my ribs and neck."

"Do you feel that sensation all the time?" Andy was startled at the descriptions Parley was giving him.

"No. I feel it a lot, but not all the time. Of course, there are other painful sensations . . . So I'm always feeling some type of hurt."

"Are you telling me that literally every second of every waking minute you feel some type of pain?"

"Well, when you say it like that, it sounds impossible to endure, but yes. I wake up in pain and massive stiffness. I wake up so much I think that's how I developed insomnia."

"Well . . . How can you possibly even be alive? I believe you. I do. It's just that no one can live through that type of pain, can they? Do you?"

"When you say it like that, I guess that's why so many people don't believe chronic fibro pain is even possible. But, that's the truth." Parley was emphatic.

Andy was dumbfounded. He just sat there for a few moments in continued disbelief. He thought how he used to hurt so badly after his surgeries and chemotherapy. As he started to understand the suffering from fibromyalgia he started to entertain the idea that if he had to choose between fibromyalgia and an ordeal with cancer, he would choose cancer. By choosing cancer, he reasoned, he would either get better or die. He wouldn't go on and on, minute by minute, day by day, week and week onto infinity with some type of constant, never-ending pain.

Andy lifted his head up and looked at Parley in the eyes. "You are really telling me the truth aren't you?"

"I got no reason to lie and I have no reason to sit around all day. I had the best life anyone could possibly have. I basically got paid to hunt and fish. Why would I want to give that up?"

"I hear ya. I do."

"Why I am asking is that some of that hurt you're talking about sounds like some of the pain I was feeling after my surgeries and while I was doing chemo. I thought those sensations would kill me. The ache, the hurt . . . Was a living hell, but it finally went mostly away. I have my flare ups every once in a while, but I have days of no pain. You don't even have a second without pain."

"I'm living through it and it's hard to believe sometimes."

"It feels like that sometimes. Before Hank diagnosed me, I had no relief. Now through Hanks diagnosis, I have pain pills and a lot of other medicine to treat most of my symptoms. I still hurt and there are flare up moments that seem like they will never end, but the intensity of the pain is a little less for me now."

There was a lull in the conversation. Parley shocked himself when he realized how deep this conversation was and with a total stranger. Of course he had never spoken to someone who was so empathetic and understood terrible pain. It was validating.

Chapter Twenty-Four: Sleep

The only thing you have any real control over is the way you respond to life. CallahanWriter

Spring 2013
Lake Shaft City, Wyoming

After a long sleepless night with insightful conversation, Parley and Andy were exhausted. Bert took Parley home while Andy took the elevator to his room. Andy was finally able to climb off the wheelchair and into his bed for a good long nap. Parley, on the other hand, was fit to be tied. The whole situation brought up bad memories from the past when his insomnia was untreated. His body was demanding and confused. Though demanding sleep, it would only allow a short two hour nap, which was far from enough rest.

He didn't know what to do to. He didn't know if he should take his night time medicine during the day and then take it again at night when he normally went to bed. He spent the rest of his day in a stupor with a thick pounding headache.

It had been a busy day for Miranda, but things slowed down just enough in the mid-afternoon that she was able to make her and Parley lunch.

"What did you do last night when you found out that you didn't have your night time pills?"

"Andy and I spent most of the night talking?"

"Andy stayed up with you?"

"Not at first. He was having a hard time not being able to sleep. He came down to the back room looking for some hot chocolate. I was awake and he stayed down with me and we talked."

"What did you guys talk about for so long?"

"Oh good heavens, I can't fully remember. Some of the time we talked about what having fibromyalgia was like and we talked about his experiences in the hospital, his surgery and chemotherapy treatments."

"I've been wondering about that cancer thing he mentioned. Did he say anything about it, as far as did they get it all, will it come back or is it gone for good?"

"He didn't say and I didn't dare ask. What if he's in partial remission and he's going to be dead in three months? What do you say to that?"

"You don't suppose– I wonder if . . . If that's why he is traveling with such flexible plans. He doesn't know where he's going when he's done here. Maybe he doesn't have that much time . . ." Miranda covered her mouth with her hands.

After a pause, Parley said, "I don't know how you politely ask someone if they are going to live or die?" Miranda nodded her head in agreement.

"Does he have any family I wonder?" Miranda was wiping a tear from the corner of her eye.

"I've never thought to ask. I guess we should relax about all this, all these questions. He's practically a stranger after all. A perfectly nice stranger . . . We hardly know him."

"How can you say that? You guys spent all night talking to each other."

"That's true, but I've only known him for a day, just twenty-four hours. There's more that I don't know about him than I do know about him. I'm just saying we shouldn't overreact."

"You've spent way more time with him than I have, but he doesn't feel like a stranger. There's a comfortable feeling about him. It's like I knew him all along, even though we've never met."

"Now that you mention it . . . There is a certain ease about him. We were quite open about the stuff we talked about. It's the kind of stuff you don't normally share with others until you know them well enough to know if you can trust them."

"That's a good way of putting it and like I said, you've spent way more time with him than I have, but I feel a connection with him." Miranda relaxed in her chair and crossed her legs. She went on, "I wonder if God led him to us so that we could help him?"

"Hold on, you're moving way too fast. First of all, we hardly know him. Maybe he has a family, it's conceivable he is in a full remission, perhaps we're making way too much out of this. We need to get to know him and not jump the gun until we do know about his situation."

"You're right," Miranda was nodding in agreement.

"I'm getting tired," Parley checked his watch. "Wow, it's 9:00 p.m. and I feel tired."

"That is strange," Miranda agreed. "Usually you have to take your medicine in order to get drowsy enough to sleep. Maybe it's because of such little sleep last night?"

"Maybe. I don't want to make too much out of it and get stressed out and then not be able to sleep."

"Why don't you take your medicine and relax? We could watch a movie and if you fall asleep great. No pressure."

"That's a good idea. What about the kids, when will they are getting home?"

"I don't know, they have a school night curfew of 10:00 p.m. so they'll be home soon. Don't worry about it. I'll make sure their home safe and the doors are locked. Just relax, take your pills and don't worry about anything. Want some popcorn for the movie? What movie should we watch?"

"Popcorn sounds great with an ice cold Coke. I guess it's your turn for a romance flick." Parley exaggerated a nod of exasperation. Then he gave a faint smile.

"We can watch one of your cowboy westerns if you want– "

"No, no. It's your turn."

They went through a song and dance routine whenever they watched a romantic movie. Parley had to make a big deal out of it to save face, then he was content to watch the chick flick. They both knew he liked the chick flicks. They weren't his favorites, but he didn't mind watching them.

Everything went just as Miranda planned. Parley took his pills and fell asleep less than an hour later. He slept for six hours, waking up to the usual excruciating pain that he always did. He was too stiff to get out of bed and find his medicine. He knew they were somewhere on his night stand. He stretched for the pill bottle. He couldn't reach it. He was hurting, but now he had to decide if his pain was bad enough to suffer through the extreme morning stiffness of getting up and moving. The ache overrode the stiffness. Where are my dumb pills?

He let out a long, low groan as he forced himself to move through the pain of stiffness in his joints. How many people in the world have to go through pain to get out of bed in the morning? Why me?

He was now sitting on the edge of the bed. He still had to stand up before he could move around to find the pill bottle. He took a long, deep breath and pushed himself off the bed with his hands. There was a moment in time where the only thing between falling down and standing upright was sheer willpower to push through the raw ache of his hips, knees, and ankles.

He looked on his night stand. No pills. He looked at the top of the dresser drawers. No pill bottles. He walked to the master bathroom. Nothing. He was forcing himself to think as clearly as the agony would allow. When was the last time I took a pill? Where was it? His mind went blank. Come on, think, dang it, think. Where are my pills? A terrible thought came to him. They are back in the den. Dang it. The few steps between his bedroom and den were laughable to anyone, anyone other than someone with chronic pain and morning stiffness.

Am I in that much pain? Do I really need to go that far to get my medicine? The pain will only get worse. He took a deep breath.

The trip to the den took a few seconds, but the pain made it feel like an hour. There were a few pill bottles in his den but no pain pills. By now his muscles were pounding and burning in agony with every beat of his heart. He was getting nervous. He had to have his pain pills. All the more reason to find them now. Even then, when he found them, it would take about an hour for the medicine to kick in. He shuffled painfully back to his bedroom. He looked again at the night stand. His eye caught a glimpse of a translucent orange bottle. It was on the floor behind the night stand. He leaned over as far as the strangulating ache would allow. Finally, his bottle of pain pills.

Chapter Twenty-Five: World Famous Hot Chocolate

Life is a series of choices, how you choose and what you choose determines how you live. CallahanWriter

Spring 2013
Lake Shaft City, Wyoming

I hate my life, all of this suffering, pain, and misery.

"How ya feeling sweetie?"

"Lousy, same pain, different day."

"I'm sorry." Sorry for asking.

"I can't do anything without all these little pills. Pain pills, muscle relaxers for the day, muscle relaxers for the night, anxiety medicine, anti inflammatory's, pills to take more pills."

"I get the picture," Miranda tried to change the subject. She wasn't in the mood for another one of his frequent tirades. "What do you want for breakfast?"

"I'm not hungry, but I got to eat so I can take my stupid pills."

"Remember those stupid pills are helping you– "

"I know. I'm just in a sour mood. Just . . . What ever's easiest. I'm sorry."

"I know, me too," conceded Miranda.

~

Andy and Bert got everything worked out for his prosthetic foot. They had to send it to the hospital who would then send it to the manufacturer who would then decide to repair it or replace it.

"So where's Nick? I haven't seen him since I arrived," asked Andy.

"He's on vacation."

"With his family?"

"Yeah, he took his family to Oklahoma to go noodling, that's where you catch– ”

"Oh, I know what noodling is," Andy shook his head with fond recollection. "I've done it several times when I was in high school and a little during college."

"I've heard of it, but I've never done it. What's it like?"

"It's a rush. It hurts if you don't use gloves. Some say it's not noodling if you wear gloves. Those huge catfish have sharp teeth. I might still have a scar from a huge catfish I once caught" Andy examined his left hand. "Right there. It's not very big." Andy pointed to the small white scar for Bert to see. "You can get some very big catfish when you noodle. It can be tough. You catch it with your hand and then you have to wrestle the fish in your arms and not let it wiggle free."

"That sounds like a lot of fun. I can't believe that I have never done it before," said Bert. "I'm looking forward to Nick's report when he gets back."

"Is Nick the type to take a lot of pictures?"

"Not so much, but Heather, his wife is an avid shutterbug."

"I hope I get to see a few pictures of Nick in action," Andy said with excitement.

"I'm really in the mood for some of your wife's hot chocolate and one of those huge scones."

"That does sound good. I think I'll join you."

Andy was sniffing at the hot chocolate and enjoying the rich decadent smell. "I've been meaning to ask, what's the deal with this hot chocolate? I noticed on the menu that they call it Betty's World Famous Hot Chocolate? What's that about? I know it takes like heaven but is it famous or something?"

"Funny story," Bert answered. "It's a recipe that goes back several generations in Betty's family. The only people that know the recipe are Betty and Miranda. We keep a copy of the recipe in the safe. We've thought about marketing it, but so far it's only available here. The 'world famous' part deals with Parleys' internet blog. I still don't know exactly how his blog works, only that we get people from all over the world vacation here and they say they heard about us from his blog and Miranda's blog."

One time, mmm . . . Eight, maybe ten years ago a blog fan brought his family from Italy. They fell in love with Betty's hot chocolate. They were here for two weeks and they drank it with every meal and in between meals. They drank so much it probably turned their blood brown. So anyway, they get back to Italy and they made a very nice feedback on Parleys' website. It was a great review about the whole resort, fishing, boating all of it, but they made a huge deal about the hot chocolate.

Then other people from Spain, France, England, Ireland, and even Russia replied to that hot chocolate comment. People were also starting to mention it on Miranda's blog. So Miranda talked about it on her blog some, then someone came up with an idea to have a contest to see who made the best hot chocolate. We have a chili contest in October and so we added a cocoa contest. Since Betty, Miranda, and Heather are three of the five judges, they couldn't compete. So for fun, after the winners were announced, we selected twenty people from the audience and had them blind taste the top three winners against Betty's recipe. And all twenty judges voted for Betty's recipe."

"Did you film the contest?" Andy asked.

"Yes we did and we posted it on Miranda's blog and the resort blog. That added to the international reputation. The next summer season we started using feedback cards all over the place and forty-percent of the international visitors mentioned the cocoa in their comments."

"So now it really is world famous. People from Japan, to Australia, Hong Kong to China, and most of Europe were on those cards."

"That's an amazing story," Andy said as he swallowed the last sip from his third cup of cocoa. "Why don't you sell it in grocery stores and other places?"

"We thought about it, but then Parley got sick and Nick's workload got heavier and I don't know the first thing about marketing. Betty and Miranda are too busy."

"If you did sell it, would it be liquid or a powder mix?"

"I don't know. We never got that far."

~

Parley was feeling well enough by early afternoon to try going to the resort. In the past, the resort had been his home away from home.

Since being sick, the resort served as a stern reminder of Parleys' inability to live his life. At first, when he did come to the resort everyone, including Bert, Betty and Nick thought he was all better and he could resume his work. They thought that if you were sick, you needed to be home in bed. Since he was at the resort and not in bed, he should be feeling fine. They couldn't understand how he could claim to be in so much pain and still be able to get out of bed and come down to the resort.

Between the reaction of his family and the physical difficulty to make the trip to the resort, he found it harder to want to go there. Most of the time it was too much effort. His family came around and started to understand more about his condition, but as his health continued to grow worse and Parley found that it cost him too much pain and energy. It was hard, if not impossible to find the motivation needed to go to the resort. Since his diagnosis and the handful of pills he was taking daily, things had improved to a degree. It was easier to get motivated to make the trip.

Thinking about Andy and how well they had gotten along, Parley was feeling motivated to go to the resort and meet up with Andy. He wanted to get to know him more before his foot was returned and he decided to get on with his travels.

Parley was a friendly and outgoing guy and in his day, but as he got sick and then sicker still, he lost a lot of that outgoing nature. Now he thought maybe it was returning since he had met Andy Zimmerman, a war hero. He almost felt like they had bonded during that long night of engaging conversation.

Chapter Twenty-Six: Time Flies

You are not only responsible for what you say, but also for what you do not say.
Martin Luther

June 4, 2013
Lake Shaft City, Wyoming

"Can you believe it, Ted and Emily are graduating high school in two days,"

"Where did all the time go?" asked Parley.

Shaking her head in disbelief, "I don't know. I just don't know," Miranda said, emphasizing every syllable.

"I guess we'll be having two college kids this fall, that makes us old," Parley said wistfully.

"At least they're a good couple of kids."

"Yes, thanks to you."

"What do you mean by that? We both had a hand raising them."

"Not really, not these last five years. Five years? Wow. I can't believe five years since this chronic pain started. It's been a long five years. It seems like a lifetime ago when I try to remember back to life without fibromyalgia."

"What do you mean you didn't have a hand in raising them?"

"It's just the last five years. . . Being so sick with this mysterious chronic pain that ends up being fibromyalgia. They grew up without me. They couldn't just stop growing up waiting for me to get well. I wish they were still little and I could have a second chance with them."

"Even still," Miranda paused, "still, you've had an impact on their growing up."

"If I did and I'm only saying 'if I did', it wasn't much of an impact on their lives. Look, I didn't help them learn how to drive. I haven't been fishing or boating with them for. . .I don't know how long it's been. I've been sequestered in the den away from them as they grew up. I haven't been to church with them hardly at all lately. They're good kids, I know and that's all thanks to you. I just wish I could have been part of it."

"I guess I know what you're saying and maybe I haven't communicated very well with you, but those kids, they talk about you, they have fond memories of you. You've had an impact on them and you can tell by how they talk and what they say about you."

"What exactly have they said?"

"I can't remember their exact words, it's the stuff they mention in passing tells me you've had an impact on them."

"They're going to be gone in three months, I wish I could spend some time with them, maybe create a few more memories. This fibromyalgia, this painful joke of an illness, it's ruining my life. It takes away my ability to do normal daily things and it takes away the opportunity in creating memories with my kids and even with you. All the memories you have of me the last several years are based on me being sick."

Knowing Parleys' moods and his way of thinking, Miranda knew there wasn't much that could be said to make things better, at least not right away. *Maybe we can get him some nacho's on the way to the resort. He like the greasy convenience store kind.*

"Even with the pain pills and other million prescriptions you're taking, you're still in constant pain, but overall, there's an improvement, isn't there?"

"Yeah. . .Yes, technically yes. It's a matter of intensity. The pain is less intense. The overall misery isn't as bad. I wish the fatigue would get better, that would help with the overall misery issue." Parley shook his head. "What are you getting at?"

"Why not try to do some of the things you haven't done with the kids lately like going fishing on the big boat. Maybe it's time to push it a little and see just how much better you really are? The big boat is heavier and more stable in the water than the fishing boat. If your pain get's worse then you pop a pill. If you get wiped out, then you lay down and rest. Meanwhile the kids are having fun and you're there with them. What do you think?"

Taking a cleansing breath, Parley shook his head. "I could try it, I guess. I wish there was some other type of pain pill I could take for special occasions."

They were driving to the resort in Miranda's car. They were coming up on the Gray Dairy convenience store. "Hey sweetie, want some nacho's? I can pull into Gray Dairy."

"Sure, that sounds good."

It always does. Miranda smiled.

As Parley was getting out of the car door, he said, "I still like the idea of adding a snack bar with the gift shop. That way we can offer ethnic food and hot dogs and junk food without ruining the ambience of the Café. Then I could finally have my nacho's at the resort."

"You'll need to talk to Bert about that."

"Yeah, but without you backing me, everyone else will just laugh at me."

"I might could be persuaded to change my mind," Miranda smiled.

"Do you want anything from the store?"

"Yes, I want some too, and don't laugh at me. I'm in the mood for them. I've got a hankering for them," said Miranda.

Parley was shaking his head melodramatically as he walked into the convenience store, teasing her about wanting nacho's. They were a favorite of his, but she usually didn't care for them much.

Miranda was a little surprised he was going into get the nacho's. *He must be feeling a little better than usual.*

A few minutes later, Miranda saw Parley backing out of the front doors with a box of nacho's in each hand. She rolled her window down to take them from Parley so he could get back in the car. They sat in the parking lot eating the nacho's and listening to the radio.

"Miranda, do you think God is mad at me?"

Startled at what Parley said, she turned down the radio.

"Where did that come from?"

"Why is all this happening to me? I thought I was living a good life. . .I spent five minutes going into the store for nacho's and now five minutes later I feel like I might be dying. The misery and the agony can swell up in an instant. It's like someone is peeking around the corner watching me and if I show the slightest improvement they flip the switch sending me into a deeper abyss of pain or fatigue or even both. I never know what to expect. I never know how to plan." He looked at his watch. "I should have taken my pain pill a half hour ago. I can't even keep that straight."

"I don't see how you can think God is mad at you. You might not want to hear it right now, but look at your life. Even though your health is terrible, you're otherwise very blessed. We have a good marriage, we've got great kids. We're not poor. I know things could be better, but they could also be a lot worse."

Parley knew that what she said was true, but it bugged him anyway. Every time he complained which was a lot, she would have something positive to say. He wasn't sure why it bothered him, but it did. *There are a lot of evil people out there, why couldn't they be stricken with something like this? Why does it have to be me?* Parley was feeling picked on and worthless.

For some unknown reason, sometimes Miranda's optimistic cheery attitude bugged Parley. On the other hand, he was grateful for her positive attitude, but sometimes he just wanted her to join with him in being mad at fibromyalgia. He understood the importance of being positive, but sometimes he just wanted to be mad at the disease that had ruined his life.

Miranda turned her car back on and pulled out of the convenience store parking lot. They drove in silence the rest of the way to the resort.

Parley was feeling frustrated with himself. He was feeling a little bit better than usual, but his attitude was terrible. He was feeling down on himself as he thought about how alone and isolated he felt from the world. Even though he had a supportive family, he still felt alone. He felt forgotten because now that his old life was relegated to the past, people that called him or sought after him never came around anymore. The fact that no one could really understand the pain and suffering he went through made him feel alone and isolated.

As they were pulling into the parking lot Parley had a thought come to him. For the first time since he had been sick with chronic pain and fatigue, someone had actually come close to understanding him and that person was Andy. He thought about their conversation the other night. Until now, he hadn't fully appreciated the value of that all night conversation.

Andy was having fun browsing in Bert's Outfitter shop. It was a huge store with a vast inventory. Most of that inventory was enthralling to him. There was a ton of camping gear, fishing tackle, a big selection of bows and arrows, rifles, shotguns and handguns. He had never seen so many knives in one location in his life. He thought about what kind of customer this store appealed to? Campers, hunters, boaters, fishermen and survivalist. Anybody interested in the outdoors would consider this a temple or a place or worship. The store was almost like a convention with the vast collection of outdoor related inventory. Andy felt as excited to be in Bert's Outfitter store as a kid in a candy store would feel.

Andy felt for his wallet. He decided to go over to the gift shop and find a paperback to read. As he wheeled himself over to the gift shop, he felt a flare up of phantom pain. He pulled over to the side of the store and pulled out a small pillbox. He dry swallowed a pain pill. He found a wall of books for sale. Novels, non fiction and no surprise, a lot of outdoor theme books. He looked at the best seller display and quickly found the perfect novel for his current mood. Hopeful. He had been thinking about the all night conversion with Parley and that made him feel hopeful. He didn't know why and he didn't really care. It was nice to feel happy and hopeful. He was glad to find the perfect book. As he handed the cashier his money, he was waved though the check out lane and smiled at. Apparently all of the Burnrise employees were instructed not to take his money.

As they were walking down the hall toward the back room Parley asked, "Why don't we invite Andy to go with us to meet Hank this afternoon?"

"That's a good idea," Miranda said as she thought, *hmm, Parley is really making a friend out of Andy. Nice.*

They spoke with Andy about going to the Reservation. He was trying to be tactful and figure out a way to say no when they explained that they had a couple of slips that were wheelchair friendly. Once he knew it wouldn't be so bad getting on the boat with his wheelchair he accepted the invitation.

Chapter Twenty-Seven: The Boat Ride

There is no pain so bad, no hope so lost, no despair so deep, that the God of Heaven cannot heal. CallahanWriter

June 5, 2013
Lake Shaft, Wyoming

The water in the lake was as still as the air above it. With no hint of a breeze, the sun was out and warming up the earth below, thawing it out after a long and hard winter. The skies were a powder blue smudged with ivory clouds ebbing and flowing in the afternoon sky. The family boat was churning through the smooth water, leaving a perfect wake in its path as it made its way across the lake toward the Washakie Reservation.

The weather system over the Lake Shaft recreation area could and frequently did change its mind in a heart beat. What started out as a smooth run across the lake in a perfectly framed springtime afternoon turned suddenly to sharp gusts of winds that churned up the water and pushed the clouds around like pinballs. Some clouds turned watery gray other heavy rain clouds were blown into the mix.

Parley was happy with the smooth ride on such perfectly calm waters and a little surprised at the sudden turn of events. Now the lake was choppy with one to two foot swells breaking the lake's surface. This turned the smooth ride too blustery and rough. The boat was now bouncing and skipping through the whitecaps and pounding on the hard water, causing his back to jar each time the boat landed. They were in no danger of a storm or capsizing. They were just tossing at the capricious nature of the wind. Experience told them the wind gusts would blow themselves out soon unless there was a rain storm in the mix, then things would get worse. The three-day forecast said there would be nothing but fair skies so there was no worry about the sudden conditions getting any worse.

There were more than two miles out when the wind storm

surprised them. The brave warrior Andy had a look of concern written on his face. Parley twisted at the hips and looked over Andy's life jacket. He yanked on a few straps to see how tight they were. They were fine. "Why are you checking by life vest? Are we in danger?" Andy yelled above the sound of the wind.

"Not likely, but we take safety very seriously. It always pays to be prepared. Remind me to tell you a story about life jackets once the wind dies down and we can talk without yelling at the top of our lungs."

Andy didn't want to fight the noise of the wind so he nodded in agreement. He squinted his eyes to take a look across the lake. The towering lodgepole pines were gently swaying in the wind.

As The Family Boat cut through the water against the white caps, the bow was lifted up. As the props pushed the boat forward and the wave finished their roll, the boat dropped against the water. The energy of the impact when the boat slapped the lake traveled up Parley and Andy sitting in the boat. That raging energy sent its force up Parleys' spine, which in turn irritated the sensitive nerves woven through his back muscles causing him terrible pain and intense agony all along his spine and around his torso to his ribs. The energy shot misery to his neck and head, causing terrible, but short-lived headaches. His back felt like buckling under the pressure of the pain.

I wish Miranda would slow down. I might die from this raging ache and misery. He tried to get her attention and failed. Between the breeze soaring past his ears and the roar of the motor adding to the noise, Parley couldn't yell at Miranda to slow down. His hips, back, and neck were too stiff to turn his head and shoulders enough to wave and get her attention. This sudden hurt wasn't the kind of pain his pill would help. It was temporary pain that would ease up if Miranda would slow down and quit slapping the water so hard. Parley looked at Andy wondering if he could be any help. He saw Andy taking a pill from his little plastic pill box. Parley took a deep breath and tried to relax.

Andy started off enjoying the boat ride. The smooth ride was pleasant and now it was adventurous with the choppy whitecaps, the bouncing boat, and the roaring wind. He had been enjoying the view and the scenic landscapes along the shorelines. There was an occasional beach made from soft tan soil. Most of the shoreline at this part of the lake was made from thick lodge pole pines and quaking aspens. Before the wind got nasty there had been some ducks and geese near some of the shoreline. It was a landscape view perfect for the cover of an outdoor magazine. He happened to glance Parleys' way and saw him fumbling for his pill bottle. He was trying to pull the translucent orange bottle out of his pants pocket with one hand and holding on to his seat with his left hand. There was no way for Andy to move over to help him.

Suddenly the sound of the roaring motor stopped and the boat slowed to a crawl. Miranda had caught through the corner of her eye, the struggle Parley was having while trying to get his pill bottle out of his pants pocket. She stopped the boat to help him. Just as she got to Parley he got the bottle out. He was grateful for the boat slowing down.

As he was removing the lid and fishing out a chalky colored white pill, he asked Miranda, "Why did you stop?"

"I saw you having trouble getting your pill bottle out so I stalled the motor to help you."

"Thanks for that. I was trying to get you to slow down, but I was too stiff and in too much pain to turn enough to get your attention. Can you go way slower? The pounding of the boat is killing my back. My neck and head feel like they might explode any second. When the wind picked up and turned up the whitecaps the boat started hitting the water way too hard and that started my back muscles to ache."

"I'm sorry. Sure, I can go slower. I wasn't looking at either of you for a long time. I was just stuck looking at the horizon. It's beautiful out here this afternoon. I'll keep my eyes on you gentlemen and I'll go slower. Do you or Andy want anything while we're stopped? A drink or snack?" They were both fine and waved her off. Parley wiped a layer of sweat off his forehead. Miranda started up the engine and went much slower. She glanced at Parley and Andy to see if she was at the right speed. Parley responded with a thumbs up.

The sound of the motor finally allowed conversation between Parley and Andy.

"Oh, right. Life jackets. You said to remind you about life jackets when we could talk."

"Shoot, that's a heck of a story. Years ago, we were having a family day here at the lake. Emily was little, about four or five. . .Maybe six years old. She was anxious to get out on the lake with the jet ski. I rushed to put my life jacket on. I was thinking it was a waste to bother with my vest, but I wanted to be a good example to Emily so I put it on. But not very well. We were on the lake and she wanted to go from behind me to in front of me so she could steer. Before I could help her, she was standing on the sideboard and just as I leaned to grab her, the watercraft leaned too far to the side and we both fell off the jet ski and into the lake. I felt myself slide through the vest and into the ice water. My vest wasn't on securely and so it wasn't helping me. I panicked and I was worried that the same thing might be happening to Emily. I managed to hook the life jacket with the crook of my arm and stopped my descent. Praise the Lord. I found enough energy to climb back into my life vest and found Emily just treading water afloat with her jacket tightly around her. Ever since I've been a control freak about life jacket safety."

"Wow," exclaimed Andy, "I can see why you would be so into it."

Miranda was at the helm of the boat making an effort to maintain a slow steady speed. Why was I going so fast? Miranda felt bad for driving the boat so hard against the white caps. She wasn't known for high speeds. She realized it felt good going full throttle. She had been going fast and clearing her mind, now she went, slower, allowing the thoughts she was running from fill up her mind.

She had been burning the candle at both ends for so many years, she had never really thought about how things were affecting her. She was in survival mode. It was strange that she instinctively rode the boat so hard that the high speed and the wind whipping her hair was so relaxing. I wonder if I'll get any alone time with

Hank? Lately, she had been realizing how hard life was since Parley had been so sick and for such a long time. She had been so tasked driven that she never thought to slow down and smell the roses. Now she was seeking a thrill to let the stress sneak out.

I can't be thinking like that. I've got to keep it all together. The twins are graduating tomorrow. We're going to have a reception for them afterward. Parley can't help. I've got to be strong. It's all on me to keep things going, to keep our heads above water . . . It's always on me . . .

She was feeling a little unsettled with these new feelings she was just now acknowledging. *Where did they come from? Why am I just now feeling them? I hope I can be alone with Hank for a while.*

After a while, the pain pill started kicking in for Parley and he was feeling the intensity of the pain let up a little. Enough to make a difference. He was looking around as they slowed down and entered the Slow Wake zone in the Reservation harbor. He was having some memories as they passed different landmarks on the shoreline. He reflected back to that spectacular video of the eagle catching a fish. He thought decades back at the boyhood fun he had with Hank and Nick on these shores fishing and playing, being wild boys.

Why is this happening to me? It should be me at the helm. I'm the one who drives the boat, I'm the one that goes fast, I'm the one who is supposed to be supporting the family. I'm worthless. I-can't-do-anything. Why is this happening to me? What have I done to deserve this? Parley was feeling angry. He didn't know who he was mad at, he only knew he was angry.

Parley glanced around at the shoreline and the wet horizon down the channel. He looked at the cotton white clouds bumping into each other. *How can nature be so beautiful and active while I wither away with this . . . With this, affliction?*

He wondered about the multiple personalities of fibromyalgia. He could be feeling almost fine one minute and be in the throes of agony the next minute. He could feel good enough to go to a movie with Miranda and then his pain or fatigue would take a bad turn forcing them to come home early. He never knew what to expect and as a result never knew how to plan his life. He could wake up feeling on top of the world, one morning and go to bed that night feeling like he would rather be dead than in so much agony. Living this kind of life was difficult. It had a tendency to make even the most optimistic person pessimistic. How do you have a good attitude when you can't plan your future even thirty minutes out?

Parley noticed that just as the intensity of his pain was letting up, they were slowing down even more as they went past the speed warning buoy near the shore of the Washakie Indian Reservation. Parley still hurt all over, the usual wide spread fibromyalgia, muscle pain, but he was at least conversational.

Parley and Andy finally were able to start up a conversation. Parley told Andy about Hank Standing Elk and how he was the one who finally discovered what was wrong with him and was able to provide help with pain pills and other types of medicines. Andy was impressed with the story.

"I had a Marine buddy who was a Shoshone Indian from Wyoming. We served together in Iraq on my first deployment. He was KIA."

"What was his name?"

"Corporal Lester Greene."

"The Washakie reservation is mostly Shoshone Indians. I wonder if he came from that tribe?"

"I have no idea," Andy's voice trailed off as he seemed to be lost in his painful memories. "Lester was the first friend I ever had who was killed in battle. Well, actually he was wounded in battle, they got him off the field alive, but he died in Germany during surgery." Andy's head was leaning forward as he spoke, but at the end, his voice was noticeably softer.

"I never thought about that aspect of your sacrifice." Parleys' voice reflected his surprise.

"What do you mean by that?" Andy was curious. He coughed his weak voice away.

"I've always respected and appreciated what you and your fellow soldiers have sacrificed by your service. But, until now I never appreciated another sacrifice you guys have made. The emotional sacrifice of mourning the loss of your friends when they get killed in battle. That's no small thing."

"That's a – well, hmm . . . I've never thought of that. I've never put it in a context like that, but you're right. I don't know off hand how many friends I've lost, one was too many and it's been way more than that," Andy's voice was starting to get a little shaky and a little raspy. He took a deep breath as he quickly scanned his memory for an idea of how many losses he had personally experienced. Shaking his head, "I'm not sure I want to know how many friends I've lost over the years. Shoot, after one or two deployments you tend to be less friendly. You become harder to get to know and you don't go out of your way to make friends. Why make friends out of the guys who could end up dying in a day, a week or a month later? You put up a protective barrier."

"Hey boys," Miranda shouted as she slowed the boat even more. "We're about here."

"There's Hank, waiting for us," said Parley as he nodded his head in the direction Hank was standing. "I think you'll like him. He's a great guy. I've known him since grade school."

"Looking forward to meeting him," responded Andy. Within a matter of minutes, they were docked and tied up. Hank came aboard to assess the situation with getting Andy out of the boat and on the dock. The Reservation wasn't as handicap accessible as the Burnrise Family Resort.

"Gunnery Sargent, Andy Zimmerman, meet Hank Standing Elk. Hank, this is Andy. The one we've talked so much about."

"It's an honor to meet you Gunny." Hank held out his hand. Taking his outstretched hand, Andy said, "call me Andy. It's nice to meet you. I've heard quite a bit about you. According to Parley, you're some kind of medical genius diagnosing him and treating him for his fibromyalgia."

They warmly shook each other's hand. "This will be easier than I thought to get you onto the dock. All we'll need to do is unlatch this gate here on the side of the boat and I'll pull you over the little bump between the boat and the dock. The water is calm, so that will help, it'll be slick as a whistle." Hank's smile was reassuring.

Chapter Twenty-Eight: The Man With A Cane

I can spend my energy fighting the past, fighting something that cannot change, or I can let go of the past and spend my energy fighting for my future, fighting for something that can be changed and controlled. CallahanWriter

June 5, 2013,
Washakie Reservation, Wyoming

"So how have you been feeling this past month?"

"Same pain, different days. The days just run into each other. It feels like one long painful day."

"With all these pills and there is no difference, at all?"

Parley exhaled a deep breath. "Yeah, there's a difference, there is, but every day is still agonizing. The hurt or ache may feel different from day to day, it fluctuates, but it still hurts. On the rare day that the pain is noticeably less, I try to celebrate by doing something fun, but then I suffer for it the next day."

"How do you suffer for it the next day? What does that mean?"

"It seems like the next day is worse than it would otherwise have been."

Hank jotted down a few notes in Parleys' record and then put his pen down and looked at Parley and said, "I have two things for you to try this next month, well maybe three things to try. The first thing is every day I want you to keep a symptom journal. I want you to write down what you did and how you felt. Rate your pain after doing something. When there are other symptoms, make a note of them as well. For instance, write down that you took a shower and got dressed. Then write down your pain level. Also record when you take your pain pills and notice how long it takes for the pill to kick in and what your pain level is when it does. The point behind this is to become more aware of your day and how you feel. I think, well at least I hope things are better than you realize.

There are other things you may notice when you keep this journal and we can talk about it if and when you do. The second thing is to exercise."

"What? Wait a minute, are you kidding me? I can't exercise with all this pain and stiffness and fatigue, what are you talking about?" Parley was growing livid.

"Hold on, let me explain. I'm not talking about running five miles, swim two miles and row a boat across the lake. I'm talking about swimming or other water-based exercises or even other low impact exercises like walking, weight lifting, yoga, you know, stuff like that."

The look on Parleys' face went from irate exasperation to a more mild consternation. He took a few cleansing breaths and said, "Go on."

"There have been several recent studies that show low impact aerobic exercises are actually beneficial for patients with chronic pain illnesses like arthritis, fibromyalgia and similar illnesses. People seem to benefit from moving their joints and stretching their muscles and breathing deep."

"Are you serious?" Parley emphasized single every syllable. "You're joking, right?"

"No, I'm not. I've already started experimenting with a couple of chronic pain patients and so far the results are encouraging. But you need to start slow. The studies make many good points about moving your body in spite of being in chronic pain. Sometimes it can improve the fatigue. It's been known to increase an overall sense of well being. Sleep can improve as well. A lot of people in these studies were surprised at how the pain improved."

"Do you know what you are suggesting? What you're saying? Well. . .It's like telling a thirsty man to not drink water until he's not thirsty. That would make no sense and neither does what you're saying."

"Remember, I'm talking about low impact exercise and starting slow and progressing slowly so you don't over do it. I'm not saying it will be easy and it won't take away all your pain, but it will help."

Parley was shaking his head in disbelief. "Look here," said Hank. "You got sick with pain. Then we start you on pain pills and muscle relaxers. That helped a little. Then we started treating other symptoms over time. As we did, your overall health got a little better. Each time we added something, things got a little better, except for those nerve pills that made you sick. We stopped those. I wrote up an outline to follow as far as exercising the next month goes. I'm going to look around to see if there is a physical therapist with an understanding what I want you to do. If I find one then I'll let you know and you can work with him or her like having a specialized personal trainer. So. . .What do you think about that?"

"I keep waiting for the punch line. I haven't heard it yet. So, are you really serious?"

"Shaking his head in exasperation, Hank replied, "Look buddy, "I am trying to help you. Like I said earlier, I've already started this with a couple of patients and I've read several studies on this subject. I really think it makes sense and I think it will help you. I can't say how much, but if it takes your pain down even one to two points I think it's worth pursuing. Remember, there is no known cure and all we can do is try everything that seems reasonable in hopes of managing the pain the best we can."

"Parley, what have you got to lose? You know Hank wouldn't suggest anything stupid. Come on sweetie, have a little faith in Hank. After all, he is the only one who has been able or willing to help you." Miranda was wearing her stern face.

Letting out a deep and frustrated breath, Parley asked, "what is the third thing you want me to do?"

"Does that mean you'll try the exercise?" asked Miranda.

"I got nothing to lose, just pain to gain." Shaking his head, Parley finished by saying, "I'll give it a try, not necessarily a big try . . . But I'll give it a try."

"So the third thing is more of a suggestion. That is to go online and look for support groups that deal with fibromyalgia. There are a surprising number of them in the form of blogs, social media and various websites. I had three patients tell me about the emotional boost some of these sights were. They allow you to interact with others who have chronic pain, fibromyalgia, and chronic fatigue."

"That seems like the least crazy idea you've had today," Parley replied with a little attitude.

"I'm sorry for the way Parley is acting today Hank. You know he's just frustrated." Shifting her gaze at Parley, she went on to say, "Parley that was a little rude. Hanks your best friend."

"I'm sorry. I think Miranda is right. I'm just feeling burned out I guess." Parley shook his head in despair.

"I guess you're entitled to the occasional bad attitude day," Hank said with some sarcasm. Hank gave Parley a light punch in the shoulder.

They left the exam room and went back out to the waiting room and chatted for a few minutes as Hank waited for his next appointment. Hank and Andy were getting to know each other when the bell over the door rang and a man limped in through the opened door. Naturally Andy turned to the source of the noise.

A tall man wearing a bright turquoise shirt with shoulder length dark hair came hobbling into the foyer with a cane. He limped his way to White Flowers desk. On his way he happened to glance over to a group of people on the other side of the foyer. He recognized Hank talking to three people. *Oh. That's Parley Burnrise. That must be his wife, and that, that . . .is that Andy Zimmerman? No. It can't be.*

In the middle of his sentence Andy stopped talking and stared at the man with a turquoise shirt who just came in. Hank, Miranda and Parley watched Andy with interest as he looked at the new arrival. That same man was staring back at Andy.

Hank, Parley and Miranda were looking back and forth at Andy and the man with a cane who Hank knew as Lester Greene, one of his existing patients.

"Andy, do you know that man?" Asked Miranda. "Andy?"

Andy seemed to be in a trance or lost in thought or otherwise unresponsive. "Andy?"

Andy's mind was swimming in a sea of confusion, shock and

disbelief. He knew that man with a cane as Corporal Lester Greene, an old Marine friend who died in battle. *Is that Lester? Could it be him? Lester is dead. Did Lester have a brother or a twin? An identical twin? Who is standing there? Is it Lester's ghost? How could it be Lester? It can't be him. Who am I looking at?* All these confusing emotions and thoughts occurred in an instant. *He's looking at me. Who is he? Do I know him? That's him? He's dead. He is supposed to be dead. They said he was dead. He died in Germany.*

Strange emotions were swirling around in Andy's head. The shock turned to anger and back again to shock. From shock, they went to disbelief, then to anger. *Is this some impossible imposter? I saw him get shot. I know he got shot. I know he's dead. They said he died. He's limping. Is it a lookalike? How could it be him?* All of theses thoughts and feeling erupting in Andy's mind.

His spine turned to jelly. His hips become clay-like as his brain started to swim. For the first time ever he is glad to be sitting in a wheelchair. At least he wouldn't get hurt if he passed out from shock, fright, or disbelief that he's feeling. Andy suddenly realizes that he is staring at a ghost, a ghost that is limping toward him. He needs to turn away, but the signals from his brain go unheeded as he stares at a dead man who is very much alive, with a limp, right where he got shot. *Could it be Lester? Impossible, it looks like it, but could can't be? Could it be?*

"Is that you Sargent Zimmerman?" the dead man asks.

The dead man speaks. The dead man is talking. It has to be corporal Greene. It sounds like Lester's strong, deep voice. Lester is dead.

Andy took Corporal Greene's death hard. It was the first friend Andy lost in battle. He carried that scar throughout the rest of his time in the marines and now that scar is a living, talking walking ghost limping toward Andy.

"Lester? Is that you?"

"Yes, It's me Sargent Lester Greene, or, well, you knew me as a Corporal."

Andy's voice had a mind of its own. Andy tried to respond,

but his brain forgot to tell his voice. Trying to gain his composure, Andy said, "you're dead. Um, I. . .You're. . . They said you died in Germany. Is that . . . Really. . . You Lester?"

"I'm not dead and ya it's me, Lester Greene."

"What happened, how come you're not dead?" *That didn't sound right.*

"I got wounded in that battle, the one where I got shot. They took me to Germany, but I'm not dead. I was medically discharged six months later on account of this limp."

"They told us YOU DIED!"

A little impatient with all this talk of death, Lester said, "I'm sorry to disappoint you, but I never died. I'm totally alive. Sometimes I wish I wasn't, but yeah, I'm still breathing."

Hank, Miranda and Parley were looking on with curiosity. They felt like they should turn away and give them a private moment, but the drama they were witnessing was too amazing to look away from.

"I'm shocked, I'm . . .   Blown away, I'm glad you're alive. I'm . . . " Andy was at a loss for words. He couldn't stand up. He helplessly held out an arm, offering his hand to Lester. Lester was taken back by Andy's response until he saw Andy's outstretched hand and really, just now, noticed that Andy was in a wheelchair. He took a deep breath of relief, fidgeting slightly, he shook Andy's hand.

It was a touching moment for Hank, White Flower, Parley and Miranda as they witnessed two disabled veterans reunite. This is the stuff of movies. They were reunited the best they could with two disabling wounds. The four witnesses were not ashamed as they all wiped quiet tears away from their face. This was a sacred moment.

The reunion was etched in the memories of time and that's where they stayed. Once they regained their composure they returned to their previous Marine like dispositions

"You look like crap Sargent Zimmerman. I mean Andy. What happened to you, you're all thin and beat up?"

"I'll let that slide Corporal since I thought you were dead and all."

"I was promoted to Sargent before being put out to pasture."

"Well, if you want technicalities, I made Gunnery Sargent before they threw me away."

"What in the world brings you out to the Washakie Reservation?" Asked Lester.

"I still can't believe you're alive. They told us you died during surgery." Shaking his head in disbelief, a shocked Andy said, "All these years you've been alive and I've been mourning you. It's a shock."

"All this time you thought I was dead. No wonder you never looked me up during all those years. I thought you might have been killed, but I looked you up and could see you were alive and kicking," said Lester.

The four witnesses went to the other side of the waiting room in an attempt at giving these men the appearance of privacy which was impossible because the foyer wasn't that big.

"Why didn't you email me or call me?" asked Andy.

"I was ticked off that you never reached out to me while I was in the hospital in Germany and in Walter Reed."

"I would have if you were alive, I mean, if I knew you were alive. I'm sorry man. Really sorry. You're alive! That's awesome." Andy was smiling from ear to ear as he started accepting this new reality.

"I'm alive all right," Lester shook his head with a smile.

"Why would they tell me you were dead? I even amended one of my reports on that battle where you were shot. No one ever corrected my report."

They both took a moment to breathe and collect their thoughts as they stared at each other.

"I think I'm still in shock. Part of me thinks I'm talking to a ghost. It hasn't completely sunk in."

"Really though, you don't look so good, at least compared to all those years ago. You know what happened to me. What happened to you?" asked a concerned Lester.

"IED, got my foot and leg blown off. While they were cutting more of my leg off, they discovered a tumor. They had to cut more leg off. Then chemo and radiation treatments. I think I look pretty good compared to when I left Walter Reed."

"Andy, it is so good to see you . . . of all the people in the world . . . I run into you. What brought you out to the Washakie Reservation? Of all the places in the world and I run into you here."

Pointing to Parley and Miranda as they were talking with Hank, "I'm with them. I've been staying at the Burnrise Family Resort on the other side of the lake. They invited me to come out here to meet Hank. He is Parleys' doctor."

"I've got an appointment with Hank myself. I like him. He's real good. I know Parley, actually I don't know him, but I know of him and I know that he and Hank have been friends forever. Parley is sort of a legend around these parts."

Lester and Andy got lost in conversation. Hank took the next patient to give them time to talk and catch up.

Chapter Twenty-Nine: Dinner

You have no control of the past except to learn from it. But you do have control of the future to have hope in it. CallahanWriter

June 5, 2013,
Washakie Reservation, Wyoming

By the time Hank had finished with his appointments and a couple of walk ins he came back into the foyer to grab Lester. When he did, he saw an active conversation that also included Parley and Miranda.

"Lester, you're up. I hope you didn't have anywhere to go, I skipped over you with all my other patients so you and Andy could have some time to catch up."

"Thanks. It's been great catching up. Andy, will you be here when I'm done with my appointment?"

Andy glanced at Miranda and Parley quickly, then back at Lester. "We can stay a while longer," said Miranda.

"Then yes, I will be waiting for you."

"See you in a minute or two."

"Lester seems like a great guy," observed Parley who was rubbing his thigh trying to work out a cramp.

"I still can hardly believe he's alive. I've spent . . . I can't remember how long I've been mourning the loss and that whole time was a waste, that whole time he was alive. I don't know if I should be mad or grateful?"

"I'd be grateful, being mad doesn't change anything and being grateful is a positive step forward," Miranda replied.

"That's a great way to look at it," observed Parley.

"It really is," Andy agreed.

"It's kind of a do over or a second chance. You don't get many of those in life."

"Man, this is so great. Lester Greene is alive and well. There's something different about him, but then again, he's still the same old guy. I just can't seem to put my finger on it, but there is something . . . Just a little different." Andy was still shaking his head in amazement.

"Maybe it's just the shock of someone coming back from the dead. Think about it. As far as your memories and feelings are concerned, Lester is alive after all. That's got to be, strange?" Miranda was shaking her head in bewilderment as she thought about it.

"I wonder what he's up too with his life now?" Asked Andy.

"You don't know? You guys were talking nonstop."

Laughing about it, Andy said, "geez, I know. There's a lot of years to catch up on."

"Okay, I'll try this new medicine," Lester said as he and Hank walked out of the exam room. "You're sure I can add this to what I'm already taking?"

Taking a deep breath to keep his patience, Hank said, "When have I ever led you astray?"

"I know, I know. I just hate taking medicine."

"Which do you hate worse, being sick or taking medication?"

"Okay, okay," Lester grumbled. "I'll do it."

"Well, now, I guess you boys can get back to your reunion, at least for a few minutes. I've got a few things to do before I lock up so talk away."

"So, Lester, Give me your phone number before either of us forgets. I've got a lot of calling to make up for during all the years you were dead to me. I lost you once, I don't want to lose you again. Oh, and here is my number." He handed Lester a piece of paper.

Lester grabbed a piece of paper from White Flower and scribbled his number down. "Enough of this death talk."

"Is there somewhere we can go get a bite to eat and keep the reunion going?" asked Andy. "Somewhere that's wheelchair friendly."

Just as he asked the question the front door bell rang. They all looked up to see Rita walk through the door.

"Rita, you'll never guess what happened today," Hank said

with a tone of excitement.

"Well, it sounds like good news, at least."

"Lester and Andy served together in the war. They're having a long last reunion right now."

"Andy? Oh yeah, Miranda and Parleys' Andy. That must be you," Rita said as she walked over to Andy.

"Nice to met you." She held out her hand. Andy shook her hand while sill looking at Lester in case he vanished into thin air again. He was also wondering what was wrong with Lester. He was now certain something was different with his long lost buddy.

There was general chatter among the group for a few minutes as Hank scurried around the clinic and checked off a few things with White Flower.

Andy could see Hank was about done and he didn't want to leave for the resort without at least a little more time with Lester. Just as soon as there was a lull in the conversation he asked again, "Is there somewhere we can go and get some dinner so we can keep this reunion going?"

"Yes," said Rita emphatically. "Our house. If Miranda will help me cook dinner that is."

"Okay by me," Miranda said. "The kids are going to be out late anyway. Is it okay with you sweetie?"

Parley felt for his medicine bottles before responding. "Fine by me."

"I'll take Andy with me. We can put your chair in the back of my truck," Hank offered. By the time they were in the parking lot all the travel arrangements were made. Within thirty minutes they were in the backyard of the Standing Elks and Hank was firing up his grill. Lester and Andy were sitting on lawn chairs under a tall oak tree watching a few of Hanks horses in the pasture just beyond the back yard.

Parley had just taken another pain pill and was sitting in a chair close enough to talk with Hank. "I don't know just how close these guys are, but wouldn't it be strange, I mean think of it. I see you get shot, then I'm told your dead and several years later I find out that you're alive."

"That blows my mind to think about it. It seems like it would make for a good movie or something. It's nice to see them reunite." Hank added more barbeque pork to the grill.

"Yeah, looks like Andy may be getting over the shock of seeing Lester alive."

Andy and Lester came to a natural pause in their reunion as they each thought about how to direct the next segment of their conversation.

"So, Lester, what are you up to now? Married? Kids? Work?"

"No, no. none of that. I dated a nice woman for a while, but she couldn't put up with me. I don't really blame her. Who wants to marry someone with such heavy baggage?"

"What do you mean by that?"

Pointing to his leg and cane, Lester said, "I'm in pain all the time. Disabled." Lester slowed down, took a deep breath and added, "and PTSD."

"There are a lot of programs out there to help wounded veterans get work, have you tried any of them?" asked Andy innocently.

"No. I haven't been off the Reservation for several years. I like it out here. It's quiet, people don't bother me . . . " Lester's voice trailed off, followed by some confusing silence. Andy was surprised at Lester's attitude. This wasn't the same friend he had as they went through basic training together. They trained as infantrymen in the same unit. They went to Iraq together. Other than a special assignment Lester went on for three months, they had been together their entire time in the Marines to that point in their service.

Parley decided to go sit with Andy and his old friend. *I need to get off my feet. They burn and are prickling.* Parley picked up his Coke and hobbled to a nearby lawn chair and sat down. "Mind if I join you gentlemen?"

"Go ahead, sit down, take a load off. This is my lucky day, I get to be reunited with one of my best friends and I get to meet Parley Burnrise, all in the same day," Lester seemed genuinely pleased. Parley was taken back by what Lester said. It had been a long time since Parley was serious with his blog. He hadn't met anyone because of his blog. He was surprised people from overseas still came to the resort because of his blog, now, after all this time he meets a fan. That's two fans, he had met in such a short time and they were both Marines.

"So you're not married, but what about work? Do you have a job?"

"No." Lester's voice was defensive.

"If I remember right, you were only a few classes from graduating. You were planning on taking those last few classes before leaving the Corp so you could have both Corp experience and a fresh new degree to start life up after your second hitch."

"Yeah, well . . . I didn't. I don't know, everything seemed to change for me after my first deployment, after my first kills . . . "

"What do you mean by that? I was with you. It was our first deployment together. Oh, yeah. Wait a minute. You're talking about the special three-month assignment?"

"Yeah, the thing I'm not supposed to talk about."

"So what do you mean things changed for you?"

After a few moments of thinking and a few purposeful breaths Lester started, "We were trained to be tough, the kill or be killed mentality. I thought I was ready. I felt ready to fight. Then I get that assignment and I get my first confirmed kills . . . " Lester's deep voice cracked a little. He tried to compose himself with a few deep breaths. Everyone patiently waited. Lester coughed a few times and cleared his throat.

Shaking his head from side to side, he started, "It's one thing to take a persons life with a rifle or a grenade, it's a whole other thing when you're fighting for your life with a person who is fighting for their life. The last one to stop fighting wins . . . Wins and is rewarded with their life and the haunting memory of taking a life in order to go on living life. When you're fighting close-quarters, no one is thinking about patriotism or the flag. All you're thinking about is killing the other guy so you can live. The last thing you remember is feeling their fury slow down, their strength lessens in intensity, until you feel their life slip out of their struggling body. They go limp, you think. You don't dare let up because their strength can come rushing back and they can stick you with a six-inch blade and watch your life drain out slowly. You can't afford to take any chances. When they start to turn a faint grayish-white, well, then you know . . . " Lester said, his voice empty.

This haunting imagery was shocking to Parley. Haunting and shocking. Andy, who had neutralized many of the enemy was even shocked, not having been in hand to hand combat, he could only imagine. He had seen one enemy soldier die of a well-placed bullet. He saw the man struggle to live as he bled out. His eyes never closed. He stared death in the face and when death won, it forgot to turn out the lights. That memory haunted Andy, until now. Hearing Lester talk about hand to hand combat put his memory in perspective. Parley and Andy just listened.

"After that, I met up with my Sargent, who was also in a fight. I drew my side arm and tried to intervene. I was nervous and couldn't hold my hand steady enough to shoot without risking the life of my Sargent. As I was trying to figure out how to jump in I saw my Sargent roll on top of the guy. He slid his forearm on top of the guy's neck. He was pressing his forearm down on the guy's neck trying to crush the guy's windpipe while he used his other hand to fight off the enemy's free hands. He was trying to put his upper body weight into his forearm. In a few seconds the enemy soldier started to slow down, he coughed and gurgled. Then he went limp. My Sargent pushed a little harder to make sure the enemy was dead, then something dark and gross came out of the man's mouth. That's when my Sargent rolled off of him and tried to catch his breath."

Parley was just nodding as if he understood. He wasn't sure if he wanted to. Andy seemed to fully appreciate what Lester was saying. Parley was trying to figure out how to jump in and shift the conversation in a more pleasant description.

The new silence was quickly interrupted by Parleys' cell phone. Parley managed to say hello, just after the third ring.

"Hello."

"Hey son, just calling so you could tell Andy, there's a

package for him. I'm almost certain it's his new foot."

"That's fantastic. I'll tell him."

"All right then, we'll see you when you get here."

"We're having dinner at Hank and Rita's place. We'll be home late."

"I'll put the package on the table in the back room so Andy can pick it up there when you kids get back."

"I'll tell him."

Okay, thanks son. See you tomorrow at the graduation."

"Thanks, see ya later."

"Bye now."

Parley turned the phone off and put it back in his pocket.

"Andy, that was my Dad. There's a package for you. He thinks it's your foot."

"Oh sweet. Thank the Lord, that's good news."

"He's putting the package on the table in the back room. You can pick it up there when we get back."

"That's fantastic."

Parley was happy for Andy. He shifted himself in his chair trying to ease the stiffness and dull ache.

"You have a foot waiting for you back at the resort?" asked a confused Lester.

"Yes, a prosthetic foot for my left leg. With it on I can use crutches instead of being in this chair."

"What about a prosthetic leg for the other side?" asked Lester. Parley had wondered the same thing, but had not thought to ask Andy about it. He was glad Lester asked the question. He was curious about the answer.

"It's a long and complicated story."

That answer was a polite brush off that both Lester and Parley understood, as well as Hank, who was still at the grill and in listening distance.

Quickly redirecting the flow of conversation, Andy asked Lester, "You were talking about how things had changed after your special assignment? How was that? What type of change?"

Thinking about it for a moment, Lester said, "Killing

someone in war is legal, if you follow your rules of engagement. That means you're not supposed to feel bad for taking the life of an enemy, but you do, or at least I did."

Parley noticed Andy was nodding his head in agreement. He felt bad about the turmoil these war vets had to go through emotionally. *It's got to be hard physically for them and then you consider the emotional toll.* Parley gently shook his head.

"Killing someone changes you, especially when you see the person you shot. Especially when you're up close and can feel it. You're glad to be alive, that is until the adrenaline is gone and you're back at base and feeling safe. Then the nightmares begin and as you relieve it a million times you realize you not only terminated someone out on the field of battle but you lose a little of yourself. At least that's what it feels like."

That profound statement left Andy and Parley silent again. Parley felt bad for Lester and Andy, who had been in the terrible situation to have to kill people even if it was in the name of war. Andy was thinking about all the kills he had made. He knew he had killed far more than his official record indicated. He had fired his rifle on full auto into small groups of combatants and watched many of them drop. He knew some were only wounded, but many of them died. His official record just recorded his sniper kills. Killing women and children was devastating. Watching someone bleed out and die right in front of you was terrible. He still couldn't imagine what it would be like to have your hands on the enemy in a close quarter fight and feel them take their last breath. His heart ached for Lester.

He still didn't know how Lester's life had changed since that special assignment, but he now knew enough not to push it with Lester. It couldn't be easy to talk about, even if talking about it might be healthy. He would suggest Lester get some counseling when the time was right.

They were ripped out of their deep conversation by a call to the picnic table. Hank offered grace and for the next several minutes the large picnic table was pandemonium as the serving trays were passed back and forth as everyone piled their plate deep and wide.

Parley was too sore to involve himself in the chaos of the food distribution ritual at the picnic table. He waited for things to slow down and hoped there would be enough food left for him. As he watched the piles of food dwindle, he thought about the pain Lester and even Andy to some extent must be going through dealing with the baggage they carried. That brought that old familiar verse from St. Matthew to mind. "Come unto me, all ye that labor and are heavy laden, and I will give you rest."

Parley had felt that verse work, to some extent in his own life. He wasn't exactly sure how, he had felt peace with that verse on more than one occasion. It wasn't continuous, but it had an impact on him. He wondered how religious Lester and Andy were. He knew Andy was Christian, but he had no idea about Lester. He wished that he could somehow explain that verse to them in a way that made sense. In a way that could help them, especially Lester. If anyone was laboring and heavy laden, it was Lester and maybe to some extent Andy.

The more he thought about it, he realized that he was still laboring and he himself was still heavy laden. He felt there was still more of that verse that could be applied to him. He wished he could understand it more so he could benefit from it more than he already had. He looked at Lester, he was happy to have met him and sad for the burdens he was forced to carry by serving his country in battle.

After satisfying his initial hunger, Andy glanced out of the corner of his eye. He saw Lester enjoying his food. He was profoundly grateful to have a second chance with him. He was feeling that maybe this was his service project that he had been looking for.

He thought back to Atlanta when he met Jackson. Though only a few weeks, it seemed like a lifetime ago. Now here he was, eating dinner with an old friend on an Indian Reservation in Wyoming. He smiled to himself as he thought how fickle life can be and yet how fun it could be. Then he frowned as he remembered that he wouldn't be able to enjoy too many more of these serendipitous events.

Chapter Thirty: Forgiveness: The Art Of Letting Go

May the God of Creation, bring peace to your soul
May the Son of Saving Grace, bring strength to your spirit
May the Spirit of Redeeming Love, bring healing to you and yours
This night and every night, for always and forever.
Irish Blessing – CallahanWriter

June 5, 2013,
Washakie Reservation, Wyoming

Hank gave the dock a big push and then quickly took the helm of his boat. He and Rita had decided to be spontaneous and spend the night with Parley and Miranda. Otherwise, they would have had to wake up early to make the ride across Lake Shaft to attend the Burnrise twin's graduation. They grabbed their oldest children and jumped in their boat and followed Rita and the boys toward the Burnrise Dock.

Lester had reluctantly accepted an invitation to come out to the resort and spend a few days with Andy. Lester and Andy rode with Parley and Miranda.

They settled in for the slow ride to the other side of the lake. Miranda remembered the need to go slow to help manage the impact the bouncing boat could have with Parley.

Lester had felt some long lost emotions resurfacing when he spoke about some of the things he had to do while deployed on that classified assignment. He hadn't really told of any of the classified experiences other than some of the combat he was in. He would never reveal the classified nature of the assignment, but it felt good to talk about some of what he did. If that got him into trouble with the military, well, he didn't care anymore. He had kept it bottled up for over a decade.

Lester compared his experiences with those of Andy. He couldn't know just how bad his other deployments had been, yet he did know of Andy being wounded in each of his deployments. Surely, it had been rough on Andy. He and Andy both shared a substantial disability from the war, but in that case alone, Andy had it far worse than Lester. He admired Andy and how he appeared to be handling his life, at least the part of it he could see. He wondered how Andy seemed to have such a good healthy attitude about life. He had been wondering for the last few hours what Andy's secret was. He didn't seem loaded down with the nightmares of war, all the killing, the pain and loss.

Finally, he looked at Andy, swallowed and blurted out. "What's your secret?"

"Huh? What secret?"

"Your secret to living after all you've been through. I know better than most what you have been through and then, in the end you become a double amputee." Lester was shaking his head in disbelief, "you seem to have it all together. What's your secret?"

Andy didn't completely understand what Lester was getting at, but at the same time he was starting to think he had found his service opportunity. He took a deep breath and mentally rolled up his sleeves. He didn't want to steer his old friend wrong, he didn't want to put him off, or shut him down, but he wasn't sure what to say or how to say it.

If he said nothing, he could lose Lester. If he was preachy, he could lose Lester. He wasn't prepared for this type of situation. In the past, he was able to do his service in the way he lived and what he did. He always seemed to have plenty of time. His service was in doing, not talking. Talking with Lester, in this situation seemed so sudden. It seemed like it had to happen now, as if there was some sort of urgency. *Maybe I don't have as much time as I thought I would, to do my one good last act of service.* Andy was a little taken back by that thought. He was glad that these thoughts were instantaneous because he felt like he had been quiet too long and needed to respond quickly. He was freaking out a little in his mind.

"What do you mean? Give me a for instance?"

"It's the way you are. The way you're acting. Granted, it has only been a few hours since our reunion, but based on the past and now, you're still upbeat and you seem to have a positive outlook on your life. You don't seem all messed up. You don't seem angry. It appears like you have it all together."

Parley was enjoying getting to know Andy, and now Andy was reuniting with a long lost friend in Lester. Parley was wondering if he should give them privacy, yet there weren't many places for him to sit in the boat other than in the small galley. He took a pain pill. He rubbed his arms as he noticed the dropping temperature.

The night air at spring time on Lake Shaft could get quite cool. Parley hoped there were blankets in the storage locker. He managed to stand up in spite of the debilitating stiffness that overpowered him. His involuntary groans caught the attention of Andy and Lester. He found some blankets and handed each of them one and hobbled to the base of four steps that lead to the helm and tossed Miranda one.

He went back to his seat and shook his blanket open before setting down. "I don't want to intrude in a private conversation, but there's no where to go on this boat."

"Oh no. Don't worry about it. Any friend of Andy's is a friend of mine. Andy is picky about who he makes friends with. He trusts you, I trust you," said Lester.

Parley was pleased with the response from Lester. As Andy was struggling in his mind about what to say and how to say it, his mind flew back to the many group therapy sessions he had gone too in the hospital. Some because he needed help, some because he was supporting his chemo buddies and some he went to because he was bored.

Taking a deep breath, Andy asked, "What makes you think I have it all together?"

"It's just the feeling I've been getting since we met up at the clinic. You seem at peace with life. You don't seem to be angry. You're out traveling around on crutches. You don't seem like you're wallowing around in anger and despair like so many of us vets."

"Until now, I wouldn't have guessed you were wallowing in despair. You seem to have it all together, as far as I can see," responded Andy.

"Comes and goes. I have good days and bad days. I haven't left the reservation for years."

"I'll do whatever I can to help you Lester. I will, Semper Fi. I'll talk to you for as long as is needed, but I don't know what to say, I can't just pull out some wise words out of a hat." Andy was wishing he knew exactly what to say."

"Life isn't the same," said Lester. " I can't go back to my old life before signing up with the Corp. I got this bad leg and chronic pain. I'm on all kinds of pills. My life isn't normal and it bugs me. It irritates me. . . It makes me angry. I'm angry and I don't know what I'm angry at," Lester sighed and ran his fingers through his thick dark brown, shoulder length hair.

"I'm mad too. Every morning I wake up and either climb into a wheelchair or I strap on my foot before I can do anything. Life isn't the same that's for sure," Andy agreed.

"It doesn't seem to be getting you down, not as I can tell by the last several hours."

Suddenly Andy felt like he knew where Lester was coming from and what to say to Lester. At least he hoped he did. "After the IED, there was about a week or so that was fuzzy. I don't remember hardly anything, but after I was coming out of my last surgery, I remember thinking this wasn't a big deal. I had been wounded twice before and I was able to heal and get back to active duty. Then later it hit me that I would never be able to go back to my unit since I was without a leg and a foot. It was mad. I didn't know who I was mad at. I was just mad."

"Like you were mad at God?" Parley asked.

"No. I was never mad at God, but a lot of guys were. I understand where they're coming from. But no, I was just mad. Then, with the help of Father Friday, the Chaplin and some of the therapy groups I realized I was just mad at life."

"Could the anger be at the enemy?" Parley wondered out loud.

"At first I thought it might be, but then I realized they were just like me. They were fighting for their country, their beliefs. I shot at the enemy, I killed some of the enemy and they were trying to do the same to us. You can't fault a guy for fighting for his country. I came to realize it was just the circumstances of my life I was mad at. I went to work one day and a couple months later I'm recuperating from surgery and losing two body parts and dealing with cancer. Life had taken a major turn."

Andy finally shook open the folded blanket and covered himself with it. "So, somehow, with Father Friday's help and just thinking about it, I don't know, somehow it just made sense to let go of the anger and concentrate on what my new life was. It was my choice to be mad and hold on to anger and resentment, accept my new life and use my old life experiences when I could to make my new life as good as I could. At the end of the day, no one was going to live my life for me. It was all on me to make my life livable or to wallow in self pity and anger."

Lester was enthralled by what Andy was saying. When Andy paused, Lester asked, "What about the part of your life that is taken away from you. There's got to be stuff you flat out can't do any more when you're missing a foot and a leg? Right?"

"Sure there is, but I can't change it. Since I can't change the fact that I can no longer run and jump is no reason to stop living or to give my life over to a cloud of despair. Everyone has their own limitations. Some people are born without hands or feet. That's a limitation for them. There are work around's and substitutions, but in the end, we all have limitations. Do you want to stop living because of that? Human beings are adaptable if they choose to be. There is still a lot of happiness and excitement in life if we accept our limitations instead of wasting time being sad or mad at our limitations."

These thoughts that Andy was sharing hit Parley right between the eyes. He had been experiencing very similar thoughts and feelings because of how his life had changed and been turned upside down with chronic pain and all the other issues of fibromyalgia. It was like a wound that damaged your body just like what had happened to Andy and Lester. Only fibromyalgia isn't dramatic and heroic, but it is just as debilitating.

Parley was wondering what would be worse, missing a leg and a foot or a lifetime of fibromyalgia? He wasn't really sure.

"What if I liked my past and all I ever wanted to do was taken away by my injury? What if I don't have any other desire for my life? What if nothing else appeals to me? What then? What do I do?"

Andy recognized Lester asked a good question. Andy hadn't really had to deal with that issue completely because he didn't have much of a future with his terminal diagnosis. He was just looking at ending his life on a high note. He didn't have to plan a life for the next forty or fifty years. *What does Lester do? How do I answer his question?*

Andy suddenly had a great idea. He turned his head toward Parley. "Parley probably has a good answer for you. He wasn't in the military, but he's had his life taken from him with fibromyalgia and he's had to deal with the loss of his old life and figure out what to do with his new life of chronic pain. What have you had to do to adapt to your new life?"

The question floored Parley. He had been eating up all the wisdom that Andy was sharing and realizing it applied to his life. He was feeling hopeful about his future now that he was learning this new life lesson.

"I haven't, I don't know, this is all new to me. I'm in the same position as Lester. I'm still dealing with the not letting go, anger thing. I'm still wanting to deny what's going on and go back to living my old life. It was a great life. I want that back."

Andy had assumed Parley had it all together and was on top of his new life challenges. Andy then realized he had made a bad assumption.

"Well, it looks like we are all in this together," Andy said, trying to cover up his little mistake.

"I guess I have it better than Parley. At least I don't have a wife and children depending on me to have it all together," said Lester. The motor on the boat grew quiet as Miranda slowed down the boat as she positioned the boat to dock. Hank and his family were coming in behind them.

Chapter Thirty-One: Graduation

Happiness is a process that starts by letting go of what is gone,
followed by gratitude for what you have now. Find joy in the
moments as they come. Love freely with all your heart and look to
the future as the blessing that it is. CallahanWriter

June 6, 2013
Lake Shaft, Wyoming

Precisely at the stroke of 9:00 a.m., Parleys' alarm blared the chorus of We Will Rock You. Parleys' eyes burst open and his heart started beating fast and hard from being shocked awake. That was by design. Parley tuned his radio to a hard rock station with the hope that waking up to some stadium stomping, loud rock, fast tempo music would help him wake up quickly. It had the desired effect. He had no immediate desire to go back to sleep. He took a deep breath and reached his alarm clock to turn it down. It was a good song playing and he wanted to finish listening to it while he lay in bed.

Once again, he was frustrated. Fibromyalgia robbed him of everything it seemed, including the very small, simple pleasures in life like laying in bed for a couple more minutes to finish listening to a single song. He couldn't do it. His back demanded he get out of bed, now! A hard rock band comprising his hips, pelvis, tail bone, spine and neck were screaming at him the familiar refrain, "get outta bed now or ya going die, going to die, going to die. Get your body outta bed now!" He just wanted to listen to Queen finish their song. Was that too much to ask? According to the hard rock band in his body, it was.

In spite of the hard rock band called Excruciating Pain screaming at him to get out of bed, the early morning stiffness was forcing him to go slow, very slow. Between the early morning pain and the terrible stiffness, Parley hated to wake up. Sometimes he hated to go to sleep because eventually he would have to wake up in depressing pain.

Every second of every day comes with consequences. Sometimes those consequences are so minor they're imperceptible. However, the consequences of being out so late the night before were very perceptible. The boat ride home was one of the very few highlights in Parley life over the last five or six years. He had learned some inspired thoughts about dealing with life. The actual boat ride was still being felt in his spine. Every single vertebra was reminding Parley of the ride.

The boat ride was a good example of Parleys' new reality. It was inspirational and painful. *Why can't it just be a good memory?* He frequently wondered why everything had to have two sides to it? Why couldn't the boat ride just be a fond memory? Why does it have to leave me in a wake of pain? In his glory days he could enjoy his boat ride and the inspiration he so frequently had on the boat. Not any more. By an act of sheer will Parley swallowed his pain pill and got into a boiling hot shower. Hot water sometimes loosened his muscles a little and sometimes if he was lucky the hot water could ease the pain slightly. Today wasn't one of those days.

Finally, after twelve years of going to mandatory school, Ted and Emily finally graduated from high school. For the last three years the family calendar showed Thursday, June 6, 2013, marked as the twins' graduation day.

For the first time in three years of high school Ted and Emily were both up, dressed and ready to go without Miranda yelling at them. They didn't have to be at the resort grounds until ten so they had to cool their heels for a while.

Miranda was up and going as usual, but she found herself mired in a melancholy mood. She had shared her children's milestones during their senior year and she was happy for them. But on the other hand, she was wistful and anxious. In three short months they would be going off to college. Her babies would be gone, leaving her and Parley as empty nesters. *I'm too young to be an empty nester.*

Parley had missed out on many milestones and special

occasions for the kids, but today, there was no way he would miss their graduation. He had talked to Hank about this important day and he gave him permission to take a couple extra pain pills if needed to get through the ordeal.

Once he was out of the shower his only focus was to be sitting in his reserved chair by 11:55 a.m. for the graduation ceremony which started at noon.

Lake Shaft High School had held their graduation at the Burnrise Resort successfully the last three years. There was a big green field that was big enough to hold all the folding chairs. The graduating class was never more than sixty kids. The resort offered plenty of space and all the facilities for families who wanted to eat at the Café or camp on the camp grounds. Some rented hotel rooms to make it a special event.

Bert offered the land rent free to the school because the traffic more than made up for it. Andy and Lester met Hank and Rita at the Café for breakfast. Hank was pleased to see Lester with a look or contentment on his face. As Lester's health care provider, Hank knew of his problems, both physical and mental. Seeing Lester buoyed up with Andy's influence gave Hank hope things would work out with Lester.

"How did you leathernecks sleep last night?" asked Rita.

"Fantastic! Since I've been here, I have slept with the window open every night. It's like taking a sleeping pill without the side effects. The cool air with a sweet natural, earthy scent, man, it's awesome." Looking to Lester, Andy went on to say, "I'm sure you're used to it, but it's a far cry from the big city or the stuffy air of the hospital." Lester nodded in agreement. Lester marveled at how Andy seemed so positive and even hopeful sounding about something so mundane as sleep and mornings.

"When will Parley and Miranda show up?" asked Lester. He was liking the idea of getting to know the legendary Parley Burnrise through their mutual friend Andy.

"I don't know. But Nick reserved a row of seating for the Burnrise family and us so it won't really matter. Oh yeah. We need to leave the outside seat for Parley in case he needs to get up and move around," said Hank.

Everyone nodded knowingly except for Lester. "Is that because of that fibroba, fiba. . .Myga. . . What's that disease called?"

"Fibromyalgia," answered Hank. "He might just have to get up and go inside. If he does, it's easier to get up if he's at the end of the row and not have to climb past anyone."

"Makes sense," Lester nodded his head. "So what exactly is fibromyalgia . . . Its pain, right?"

"Yes, pain and a whole lot more. It's characterized as chronic widespread pain. It can affect any and all of the bodies soft tissue. I've heard people describe it to be like having all the body aches and misery of the flu, all the time. They seem to be stiff all day, but more so in the morning

"How can anyone live like that without going totally crazy?" asked Lester.

"I've wondered that myself. I wonder if that's why, in the past it's been hard for doctors to diagnose. They can't wrap their heads around the reality of the pain. I don't know, it's just something I've been thinking about.

"Wow. That's awful . . . That's terrible." Lester was shaking his head in disbelief. "I thought I had it bad with my chronic pain and disability," remarked Lester.

"So Nick is finally back from his family vacation right?" asked Andy.

"Yeah, he had to be back by yesterday because he's in charge of the whole graduation thing," Rita answered.

"I've been looking forward to meeting him. Bert said that part of their vacation was noodling. I've done that. Can't wait to talk to him about it and swap stories," said Andy.

"What's noodling?" asked Rita.

"Catching catfish by hand."

"Really? Catching fish by hand? You just walk in the river and bend over and catch a fish with your hand?"

"But there's more than that. It's a whole sport and some states have noodling contests."

"Were you ever in a contest?" asked Hank.

"No. I just had fun with it. When you get to the level of competing, well, that's when it gets really tough."

"How do you do it exactly?" asked Lester.

"The big fish hide out in underwater caves and holes made by tree roots or debris. You walk around in the lake and feel for holes and then you bend over and put your hand in a hole and hope that it's not a snake or a snapping turtle. The fish will usually bite your hand and then you pull it up and grab it with the other hand and then tie it off or put it in a basket and do it all over again."

"Does it hurt?" asked Rita.

"It hurt me. Some of the competitive old timers have heavy callouses and scars all over their hands and they brag that it doesn't hurt, but it hurt me."

"Are you pulling my leg?" Rita asked in disbelief.

"No, not at all. Talk to Nick and see what he has to say about it. You'll see."

"Maybe they took pictures or some video," Hank wondered.

Parley had taken his first extra pain pill before they got to the resort. He had been hearing Miranda talk all the way to the resort, but he hadn't really been able to listen he was so concerned about whether or not he would make it through the graduation ceremony. He felt like he had neglected his kids for the last five or six years and he probably would for years to come, but not today. This day was too big to let all the pain and agony that was fibromyalgia, get in the way of support and celebrating his kids' success. He was trying to will away the pain.

Once they got to the resort they easily found Andy. Andy was crutching around the facility's swing stepping and shooting through the crowds. His face showed a genuine happiness with the freedom that crutches gave him. He was oblivious to the fact that people stared at him with his right leg folded and pinned to the top of his right leg stump. He was energized by his new freedom.

Parley found his seat. Nick had put a cushioned folding chair in Parleys' spot at the end of the row. "That was thoughtful of Nick," Miranda said, pointing to Parleys' chair. As they took their seats,

Andy came swing steeping toward their row. He was followed by Lester, who wore crisp denim blue Levis and a bright, long sleeve blue cotton shirt with a button down collar. He also had in his arms a faded blue denim jacket.

Andy sat next to Miranda, who was next to Parley sitting at the end of the row.

"Nick!" Parley called his brother over as Nick was running around like a chicken with his head cut off making sure all the last minute details were taken care of.

"Hey Parley, Miranda. How you guys doing?"

"Great, sort of. Now I understand how Heather felt last year when Jeff graduated."

"Just don't go crying like Heather did."

"You men and your lack of emotion," Miranda playfully scowled at Nick.

"Nick, I want you to meet Gunnery Sargent, Andy Zimmerman, a war hero. Andy, this is Nick the noodler." Parley smiled at his own humor.

Andy held out his hand and Nick shook it. "It's good to meet you Nick, I've heard a lot about you including your noodling vacation."

"I've heard a lot about you. You're a real war hero. It's a pleasure." Nick finally let go of Andy's hand. "I have some pictures of a couple catfish I caught."

"I've noodled. I'd like to see your pictures."

"Let's hook up in a couple of hours and we can swap stories. I've been looking forward to meeting you. My dad has told me a lot about you."

Parley introduced Lester to Nick before Nick had to run off.

"Gotta run. See you later," said Nick.

"Looking forward to it," said Andy.

A man in a dark suit stood at the podium. The crowd grew quiet. "On behalf of the class of 2013, we welcome you. . ."

Parley had only been sitting for ten minutes and the pain and agony of his illness was throbbing and pounding and dancing around his muscles. No muscles were left untouched. This was the first time since his chronic pain that he had been in a crowd of this size. The two hundred and fifty people were so overwhelming. Parley felt that each person in the audience was sucking energy out of him creating a vacuum that was quickly filled with raging pain.

Time was crawling by in slow motion. Every word that each speaker uttered took forever to say. *All, I'm here for is to see Ted and Emily walk across the stage, shake hands with the principal and receive a diploma. Who cares what these kids are speaking about.*

Somehow, after a while the pain moderated a bit and he took in some of the words these young speakers were saying.

The speeches, all had a common theme of saying goodbye to the past and hello to an unlimited future. "The future is before us," "let us hope for a brighter tomorrow," and "there is nothing we can't do," were some of the highlights of their hopeful speeches.

Why not be hopeful, they're young and in good health. They might as well be optimistic now. Life won't let it last. . .

Parley listened on. In truth, he was excited for his kids and their future. *They're smart kids with a youthful exuberance and a huge hope for the future. Their future does look bright, at least as long as they have good health. What if they didn't have good health? What would I tell them? How would I motivate them? I'd want them to still be optimistic about their future and not shut themselves off from life. There are people with physical limitations making the most of their lives. . .*

Parleys' thoughts stung him with an accusation. *Aren't you a hypocrite? Thinking like that and the way you're living your life, blaming the past, holding on to your anger rather than fighting for a future. But what kind of future do I even have?* Parley didn't like those thoughts and he tried to think of something else. He didn't like feeling bad about himself. His mind wandered, he had trouble concentrating. It wouldn't take long to forget what he thought about.

Parley wondered what would happen in four or maybe five years when his kids were armed with their college degrees. *They'll want to get as far away as possible from Lake Shaft City and their chronically sick Dad.*

The speakers kept droning on. Parley mused about the unlimited potential this graduating class had. All that youth, all that untold energy, all that life ahead of them. He was jealous. His life was, for the most part over. Sure, he had twenty, thirty more years, but not much living ahead of him. *How do I learn to live with this constant crippling pain and fatigue? I can't even think straight half the time.*

He thought about the intriguing conversation he had with Andy and Lester the night before. Let go of the anger and use the energy that was tided up in being angry and apply it to be happy in life or being as productive as circumstance will allow. *It would help if I had a life. My life is pain, is there room for anything else?*

Parleys' attention was drawn back to the ceremony. They were finally ready to read off the seniors' names and hand them their diplomas. Parley was going to get up and leave after his kids got theirs. With a last name of Burnrise, there were only six kids ahead of the twins. He wouldn't have to wait much longer.

"Emily Burnrise," the audience applauded. Parley and Miranda clapped like there was no tomorrow. "Ted Burnrise," the announcer said. Parley and Miranda just kept on clapping. *Now I can get out of here, finally.*

Chapter Thirty-Two: A Big Day

To everything there is a season. There is a time to hold on and a time to let go. A time to kill, and a time to heal. A time to reject and a time to accept. A time to break down, and a time to build up. A time for the past and a time for the future. A time to weep, and a time to laugh. A time to mourn, and a time to dance. A time to reflect and a time to move on. A time to cast away stones, and a time to gather stones together. A time to embrace, and a time to refrain from embracing. The Preacher

June 6, 2013
Lake Shaft, Wyoming

Wishing he had a cane or a crutch, Parley walked slowly and deliberately toward the main entrance on the back side of the Burnrise building. As was his new normal, he was feeling conflicted. He felt like he had achieved something monumental by attending the graduation ceremony, but on the other hand, he was feeling bad he was leaving early. On the one hand, he saw each of his kids get their diplomas, but then again everyone was watching him hobble toward the entrance. He staggered like he might be drunk. So few people understood what he was going through and all they did was stare. He felt isolated.

Why can I be happy for small victories, he thought as he opened the door and stepped inside the great hall where the aquariums and display area were located. He still limped as he walked with an unsteady gait. He looked at the pictures on the wall and the occasional displays celebrating five generations of Burnrise history on Lake Shaft. Of all the Burnrises over five generations, Parley had the most pictures and displays. Now here he was, looking like he might drop on the floor.

The Willow Creek Display and award reminded him about five years ago when he raced down a dangerous canyon to save thirty-something people snowed in at Willow Creek Resort. He broke a few bones in the process. Those broken ribs hurt badly, but now, if he could, he would gladly trade his current fatigue and agony in for a few broken bones. Now his lot in life was the chronic fatigue and pain of fibromyalgia. He was in what should be considered the prime of his life at forty-two years old, yet he was now living the life of an invalid.

As he was limping down the hall, Parley happened to glance at a display of walking sticks from the Outfitter shop near the hallway. They were primarily sold as souvenirs, hand crafted from sturdy local tree limbs of maple, elm and pine. On a whim he went in and grabbed the nearest one. He looked for the price tag and tore it off. He gave the tag to the cashier and said, "put it on my account please." He used the stick like a cane. He still limped and staggered, but felt more control and less like he might fall. He went straight into the back room and ordered a pitcher of coffee, Lake Shaft Fish and Chips, fish from Lake Shaft, and a large Coke.

Miranda had reserved the main pavilion for the afternoon. They were holding a reception type of graduation party for Emily and Ted. After the reception, the twins would go to the school gym and party and celebrate with their classmates all night. While Parley was holed up in the back room, Andy was hanging back in a field of folding chairs waiting for the crowd to thin out. He loved the freedom of crutches, but they were a little tricky in a crowded area. Some of the people gathered around were taking pictures and milling around as they waited for their reservations at the Café. Andy was getting impatient as he waited to get up and get on his crutches. Lester had left Andy to go for a brisk walk to help burn off some of the anxiety he was experiencing in the large crowd.

As Andy waited, he gazed around the landscape of this part of the Resort. It was breathtaking. He got a whiff of clean spring air from the lake. He looked at the blue sky with billowy white clouds steadily passing overhead. He saw a giant floating turtle in the form a pronounced half circle of white puffy clouds that represented the shell with a long narrow wispy cloud that served as the turtle's neck. At the tip of the neck was a rounded triangle that looked like the head of the turtle. Truthfully, it was more like a caricature of a turtle in the billowy white clouds with traces of gray. It was interesting to Andy at how many shades of sky blue there could be. He was falling in love all over again with the outdoors as he spent time in this part of Wyoming.

He saw the crowd thinning and used his crutches as something to hold onto as he got himself onto his prosthetic foot. Quickly getting his crutches under each arm, he did a fancy side step with his prosthetic foot and the two crutches to go down the aisle until he was in the open courtyard area.

As Andy made his way to the reception area, he was keeping his eye out for Lester. He thought about the last couple of weeks and meeting Parley and his family along with an unexpected reunion with a dead man. He was now positive Lester was meant to be one of his acts of service. He had also been getting a strange feeling that somehow he and Parley were linked together. He was wondering if his blog hero was meant to be one of his last acts as well.

It was strange to think he had specific people to serve considering his past years of service was a broad service to his country. Now it was down to two people if he counted Parley. Since he still had a nagging feeling about serving Parley in some remote way, he decided to add Parley to his list.

Parley was groggy and his mind felt thick. He heard voices talking. He felt the need to wake up, but his brain felt so heavy and sleepy that it seemed impossible to keep his eyes open. He stayed awake with his eyes closed which was the best compromise he could make with his head. After a few minutes he recognized the voices of Andy and Nick. He heard them talking about something exciting. They started swapping stories of their past experiences noodling.

He could hear Andy's response to the pictures Nick was showing of the catfish he caught with his hand. Parley wanted to see the pictures, but was too groggy still to say anything.

"It was a blast," Nick said, "To catch those big fish by hand. I've got to do it again before I die. It's going onto my bucket list."

"So how big was your biggest catch?" asked Andy.

"Twenty-one pounds."

"That's pretty darn good. You could compete with a flathead that size."

"They have fishing contests for hillbilly hand fishing?" asked Nick.

"Yeah. They have big professional ones and a lot of amateur competitions. Too bad you guys don't have a catfish pond here at your resort. You could add hand fishing to your fishing contests."

Parley finally got his eyelids to stay open. He drank some ice water to help him stay awake. Normally he would enjoy the sleep, but he wanted to talk about fishing with the guys. Something he hadn't done much in the last five years. He poured himself a cup of coffee, hoping for a quick caffeine boost.

Chapter Thirty-Three: Beaten, Battered And Bruised

We can be beaten, battered and bruised, but how we feel is up to us. CallahanWriter

June 6, 2013
Lake Shaft, Wyoming

Lester had calmed down enough to make his way to the back room. When he got there, Andy and Parley were talking about noodling. It was a fascinating conversation about a subject he had never heard white people talk about before. Many old timer Indians had caught fish in the rivers and tried to pass the skill onto the young Shoshone, but the younger tribal members were not very interested. These white folks were talking about a sport of catching flathead catfish by hand, whereas it was a necessary skill required by old timer Shoshones to put meat on the table for their families. They caught trout and other active freshwater fish compared to the big and sluggish flathead catfish. Lester enjoyed the spiritual side of being a Native American, but like many his age and younger, he wasn't as interested in social customs. Yet he smiled at the traditions of his people being considered a sport and a much easier one at that. But still, noodling sounded fascinating.

"What would you guys think of us going hillbilly hand fishin' this summer when it warms up?" Andy looked at Lester and then Parley.

"Sounds interesting. I might like it," responded Lester.

"Yeah, no. I don't see how I could do it with this fibro." Parley shook his head.

"Don't sell yourself short. The water in the late summer is warm, and if they had handicap facilities, why not? It would be a blast even if we don't catch a cat."

"What do you mean late summer? Is it not legal in the spring like Nick did?"

"No. That's not what I mean. I said late summer when the

water is as warm as it's going to get. Most of those lakes and ponds where the catfish are, can get comfortably warm. I was thinking the warmer the water the better it might be on your muscles with your fibro condition."

Parley was touched at the sensitivity and concern Andy showed. That sensitivity made it harder to say no.

"I think you could do it Parley, if they have these facilities' Andy's talking about. I know they have a lot of private ponds that offer noodling. Maybe they might have some kind of handicapped access? Worth a try." Nick urged.

"What if I found pond or lake that offered friendly access?" Asked Andy.

"Why would you need handicap access? If the water is warm and you have your life vest on . . . What's the big deal? All you need is a guide who can help you find easier access to a hole that you could reach with a life jacket. I can't see how it's any more complicated than that," Nick asserted.

"Nick's right. I don't know why I didn't realize it sooner. We would need a flotation device and a guide that is willing to work with us and our circumstances, someone who can take us to an easy spot to catch a few flatheads." Andy was nodding his head.

Parley had been thinking it would be fun to have Andy around for a while longer. Now that he had his crutches he could be off any day. Making plans like this could ensure more time with him. Then he had an idea burst on him. They could take the twins and have one last summer fling before the kids went off to college. Everything in Parley's mind seemed to be ganging up on him telling him to agree to the outing.

It was as if his brain had a mind of its own. He heard himself say "I guess I could keep an open mind to the possibility."

"Great. I'll go get my laptop and start looking before you can change your mind," Andy said with a grin and a wink. Nick excused himself and went out to check on the crew that was taking down the chairs and podium from the graduation ceremony.

Andy left for his room to retrieve his computer, leaving Lester and Parley alone.

"It's kind of weird that we both grew up around here, me on the reservation and you in Lake Shaft City and we're just now meeting each other," said Lester.

"Well . . . At least things are improving between those of you on the reservation and those of us in town." Parley nodded his head.

"You're right about that. Good grief, we're all just people. People on and off the reservation make such a big deal about all our differences. That's no reason not to get along. Everyone's got a past. People become friends or fall in love and overlook the past of the people they fall in love with or want to become friends with. Why can't Indians and Whites do the same?" Lester shook his head.

"I'd like to think we're doing a lot better with that idea than we used to."

"Well, I guess, when you think about it, there is an overall mind set which seems to be slowly moving in that direction," said Lester.

"What do you do over there on the Reservation? You know, for work or whatever?"

That was a sore spot for Lester and he seemed to stiffen at the question, but the kind way Parley asked, he felt an answer slip out. "Truthfully, not much. I have a decent pension or disability I guess you'd call it. I have a lot of issues from the war . . ." His voice was growing soft as he was talking. He was treading on uncertain territory that he wasn't comfortable talking about. Sensing that, Parley let it slide.

Andy was back, now sitting at the table searching the internet for information about a possible vacation.

"Andy, were you ever angry?"

"About what?"

"I was talking about last night. That stuff you said about letting go of the anger and moving on."

"Oh yeah. Yes, I was."

"Does it really work? It sounds good, but have you seen it work in your life or in the lives of people you know?" asked Parley.

"It works for me. I saw guys in group therapy embrace the

concept. There's more than letting go of the anger. If a person can no longer be the person they once were, then they need to accept who they now are. Take me for instance. I could take all the energy that I use by being mad at my life or the circumstances that took away my foot or leg and use that same energy channeling it into a new future becoming the best new me I can be with my new set of circumstances."

"That makes some good sense. So you really have done this, this letting go and changing?" asked Parley.

"I have and I am."

"Huh? What do you mean by that?"

"It's an ongoing process. Really, I'm in the middle of doing it right now and hopefully I'll continue to do it until I die."

"That makes sense," said Lester.

"For example, after college, I joined the Marines. After losing my leg and my foot I could no longer be a Marine. I was angry for a while when I realized for the first time in my life I had limitations. But then if you think about it, what good would being angry do me? It won't bring my leg and foot back. So I've been trying to use that energy in focusing on the future."

Lester and Parley both were having an ah-ha moment, a moment of self-discovery and awareness. Lester was both excited and scared at this new information that had the potential to make a difference in his life. He excused himself to go get some more food.

Parley had a peaceful, easy feeling going on inside of him. It was the first time he had felt this way in years. For the first time since getting sick, he had a feeling of hope wash over him. There was another lull in the conversation.

"I'm going to catch up with Lester. That food your wife and mother prepared is out of this world good. Want to come with?" Andy gathered his crutches under each arm as he waited for Parley to answer.

"No. I'm not really hungry. I think I'm going to lie down on this sofa and try to sleep a little more."

Parley struggled to get comfortable on the couch. As he was tossing and turning he thought about the conversation he had just had. *We could take the RV and maybe talk Hank and Rita into coming along. We could also borrow the Resorts SUV and caravan the trip. One last hurrah for the kids and a nice summer vacation. Wow. It's been more than five years since our last vacation. Heck, I'm on the best medicines I'm likely to have. I could always just watch everyone else if I'm not feeling all that well.* Parley quickly dozed off.

Not long after falling asleep, Parley awoke with a start. His back hurt and his neck was aching. He was having a hard time turning over in the right way, allowing him to get up and off the couch.

Then he heard Hanks voice. Hank seemed to be talking to someone. *Maybe it is Lester or Andy. No, they're probably still eating.*

Hanks' voice grew louder and more clear as he came closer to the back room. Hank had a deep voice. "How long have we been seeing each other? Five, maybe six weeks?"

"Longer than that. It's been three months."

That's Miranda's voice.

"Hey guys, have you seen Parley?" asked Bert.

"No, not me," responded Miranda. "Neither have I," added Hank.

"Well, if you see him, tell him that we need him out at the pavilion if he can make it."

"Okay," they both said in unison. They continued their conversation as they got closer to the back room and easier to hear. Parley was wondering what they were talking about.

"So, we'll be seeing each other next Thursday then?"

"Yeah. Afternoon sometime?"

"Yeah," Hank agreed, "and you still don't want to tell Parley that we're seeing each other?"

"No, not yet. He's got too much going on to deal with this."

"When do you think we should tell him, then?" asked Hank.

"Not for a while yet. Are you okay with that?" Miranda asked.

"Not really. Parleys' my best friend. I think he should know."

"Not now, I'm not ready for him to know. Can you be okay with that?"

"I guess I'll have to be."

"Thank you for understanding. I guess you need to go?"

"Yes, I do." Hank leaned in for hug. "Bye."

After a tight hug, Miranda pulled back and said, "bye."

"Bye." Hank went out the side door to the dock. Miranda went to the desk in the back room and sat down. She opened the desk drawer and Parley could hear her rummage around in the drawer.

He was confused at the part of their conversation he heard. Why would Miranda not want me to know she is seeing Hank? Why is she seeing Hank? She's not sick. A sick frightening feeling came over him. He replayed the parts of their conversation he could hear over and over in his mind.

"How long have we been seeing each other? Five, maybe six weeks?"

"No, it's been three months."

And then he rehearsed the rest of what they said, *"You still don't want to tell Parley that we're seeing each other?"*

"No, not yet."

What are they talking about? It sounds like they . . . They . . . . There . . . Having a. . . No . . . No! It couldn't, they couldn't . . . They're not having an affair? He reviewed those comments over and over in his head. Then he thought about the last five or six years of his marriage with Miranda. After considering what a burden he had been, it all started to make sense. Then he got sick to his stomach. Surprisingly Parley nodded off to sleep before he could figure out what to say to Miranda.

Less than a half hour later, Miranda woke Parley up telling him they needed to go outside and get their picture taken with the twins. Heather was doing a photo shoot for their graduation pictures. Parley was feeling betrayed and upset toward Miranda. "Go on without me. I'll be there for them. It's going to take a few minutes to get up and loosen up." Looking at his watch he added, "I need to take another pain pill and muscle relaxer. Give me ten minutes."

"All right sweetie, I'll slow them down until you arrive."

Miranda touched up her hair on her way out of the back room through the sliding doors.

How can she possibly have the nerve to call me sweetie when she's stepping out on me with my best friend? Parley swallowed his pills with the last of his ice water. He forced himself to get up and push through the stiffness. *Is it really possible that Hank is having an affair with Miranda? He loves Rita . . . At least I thought he did. They have a good thing going, don't they? But then again, I thought Miranda and I had a good thing going. Is it possible I mistakenly heard them? It's too ridiculous to think they are having an affair . . . I hope.*

Parley was a little looser and he was able to reach his walking stick. He made his way out the sliding doors. He was slowly shuffling toward the Burnrise Pavilion they had reserved for the entire day. On his way he kept going over the memory of what he thought he heard from Hank and Miranda. He knew his memory played tricks on him and had been dubious for the last three or four years. *Is it possible that I misunderstood their tone and maybe their words?* He felt a little better when he thought that perhaps he misread the conversation between his best friend and wife. *What am I thinking? There's no way they would be cheating on me.*

Parley looked up at the sound of laughter and familiar voices. He was close to the Pavilion. He saw the twins goofing around in front of the camera. He looked for Miranda. He couldn't seem to find her. He kept looking as he limped toward the pavilion. Out of the corner of his eye, he saw Miranda walking playfully up behind Hank. She slipped up behind him and put her left hand on his left shoulder and her right hand on his right shoulder. He could hear her saying "boo!" in a tone of voice that was way beyond friendly and maybe even flirty. As she let go of his shoulders, her left arm seemed to slip around his neck in the form of a squeeze before dropping her hands to her side. She was standing way too close to him.

Parleys' chest felt like it might blow up. His heart sank to his feet and his face grew flush with anger or resentment, maybe it was betrayal. Whatever it was, Parley was sure he hadn't misunderstood that earlier conversation between them.

Authors Notes

Thank you for reading Parleys Quest. I hope you enjoyed it. While this story is not based on my life, however, the symptoms, the chronic pain and the fibromyalgia diagnosis were created based on my personal experiences. I set out to write a story where the protagonist had fibromyalgia as a side conflict to the story line. I did this as a way to bring fibromyalgia into the mainstream of public awareness.

I created a few characters and started the story. This is my first novel and I had no idea how powerful characters with real problems could control the story being told. Had I stuck with my primary storyline, I would have portrayed fibromyalgia as a thorn in the side of the protagonist. If you have the dreaded illness or know someone who has it, then you know that fibro is a thorn in the entire body. It is too powerful to be relegated as a side conflict.

I gave into my muse or my suffering, in this case they well could be the same thing and let the story go where it needed to go. The problem with a story line such as that is that there is no end in sight. How do you wrap up a story when a person has a mysterious illness that doctors call fibromyalgia? You don't. You can't.

It is therefore my intention to continue the story with Parley, Miranda and Andy at the pace that health and energy will allow. Since this story took almost two years to write, I can't promise a time frame for the next story. I can tell you that I am already working on the second story as I write this blurb. I have a few twists and turns for the primary characters to go through in the second volume so keep your eyes open for the next installment of the Inspiration Burnrise Saga.

Made in the USA
Las Vegas, NV
28 February 2024

86400410R00142